PRAISE FOR ANN C. FALLON'S JAMES FLEMING MYSTERIES

BLOOD IS THICKER

"Fans of Elizabeth George, P.D. James, Martha Grimes, Caroline Graham . . . should rejoice at this new entry. . . ."
—*Mystery News*

"Some mystery novels begin with such character, such eccentricity and promise that the reader's response is childish glee. Such is the case with Ann C. Fallon's *Blood Is Thicker*. . . . There's humor along with pathos in this charmingly written story."
—*Toronto Sunday Sun*

WHERE DEATH LIES

"As provocative as any murder you'll find in Agatha Christie or P.D. James. . . . Fallon's Mr. Fleming will be welcome with mystery readers for a long, long time."
—*Irish Voice*

DEAD ENDS

"With its prevailing aura of menace and rich Irish lore, *Dead Ends* establishes Ann Fallon in the forefront of today's young mystery writers."
—*Dorothy Salisbury Davis*

POTTER'S FIELD

"Complex. . . . Refreshingly different and well worth exploring for all armchair travelers and detectives."
—*Murder ad lib*

"A well-written and enjoyable mystery. . . . James Fleming is a fine Irish friend on a cold winter's night."
—*Murder & Mayhem*

Books by Ann C. Fallon

Blood Is Thicker
Dead Ends
Potter's Field
Where Death Lies
Hour of Our Death

Published by POCKET BOOKS

HOUR OF OUR DEATH

ANN C. FALLON

POCKET BOOKS

New York   London   Toronto   Sydney   Tokyo   Singapore

This book is a work of fiction. Names, characters, places and
incidents are products of the author's imagination or are used
fictitiously. Any resemblance to actual events or locales or persons,
living or dead, is entirely coincidental.

An *Original* Publication of POCKET BOOKS

POCKET BOOKS, a division of Simon & Schuster Inc.
1230 Avenue of the Americas, New York, NY 10020

ISBN: 0-671-88515-4

First Pocket Books printing April 1995

10 9 8 7 6 5 4 3 2 1

POCKET and colophon are registered trademarks of
Simon & Schuster Inc.

Cover art by Richard Ross

Printed in the U.S.A.

For my dear friend, Kathy Turke

. . . Holy Mary, Mother of God,
pray for us sinners.
Now and at the hour of our death. Amen

—from "The Hail Mary"

Chapter One

The dawn broke gray and silent in the village of Buncloda. Even the birds' morning chorus was muffled by the heavy air. From the hill on the east side of the village, the view revealed a scattering of houses and shops beneath the slowly rising fog. They did not nestle as in many Irish villages; rather, they seemed flung haphazardly around the Catholic church that stood in their midst, its stone walls wet, its spire still lost in the mist. Beyond the village on the west side lay an ancient cemetery, its lichen-covered gravestones showing black with damp. The slate roofs of the houses gleamed too with a skin of moisture, and the few roofs that were thatched lay sodden.

From the hill could be seen, running like a flat, colorless ribbon from east to west, the road to Dublin, seeming right now as far away as the biblical shining city. On the western horizon there appeared a shape, dimly moving, a wavering form that moved and paused, moved and paused. The milk lorry. On its first round of the day it stopped at each gate of the outlying farms to collect the aluminium cans of milk to be brought to the co-op dairy. Its arrival signaled the stirring of life in Buncloda.

From one of the somnolent cottages a woman emerged, head bent into the drizzle. She walked east, and her pace quickened as a second figure, with head scarf pulled tight, came out from one of the shop fronts. A third figure hurried from the mouth of a side road to join them. Moving quickly, more lithe, more energetic, the younger woman ran lightly to catch up to the other two. But no voices carried on the heavy, humid air.

The trio moved with more purpose now, their steps lighter, faces lifted to the hill that rose on the western side of the village. They walked for a short while on the main street before turning off on a side road. And the stillness was broken only once, as a young farmer herded his few cows through the gate of one of his small fields and across the road through yet another cow gate, the beasts lumbering towards the milking parlor, their breath heavy in the humid air. The young man tipped his cap but he was soon forgotten by the three women, who had begun to recite the Rosary aloud, their voices falling and rising in unison in the rhythm of the monotonous, soothing prayer.

Reaching the site, they followed a path beaten into the mud and matted grass. Now in single file, they slowed as they negotiated the steeper incline of the rising hill, here and there skirting the rocks and puddles that lay in their way.

Devoutly, they moved with heads now bent towards a small rock-lined grotto. Ensconced in this niche was a statue of the Virgin, her smooth hands pressed together, eyes upraised longingly towards heaven. The ground in front of the grotto was worn to a cementlike surface from the feet of the many previous pilgrims. Even the rain could not penetrate the hardened soil. The women moved laboriously towards that flat ground, approaching the grotto from the eastern side. Praying more loudly as they neared the statue, they lifted their eyes to the face of the Virgin.

The statue stood about five feet above their heads, its

remoteness emphasizing the distance between heaven and earth. Or perhaps the intercessionary function of the Virgin herself. It rested in a man-made niche built into the side of the hill. The statue's heavy square pedestal was set into a shelf of concrete. Its gold paint was flaking off, but no one seemed to notice. They merely remembered in their prayers the farmer, O'Rourke, and his wife, who so many years before had raised up the statue and its stone grotto in thanksgiving for the rescue of their farm.

As they finished their first Rosary, the three women glanced at each other, whispering as to which novena prayer they would say this day. As if looking for inspiration, they stared again at the statue, their eyes traveling over her benign face, her hands, the deep folds of her blue dress, which fell to the unshod feet.

Three voices, a single gasp. Stretched at the feet of the statue, resting on the ledge that held it, lay a huddled, awkward shape.

Although shrouded in some sort of gray material that blended with the gray of the concrete and the grayness of the dark morning, the shape was unmistakably that of a body, a human body, lying as still as the lifeless statue that stood above it—unknowing and unseeing.

─── *Chapter Two* ───

James Fleming, Dublin solicitor-at-law, deftly pulled his jade-green Citroen into the last space in the car park of the Old Stand Pub and Restaurant in the market town of Enniscorthy. He was lucky, for at lunchtime on a Friday by rights there should have been no spaces at all. During an Irish traditional music weekend, it was even more remarkable.

Checking his watch, he realized that his own reluctance had made him late. No last minute legal dramas had risen up to give him a legitimate excuse not to come, not to spend an ill-advised weekend with his brother Donald and their now mutual friend, Geraldine. Showing his ticket at the door, he wended his way through the large, darkened room, finding his table and nodding to his companions just as the musicians took the stage.

James was relieved that the seriousness of the audience and the intensity of the fiddle playing precluded any conversation. He relaxed slightly.

The music that poured from the fiddler's strings was both

lilting and haunting, evoking an historic melancholy that James, as a member of the self-conscious transitional generation that would drag Ireland into the twenty-first century, eschewed. And so he denied it every time that peculiarly Irish loneliness invaded his thoughts or his heart. He tried to keep his attention focused, and so wrenched it away from the mournful music and settled it on Geraldine, sitting across from him at the tiny wooden table. The press of the crowd made movement impossible, and now their knees were touching, albeit involuntarily. James, now that he could see her, hear her, yes, even touch her, knew for certain that his old feelings for Geraldine were far from dead. He averted his eyes as Donald reached—boastfully, James decided—defensively, he hoped—to cover Geraldine's hand with his own.

The long set finally drew to a rousing close with a complex series of reels that lifted the collective mood. The fiddler left the tiny platform to enthusiastic applause, and the audience left its seats for a mad dash to the bar. Donald, stouter and nearly as tall as his older, darker-haired brother, stretched his full length without knocking over the table.

"Drink?" he said vaguely to the air in front of him. Before Geraldine could answer, James nimbly stood up.

"Let me, let me. Gin and tonics all around?" James interrupted, not looking at Geraldine but remembering well her favorite drink.

"Great, James," Donald said, turning his fine, long face towards Geraldine in what James could only perceive as a dismissal.

James lingered as long as he possibly could at the bar, trying to figure out how he could extricate himself from this absurd situation. He wanted to retreat, to flee back to Dublin. Direct confrontation with Donald was out of the question. He was too aware of his own feelings for Geraldine, feelings that inspired a guilt that Donald might easily discern. Or hadn't he already? Why else his present behavior? Still in a quandary, James returned and neatly placed the three drinks on the table, making an immediate effort at hearty natural conversation.

"How's your residency going, then, Geraldine?" he said as he lifted his glass to them in the conventional gesture.

Geraldine arched her finely drawn, magnificently penciled eyebrows at James in a silent question. He dropped his eyes and studied instead the bloodred nail polish that he had known her to wear consistently. The brows, the nails, the matching lipstick all contributed to her overall style, one that reverberated with echoes of the cool, sophisticated Twenties.

"Grand, grand," she said finally. "Second year now. Much of my work is drying out alcoholics. Rich ones at that . . ." She laughed gaily. "Ironic, isn't it, as here I sit, swigging gin." She smiled at James, that familiar knowing look that implied so much. For a split second James actually forgot Donald was present.

Until Donald spoke, that is.

"She's doing well," he said proprietorially. He spoke with the authority of the fully qualified, successful doctor. "Very well, actually." Somehow this statement stalled the conversation.

"It's late," James said pointedly. "Maybe we should discuss tomorrow's plan . . ."

Donald flipped open the printed program and listed off the names of the various performers and their venues for the following day, Saturday.

James groaned.

"A problem?" Donald asked laconically.

"No, no. But I have to admit that one full day, that is . . . Look, tomorrow might be enough for me. I can't see myself sitting through Sunday as well . . ." Not in your company, anyway, he neglected to add.

Donald was nodding sagely. James wondered was this his customary wag of the head as he listened to his patients.

"James is right, Donald. One can have too much of a good thing. And I've had a great idea." Geraldine coolly flicked her ash into the ashtray and studied the cigarette tip. Readjusting her holder, she went on. "We're a hen's spit from Buncloda . . ."

Donald yawned theatrically.

"No, no, Donald. It's about a forty-five-minute drive from here. And I've a grá to see it. I can't tell you how many of my friends and people at the hospital have gone down or who know someone who's already been——"

"You do mean the place where there was this so-called apparition?" Donald was dismissive.

"Yes, I do." Geraldine looked appealingly at James, and although till now she'd restrained her habitual flirtatious manner, he saw it there behind her eyes, behind her smile. "James?" was all she said.

"Why the hell not," James answered gallantly.

"Have either of you heard the midday news on the radio?" Donald asked increduously.

"No," they answered simultaneously.

"Then you haven't heard that a man was found murdered at the foot of the statue there . . . very early this morning."

"Not at the grotto?" Geraldine cried in horror.

"Where the Virgin was said to have appeared?" James asked, for even he was aware of the event in Buncloda that had, off and on, filled the Irish papers for weeks.

"Apparently," Donald said, in poor taste.

James ignored him. "That's astonishing. Someone slain at the feet of a holy icon . . ." James was lost in thought.

"But it shouldn't change anything, should it? I'd still like to visit the scene of . . . well, you know. For Catholics like myself, it's almost like missing a chance to be part of a modern-day Knock."

"That's where some saints and Mary were supposedly seen at the little church in that village in Mayo?" snorted Donald. "I think, Ger, that was over a hundred years ago. Things have changed in Ireland——I hope!"

James rose to her defense. "Come on, Donald, I can see Geraldine's point. And I for one would like to go." He

7

smiled at Geraldine. "And the murder aspect of it intrigues me."

Geraldine looked at him uncertainly, and then bestowed on him a beaming smile.

Donald quickly spoke up. "Yes, well, a quick run over there might break up the day a bit."

"Great!" Geraldine whispered as the presenter called for a little bit of hush from the audience. And as the next group of musicians took the stage, she surreptitiously blew James a kiss.

Chapter Three

As James Fleming was taking his seat in the pub in Enniscorthy, Miss Mary Dowd was being helped from her chair in Conway's Pub in Buncloda. The small bare room at the back had been taken over and was now crowded with gardai, the police from the nearest police barracks at Gorey. The publican, Joe Conway, had just entered with a tray of steaming mugs of tea and five packets of cellophane-wrapped Mikado biscuits.

"Ah, sure, Mary, have a cuppa before you go."

"No, thanks, Joe. Too tired." Weariness was evident in the young woman's slow movements as the even younger garda, gentle and solicitous, helped her on with her raincoat. As she bent to reach for her handbag, she swooned and sat down heavily.

"Here, Mary, don't be stubborn now." Joe slid a mug from the tray across the wooden table. The policemen joined her as she sipped her tea. A bit of color in the shape of two burning red circles crept onto the whiteness of her face.

"Sorry to have kept you so long," Sergeant Molloy added as he sat down again at the table. "We needed your written statement, Miss Dowd, and we have found the sooner the better after a witness has observed something."

"I know. I'm fine, really I am. It's just that I got up at five and took no breakfast. And then the shock of it all. The tea is welcome." She looked at her watch. "Oh God, I hope they're managing up at the school!" She looked up, panic-stricken. "I'd forgotten all about the children."

"Not to worry. I spotted Father Donnelly on his way there earlier . . ."

"Jude?" Mary Dowd's eyes widened.

The older man winced at her use of the priest's first name.

"Indeed. When the news broke, one of my men went to the rectory to inform Father Donnelly and Father Maguire. Maguire's up at the grotto now. The men tell me there's a large crowd gathering there."

"Oh, God," Mary murmured. "This is terrible, isn't it?"

"I know, I know." The sergeant responded with a certain air of irony. "It's hard to say who is a bloody gawker at the scene, and who is a poor soul just come over to pray."

Mary stood up suddenly. "I'd like to go now."

"Here, one of the men could drive you home."

"No, thanks, I'll go straight to the school. If Jude is there, I'd like to . . . I should go and take over my class."

"I don't think it's wise, but suit yourself." The sergeant shrugged, and, as if she were already gone, he shouted to his junior to bring in Miss Garrotty.

The two women glanced at each other as they passed through the narrow door, a wordless exchange that Molloy could not read.

"Now, Miss, or is it Mrs. Garrotty?" Molloy said heartily as the older woman, in her late forties, settled herself in the small wooden chair. A sullenness was on her, Molloy observed.

"It's Miss all right," Garrotty said in a neutral tone.

"Goretti Garrotty, can you credit it that! My mother, God rest her soul, must have been weak in the head the day she named me that, but there it is. I've changed it to Rita, so call me that."

"All right, Rita. If you'd tell me in your own time what happened this morning?" He waited, pencil poised over his pad.

"I got up around five. The cockerel woke me, but I'd set my alarm anyway. I was to meet Mary as usual . . ."

"What does that mean, now?"

"Well, since . . . since we had our vision." Molloy noted her hesitation. "Since all this thing began in May," she resumed, "most mornings I meet Mary Dowd quite early to go up to the grotto to say the Rosary . . ."

"Why is that?"

Rita looked at him for some moments as if she were talking to a stupid child and would have to spell everything out in words of one syllable.

"Did you not speak with Mary just now?" she said at last.

"I'm speaking with you just now, Rita."

"Right." She shrugged, but continued. "Mary and I and Mr. Devane up the road had a spiritual experience at the grotto in May . . ." She said this quite proudly, almost smugly, and she raised her eyebrows as if asking him if he didn't already know all of this from the papers at least.

"Go on," Molloy said neutrally.

"Since then, these six weeks or so, Mary and I try to go to the grotto when it's least crowded. I've missed a day or two and so has Mary, but at least one or the other of us is there every day." She heaved a huge sigh, as if to say this might be a trial in her life.

"And Mr. Devane?"

"No, he doesn't come. At least with us. Perhaps he goes on his own. He's one who blends in with the crowd." She laughed. "And anyway, he has the cattle to look after, morning, noon, and night, or so it seems."

"Miss Dowd, I know, is a teacher, and Devane a farmer. What about yourself?" Molloy had finished his tea and now he hollered through the open door to the publican to bring more.

He watched Rita's face as it hardened unexpectedly.

"Yes?" he encouraged.

"You might have seen the shop on the main street? Garrotty's. My brothers run it, the three of them. They're suppliers of hardware, and agents for farm machinery. They do mechanical repairs as well. It was my grandfather's and father's before them. It started out as a blacksmith's. Bill, the eldest, still shoes horses and does the necessary when the vet isn't around."

"And you, you do?"

"I take care of them, the brothers."

"Yes?"

"The cooking, the cleaning, some of the book work. For myself, well, I lay out bodies. You know, at their houses—in the old way."

"Ah, I see."

"Mmm, there's no one around who would take it up after old Mrs. Cullen passed away. I laid her out, you see, about ten years ago now. There was no one to do it, and no family. So I did it, and I'm still doing it," she ended simply.

"It's a kindness and a service to the dead and their families, Rita." Molloy said this sincerely, and he watched her brighten considerably. "A vocation all its own," he added.

"Thank you, Sergeant. That's how I see it too."

"Please go on."

"Let me see, where was I? Right, Mary and I met on the road. It was terrible misty this morning. Very wet too. We met Mrs. Duggan on the road. She's been joining us now and then, since her baby died earlier this month. She's gone in on herself, you know, hardly talks, but she'll watch from her door and when she sees us she runs over and we all three

12

go on to the grotto. We say a Rosary usually. We don't really talk much to one another. It's too early for a chat, and then there's poor Mrs. Duggan. She says nought."

"And then what?"

"We go about our business. We're not friends, you see." She looked at Molloy sharply. "Not enemies either. We've been thrown together by circumstances. I know Mary Dowd no better now than I did in the spring, when the thing happened." She waved her hand in a rather desperate gesture.

"This 'thing' you speak of, Miss Garrotty . . . you mean your vision." Despite his professionalism, Molloy's voice trembled.

"Yes, that's it . . ." Miss Garrotty hesitated and looked for a long while at Molloy's kindly leathery face.

"Sergeant, did you ever have someone close to you die?"

"Yes, my mother, God rest her soul, passed away last year."

"I can tell from your voice that you loved her . . ."

Molloy nodded dumbly but eloquently.

"And if she came to you now, after death, in your sitting room, or on the road? How would you feel?"

Molloy shivered. He seemed to ponder for a while. "Much as I would love to see her again, I would want it to be in this life only. If I saw her now, I think, well, I think I'd be uneasy . . . aye, uneasy. Not afraid, I would hope."

"But you might be afraid: I think you know it."

He nodded again.

"Well, that's how it was for me with what happened in May. I did not seek this out, Sergeant." She lowered her voice. "It's a fearful thing. A burden to me . . ."

"Let me understand you clearly, Rita. It is all the publicity surrounding you and the others?"

"Oh, there's that." Rita was offhand. "I can hardly bear that, it's so annoying. No, what I mean is that it's a fearful burden to be chosen. I'm a simple woman, Sergeant. And

13

now I think . . ." Her voice trailed off and her face closed over. Her moment of trust and confidentiality had passed.

Molloy almost said go on, but from his years of talking with witnesses and suspects, he knew this was a woman not to be coerced. And perhaps he didn't want to hear any more of what she felt about her experience in May. He resumed his brusque manner.

"Back now to the matter at hand, Miss Garrotty. When you arrived at the grotto this morning with your companions, was there anything or anyone at all that you noticed? Any movement? Any other visitors?"

"I've gone over that in my mind while I was waiting for you to call me in. There wasn't a living soul about the place. From when I met up with Mary Dowd and then with Mrs. Duggan, I saw no one. No person, nor car nor van . . ."

"Milk lorry?"

"Wait now. No. Not even that. It was a heavy morning. The air was still and wet with the dew. I observed to Mary that the weather had kept the tourists away, and she agreed. She was even glad . . ."

"She said as much."

Rita took umbrage at this mild statement and he soothed her feelings.

"I only meant to convey that you are in agreement, that's all. I am not checking up on you, Miss Garrotty. Now just tell me which of you noticed the bundle first."

"I did. We'd been praying awhile, and I keep my eyes closed usually. As this day I did. We were nearing the end of the Rosary. Finished the last Sorrowful Mystery, you see. And I opened my eyes to glance at Mary—"

"Why, may I ask?"

"More to check if she was going to let it be at that, or did she seem to want to say more."

"More?"

"Sometimes she meditates or whatever. I don't like to leave her there on her own. While I was finishing with the

14

'Our Father,' my eye just rested on the shelf, and I saw the material of the bag, I guess. The thing struck me as being a bag. And I was startled. Since the . . . since May, I've seen all manner of things left in the grotto, on the ledge, on the statue itself, even in the trees and bushes. Letters, prayer cards, medals and beads, you've seen the like. But I'd never seen anything so large. The sky was lightening. I waited for Mary to finish and then I pointed it out to her. By standing on my toes I could reach it. I poked at it with my hands, and it was hard and big. I thought perhaps it was kindling, but why? As an offering for the poor? I didn't like it, though. It seemed weird."

"What then?"

"Surely you know all this," Rita said impatiently. "Haven't I just seen Raymond in the other room?"

"Please go on . . ." Molloy called again for the tea.

"Not for me, thanks all the same. Just let me finish, will you." Rita's manner was imperious now and she rushed her narrative.

"We all heard together the sound of Raymond's milk lorry. Mary, being younger, ran down the hill. She'd got the fright on her when I poked at the bag. And Mrs. Duggan, poor soul, was paralyzed. Raymond came right up and dragged it off the ledge. It was heavy all right. He had no suspicion of what it was, and he just pulled open the mouth of the bag and there it was . . ."

"It? Can you describe it?"

"I saw two feet, one still shod in a boot, I think, and I looked no more. The three of us took off for Mrs. Duggan's house, which is close by, and Ray stayed with the body. I called the police barracks, and I think I finally spoke to you?"

Molloy nodded. "Myself, indeed. Anything else?"

"Mary Dowd made a call, I think. And poor Mrs. Duggan made tea."

"Is there anything else you wish to add?"

15

"You know, it was as though the bag and the body fell out of the very heavens and landed there on the ledge. God help him, whoever it was."

"God had nothing to do with this, Miss Garrotty," Molloy said somberly as he left to prepare her statement for signature. "Most definitely, God had nothing to do with this."

Chapter Four

Father Donnelly watched Mary through the long, low window of the infant class at Our Lady of Mercy National School. Unobserved by the children around him, who were coloring preprinted pictures of a clown, he followed her with his eyes as she walked quickly and purposefully along the roadside and turned into the school. He noted that her usually white face was intense and drawn, pinched by the unseasonal cold breeze driving against her. Her black leather coat was belted tight as she walked with head down, preoccupied. As if somehow suddenly aware of his distant scrutiny, she turned and peered at the school. Although she could not see him through the glass, he felt for a moment uneasy, as if she had looked straight through and into his curious face. He shushed the children and left the room to greet Mary at the school door.

"Mary," he said as she hurried towards him, now breathless, "you needn't have come in today."

"Oh, Father, it's the last week of school. You know the summer holidays begin next Thursday."

17

"But they're fine. I've them coloring in a clown."

"Ah, God, they've done that one before." She paused as Jude blushed. "No, no harm. It's just I had little treats planned for all of this week. They're such dotes, so sweet and good. Especially good since May."

She laughed, deftly acknowledging that her status as teacher had risen immensely since she'd been known to have had a vision of the Virgin. Too young at four years of age to have any real sense of what had transpired in their town, they variously thought she had seen God Himself at the front of the church, or seen the statue in the grotto get off its stand and walk down the main street, or had a personal chat with Santa. A good and scrupulous teacher, she had kept the subject of her experience light and cheerful. Now she walked on towards her classroom, past the blue and white plaster statue of the Virgin in the hallway, but Jude suddenly blocked her way.

"Sorry, Mary."

She looked up at his face, caught by his stern tone. "What is it? I shouldn't delay any further."

"I don't want you to go in, Mary. I'm serious now. This is very different. The children . . ."

"What are you saying, Father?"

He was blunt. "I'd like you to stay away. There's a dead man involved, Mary. There'll be talk. And questions. It's too much for the wee ones. And a scandal for the school. As head of the board, I—"

Her stricken face stopped him cold. He watched as a deep red flush crept up into her cheeks, and he watched the stubborn set of her jaw.

Her voice didn't change. Soft and low as always, belying her expression. "Scandal? What scandal? A dead man was found . . ."

"In such circumstances!"

"That has nothing to do with me, Father."

"You found the body."

After a long pause she spoke. "I want to finish out the day at least." She bowed her head slightly; acquiescent, he was relieved to see, to his authority.

"Right, then," he said, mollified. "But if anyone approaches near to the school, I want you to leave as inconspicuously as possible."

"I hope that won't be the case, Jude," she said at last, laughing again and walking on, unbuttoning her coat and calling out to the children to be just so good, because if they all weren't then they couldn't even have a peek into the bag of sweets she'd brought in her teacher's bag.

Happy shouts of "Teacher, teacher!" rang out and brought a smile to Jude's face. But dubious—or rather, media smart—since the events of only eight weeks before, he remained in the teacher's lounge. As he'd feared, the first reporters from Wexford itself, the nearest big town, rang at the front door of the school. Jude watched silently from the front lobby as the principal teacher, an able, forceful woman, stout and square, faced them down in no uncertain terms. Reminding them where they were, she turned the reporters away, but it was enough for her and for Jude. She glanced at him questioningly.

"You see to it," he said neutrally, and taking his sheaf of letters still to be answered, he left the school.

Walking slowly, he deliberately took the short side road that ran behind the town, parallel to its main street, off which ran numerous other roads which branched like bronchial tubes fading into villi out into the deep countryside. It was also the road on which Mary lived. It led in its own roundabout way in the direction of the church. He took out his breviary and walked slowly, listening for footsteps and eyeing the front of Mary's house as he approached. No reporters, no one at all. Jude was relieved. Eventually he lost himself in his prayer, and was genuinely startled to hear Mary call his name from a few yards behind him.

"Spying on me, Father?" she joked.

"Not at all . . . more like preparing the way."

She observed his sudden intense expression and she looked away.

"I am not worthy, Mary . . ."

"Father, please, don't talk like that. It embarrasses me, more than I can say." She glanced away, but not before he saw tears welling up.

"Oh, Mary, I . . ." He wanted to say he never wanted to hurt her in any way, but always ill at ease with women when he was alone with them, he never knew how much or how little to say. He never realized that it didn't matter, since because he was a priest, they accepted him exactly as he was.

They stood awkwardly until Mary invited him in. Again he hesitated, wondering at the impropriety that might be perceived. Yet all the neighbors knew them, and Mary seemed at that moment so vulnerable. And he was afraid that the reporters would come bothering her.

"All right, yes, as I have two or three things to discuss with you. Perhaps this time would be appropriate."

They entered the small, neat cottage where Mary lived alone. While she prepared coffee in the kitchen in the back, he sat and admired the sitting room. He hadn't known Mary's parents. They'd died before he'd come as curate to the parish. Elderly parents who'd left her a fine, sound house on a good road. The insurance money had enabled her, he'd been told, to modernize, and now the interior was youthful, bright, and airy. Comfortable chairs and sofas, a large TV, CD player, computer—all were arranged in the spacious living cum dining room area. Framed art prints toned with the wall-to-wall carpet and furnishings in mauve and rose and pale pink. For contrast, a black Spanish shawl on the wall, and pottery bowls filled with flowering narcissi and tulips. Spotlessly clean, everything was planned for physical comfort and ease, for relaxation, for entertaining. The room was cold, however, and he stood to switch on the electric fire neatly built into the white open fireplace.

He sat again, realizing that he was surprised. It was not

the house he would have pictured where lived a young woman who'd seen an apparition of the Virgin. His thoughts stumbled and turned on themselves. What had he wanted to see? he wondered. Holy pictures with candles burning, statues in corners, little shrines, what?

He stood up as she entered with a tray.

"My mother would be horrified, Father," she said, laughing as she set the tray on the low teak coffee table.

"In her day you'd be in the dining room with the best lace cloth and a full tea. But I'm afraid it's store-bought biscuits and fresh coffee."

She threw herself in the chair opposite him and laid her head back on the chair's soft cushion, closing her eyes. "Oh, I'm tired, more than I realized." She leaned forward again. "I'm sorry, the coffee will give me a second wind, I hope." She poured out two mugs and passed the bowl of brown sugar to Jude.

"You know, Mary, these things I wanted to discuss will keep for later. I just wanted to explain . . . you are an innocent in all of this. I know that, of course. The board knows that. But we don't want reporters at the school . . ."

"I know that, Jude," she said very softly, her voice thrilling him unexpectedly. "I think I just wanted my life, the kids' lives, to be as it all was before. I won't go back to school except on their last day. I want to give them their gifts. Jude." She breathed his name, so softly.

Father Donnelly stood up. Mary didn't move.

"I should be going, Mary. You're tired, and I see, at least for now, there are no reporters outside. Long may it continue." He hesitated again. "Listen, Mary, we should have one of our . . . counseling sessions. I've obtained some books which I think we should look at together. You're tired now but I'd like you to ring me later, and we'll set up a time. All right?"

"Right, Jude, right." She yawned. "The door will lock after you." She said this wearily. "I'm going to forget this coffee and just try to get some sleep." She curled herself

21

childishly into the large soft chair, tucking her feet under her and pulling her cardigan close around her broad shoulders.

Jude wanted to throw a warm rug over her, but thinking better of it, he let himself out of the house. Glad of the now brilliant blue sky, he let the walk to the rectory clear his head, and his heart, of the image of himself taking care of Miss Mary Dowd.

Mary did try to rest, but the little caffeine she'd consumed prevented sleep. She stood up and moved restlessly around the pretty room, at last switching on some bland instrumental music which suited her taste. No love songs here, no songs of yearning.

She pulled back the curtains on the large front window, curtains that Jude had so thoughtfully drawn against prying eyes. The blazing sunlight and blue sky behind the houses opposite her own blinded her momentarily and she squinted. Mr. Callahan was in his garden opposite and saw her form moving at the window. He raised an old browned hand in silent greeting and she waved back. That one gesture made her sense of isolation complete.

The rest of the day stretched endlessly before her. Tired, restless, irritable, she turned from the window, unwilling to stand there now that Callahan had seen her, and acknowledged he'd seen her. If she stood there, would he say to himself, That Mary Dowd, she has little to do on this fine day. She knew that he would work in his front garden from now until darkness finally fell at eleven o'clock. Weeding, mulching, tying up, pulling down, in the endless round of chores of the interested gardener. Many times in recent years she'd wished he had his garden at the back. But no, he had laid it out at the front. So much the better to see you, my dear! And anyone else who might pass and pause and stop and chat. Worse than any reporter camped on her doorstep was Mr. Callahan in his garden endlessly, endlessly.

On a normal day, such as Mary would have had before the events of May, she would arrive home at three, her class having been dismissed to their mothers and grannies at one-thirty. She'd conscientiously tidy her classroom, lay out the materials for the following day. Snatch up tissues off the floor, sharpen the infants' stubby pencils. Physical work that took no thought at all. She'd neatly pile their copybooks to take home. She could have done such work in the classroom, but this task gave focus to her afternoon. Today, however, she was at home too early, too idle. No copybooks, no lesson planning. The thought struck her. She had nothing to prepare for the morning since she would not be going to work. Nothing for the next week either. A sense of terror filled her. She could think about tea, her evening meal, hours off. What to have? A frozen vegetable pie taken from the freezer and placed in the microwave? No task at all.

Mary walked with a sinking feeling through her pastel rooms to the rear door. Here too the sun blazed uncompromisingly on the flat grass lawn surrounded by the neat cinder-block wall on three sides. The coal bunker stood neatly beside the newer housing for her oil tank. Spartan, clean lines, she observed with momentary satisfaction. Her parents would have been dismayed to know their garden had been so transformed, but at their deaths Mary had remedied all, streamlined her life, eliminated the work and responsibility of a garden. Now, front and back, perfect squares of flat green lay like wall-to-wall carpet, like perfected Astro-Turf. A local boy ran his mower over it all at regular intervals, and that was that.

She brought her lawn chair out onto the grass in back, for here no prying eyes could watch her. She reclined, letting her face lean into the sun.

Healing heat, she thought, would burn itself into her bones. She longed for a sense of physical well-being. Although ostensibly healthy, in fact strong-boned and sinewed, she hadn't felt at ease in her body for months, perhaps years.

She must have dozed, for she recollected in a state of semiconsciousness that someone seemed to be talking to her, someone seated near her in the garden. As she came awake she thought perhaps it had been her mother, chatting to her as she had been wont to do, reading interesting bits out of the *Wexford Courier*. Or telling her of the most recent births, deaths, and marriages in the town. She'd barely listened then, and hadn't missed those chats since. She opened her eyes and studied the plain blank cinder-block wall in front of her. Yes, she'd done her best to make all of it her own, to put her own stamp on it. But she surely would have moved if her occupation had allowed it. A bigger town, a city even more desirable, where there was life and hope. She glanced at her watch although she had no need, knowing from the lay of the sun in the sky that it was around four o'clock. She dreaded going into the empty house, and so retrieved her portable radio and switched it on, lying back again in her chair. But as the local station broadcast its news update, she switched it off again. Unidentified man, cause of death at this time unknown.

Unidentified, unknown. They'd made her look at his face, and she had, through her closed lids, glancing through her eyelashes for a millisecond. Enough to know he was young, dead, and nothing to her.

What questions she might have had she stopped at the threshold of her consciousness. It was an old trick, an old habit. She could block anything from her waking mind. It was useful. It kept things straight, simple, clean. Like her house. Her garden.

The death had nothing to do with her. If it had something to do with her vision, she could not say, so she refused to travel down that road. The vision was hers, intact, internalized, protected in the womb that was her entire body. It rested whole in a deep, secure place. Not in her mind, as she knew some considered, and not in her soul, as others assumed. Somewhere deep inside where no one could reach it. Entrails. The word floated unbidden. Yes, hidden and secret, to be revealed only at her own choosing, her own discretion, her own choice.

And the less she said, the more people said for her. But

she'd learned that trick too, a long time ago. One newspaper article had claimed her silence was eloquent in itself. She smiled. She hadn't even kept the clippings. No scrapbook as her mother's sister in Galway was keeping for her, to show her at Christmas when she came down. Christmas seemed very far away. Perhaps it wouldn't even come to pass. The yearly trip to Galway. Family. She didn't need any family, especially not now.

Mary stood up suddenly. Feeling a bit peckish, she went inside at last and the sudden change to the dim interior blinded her momentarily. Her head swam and a light, high ringing sounded in her ears. She groped for a glass on the draining board and quickly drank a glass of water from the tap. "Swooning again," she said aloud; twice in one day. The heat, she concluded.

She looked at the plain kitchen clock. Nearly five. She wondered how to pass the hours before she went to bed. She wondered how, when she went to bed, she would get to sleep. She felt overcome with a familiar ennui when the doorbell suddenly rang unnaturally loud in the kitchen above the back door.

She didn't jump, but her gorge rose in her throat. She waited. It rang again. She crouched like an animal. She hugged the interior walls of her neat home, moving on all fours so as not to be seen through any window. She crept to the sitting room and carefully peered out the window from the level of the sill. Two young men were at the door— strangers—one with a camera slung over his shoulder. Reporters. She stretched full length on the floor and waited, breathing quietly. Ten minutes passed. Twenty. Thirty. The bell didn't sound again, and Mary Dowd fell into a deep sleep where she lay, exhausted and alone.

Chapter Five

It really was a beautiful afternoon, Father Donnelly observed as he walked. The dry weather had held, and the clear blue sky was deepening to the shade of azure so favored by devotional artists. Thick cumulous clouds drifted high above, with thin strands of cirrus moving from the west, and the luminescent beauty of the sky would lift the spirits of anyone who took the time to look up.

It was nearly four when he returned to the rectory, his spirit soothed by the clarity of the air and the light. As he let himself in at the side door that led directly to the kitchen, he was looking forward to his ritual cup of tea and biscuits at four o'clock. He relished the calm routine of his life and was glad he had not taken the coffee and biscuits at Mary Dowd's. He greeted Mrs. O'Leary, who, being tall, and thin, and brittle of bone and speech, was hardly a maternal figure, yet her presence in the house, and her service, periodically gave Jude that sense of well-being that being taken care of by another can inspire.

"Father Donnelly," she said crisply, "Father Maguire is waiting to see you."

Jude looked at her silently, an anxious look.

"Aye, he's in a dark mood, Father. Perhaps the tea will sweeten him. You take the tray there, Father, and I'll bring the extra pot of hot water."

Together they moved to the study, where the long windows had been thrown open. As they entered, Father Maguire, unfailingly polite in an old-fashioned manner, stood up, placed his book on the arm of the chair and sighed noticeably.

"Thank you, Mrs. O'Leary," he said as the woman left the room.

"It's a fine day, Father," Jude began feebly.

"Is it? Oh, yes, the weather is strangely fair. I'd prefer a dense fog myself. More in keeping with the events of this terrible black day . . ."

"I know the death, the body was—"

"Please, Father Donnelly . . ." Maguire put up a thin white hand.

"Have the reporters been here?" Jude said at last, pouring the tea and trying to ascertain what was on the older man's mind.

"Yes, indeed. And the phone has not stopped ringing." He inclined his head even then to indicate the ringing and the muffled voice of Mrs. O'Leary answering.

"Mrs. O'Leary has been fielding the calls. I gave her a short written statement to read to whomever rings. English radio and television have already picked up the story, and I expect the wire services to phone any minute now." His tone was weary as he spoke, now all too knowledgeably, about the voraciousness of the public's need to know. And the media's eagerness to feed it. He sat again in his favorite worn armchair.

"This is like a rerun of the events of May, only much worse, Jude. In May, the calls were speculative, there was even a sense of ridicule, or a suspicion that a hoax was being perpetrated, my God!" He whistled through his teeth in exasperation.

"Well, you know all that . . . But now, Jude, now there is a morbid curiosity as well. You should hear their questions! Was it a sacrificial rite? God defend us! Or was it a *ritual* murder? They ask unspeakable things. Can't you see the gutter press headlines? 'Man slain on Virgin's altar in small Irish town.'"

Jude shivered inadvertently. He had not looked beyond the immediate concern of this day, which to him had seemed to be Miss Mary Dowd.

Father Maguire looked at him suddenly. "Where were you all day?"

Jude reprised his actions from the moment Mary had phoned and he had hurriedly left the rectory. How he'd gone to the scene at the grotto, arriving minutes before the police. How he'd prayed over the body before it was finally moved. How he'd spoken with the pilgrims, as they arrived, and explained briefly the situation and why the area nearest the statue had been cordoned off with tape by the police.

As Maguire listened intently, Jude recounted how he'd gone to Conway's Pub, which was being used as the headquarters for the police investigation. How he'd gone on from there to the school, spoken to Mary Dowd, and relieved her of her duties for the sake of the school and herself.

Father Maguire was mollified by Jude's report of his long day, and the tension between the two men eased somewhat.

"You did well, Jude, under the awful circumstances."

Jude watched as the older priest's shoulders sagged ever so slightly. He poured him another cup of tea, and, thinking he was safe from continued reprimand, he relaxed. But he was premature.

Father Maguire replaced the cup in its saucer and took out his crumpled packet of cigarettes. Jude, who did not smoke, always thought it odd to see such a refined man of the cloth puffing on the worst brand of the untipped cigarettes, bits of ash floating about him like a small miasma.

"Jude, this cannot go on," the priest said at last. His deadly serious tone unnerved Jude, and he felt himself begin to tremble. It was a holdover from his childhood days at boarding school, and even now it would sometimes overtake him. And it inevitably happened, as he had noted over the years, when his conscience was not crystal clear.

"I'm not sure what you are referring to, Father." Jude put down his cup and began to tidy the table.

"Sit down, Father, and stop that bloody fussing. I think you know I regret my decision to let matters run their course since May. I mistakenly thought both the actions of the visionaries and the reactions of the people would peter out. But now this tragic death—"

Jude interrupted without thinking. "Father, the two events are not connected. The appearance of the Virgin in May at the grotto and this death today, well . . . one has nothing to do with the other."

"Oh, Jude, don't try to fool yourself, or me."

Jude blushed a deep red. "Pardon me, Father, and I don't like to contradict you, but I sincerely do not believe there is a connection."

"You honestly can say that a body of a dead man would not have been found this day lying at the feet of that plaster statue if Mary Dowd had not claimed to see visions and dream dreams!" Maguire's impatience was apparent, but Jude stood firm.

"That's exactly what I say. A man is dead, yes, God rest his soul. He could have been found on the road, in a field, in a doorway. It is merely circumstance he was found in the grotto."

"What you are saying is not reasonable, Jude. This death will bring notoriety to Buncloda, to the parish, possibly to the Church itself. It is the kind of notoriety that I feared in May. And it is the kind of disservice to the Church's image in Ireland, indeed in Europe or America, that I so wanted to avoid. And yet, here we are . . ." He sighed without anger, but with a great sadness.

"I reiterate what I said in May, Jude. This should have been handled by you *and* viewed by you as a private religious matter between the three seers—as you're so fond of calling them—and God."

The older man stubbed out his cigarette and coughed mightily.

But Jude took no note, anxious to press his point. "Father, they sought no publicity . . . if I might remind you."

"What about Mary Dowd?"

"No, Father Maguire. She came to me in strictest confidence that first night. She'd spent that entire day at the school, and betrayed nothing of her experience. And it was only after she spoke that Miss Garrotty timidly referred to it. Then there were her brothers. From them it spread via their shop and its customers—"

"All right, all right. I understand better than you, Jude, the power and speed of a good story in this unique country of ours."

"Yes, Father, that's it exactly. That's how it spread—through the people themselves. And it was not a 'story' at all. It was a vivid spiritual experience for those three poor souls . . ."

"Why poor souls, Jude?"

Jude hesitated. His slip of the tongue revealed to himself his own ambivalence about being a part and yet not a participant in the visionary experience of his three parishioners. He sighed as he stood up, walking to the window to close it against a stiff breeze that had blown up.

"Yes, I suppose I do think of them in that way. I have tried since May to imagine myself in their place, to walk in their shoes, as the saying goes. I do believe it would be a crushing burden to me to have been granted a vision of the Virgin Mother . . ."

"Why a burden, Jude?" Maguire's voice was encouraging,

his former anger dissipated as he observed the troubled younger priest.

"I imagine that guilt would be the reason I would see it that way."

"Guilt?"

"Yes, I would feel so unworthy, unworthy to receive so great a gift. And therefore I would feel guilty." He chose not to mention the powerful envy he felt towards the seers, and the guilt that caused him.

But Maguire took him at his word. "You would feel guilty for receiving a gift you had not earned, is that it?" he asked kindly.

"I think so."

"But you forget the true meaning of the word 'gift,' Jude. A gift is never earned. It is given at the giver's discretion, freely. Perhaps you are confusing gift with reward?"

"Oh, I take your point, Father, but it doesn't alter my sense of guilt. To be frank, I've been feeling weighed down as it is." He was beginning to feel weary.

"Perhaps you're feeling this way because you encouraged this situation to develop and continue here in the parish?"

Jude blushed with anger. "No, I'm sorry, Father. You seem to want me to express regret over this whole affair. I cannot. That would be deceitful. I believe this is the single greatest event to happen in this town since the dawn of time! And the single greatest thing that has ever happened to me. To be in almost daily contact with people who have seen the Virgin manifest Herself. It is beyond touching a relic or visiting a place sacred to the memory of Our Lord. It is a living and breathing thing, and it happened here right in what is now my very home."

"Jude! Your eagerness to transform Buncloda into the Knock of the south is, I believe, clouding your judgment. Have they—your seers—really seen a vision? That is the key question, Jude, which you constantly neglect to address. I've spoken to all three of them, remember?

31

"Miss Dowd, for example, thinks she saw the statue's hands move, perhaps in an opening of the hands, a showing of the palms. But well you know, Jude, that this is an image familiar to all of us from the Miraculous Medal. And if not from that, then from the hundreds of holy cards and statues and pictures in books that these people have seen since they were children!" Maguire was clearly exasperated.

"Because it was a familiar gesture does not invalidate it, Father," Jude said in rebuttal. "Surely the Virgin can choose to appear in any guise familiar to the seer. To make certain, perhaps, that she or he recognizes what he is seeing."

"Are we now speculating on the Blessed Mother's thought processes as She chooses what to do from a range of options? Listen to yourself, man! Or at least to me . . . I also spoke with Miss Garrotty. She saw something different. She said more than once that she saw a light."

"Yes, a light, a bright light that filled her with peace. I know their statements by heart, Father Maguire."

"All right, Jude, then where does she say she saw the Virgin?"

"She has indicated as much to me, Father . . ."

"And not to me, is that it?"

"Let me ask you, Father Maguire. Have you been receptive to what they have to say? Have you been approachable?"

"I have been objective, but I think that you see anything less than my complete acceptance of all of this as some kind of hostility. But I am attempting to assess these parishioners' experience. I have vows to honor here, Jude. They are my flock and I am their temporal shepherd."

"But they perceive you as judgmental."

"They do, or you do, Jude? Is that their word or yours? Is it not that you feel that I am being critical of you, judging you, in some way?"

Jude didn't answer. A small gong rang from the dining room off the hall.

"That's our evening meal, Jude," Maguire said, looking at

the clock on the mantel. His stern tone eased a little. "What are your plans after this terrible long day you've put in?"

"I thought I would lead some prayers at the grotto, for the dead man. I was planning to use the incense. To sanctify the area?" He looked hesitantly at Maguire.

"Yes, that'll be fine. I'll be on duty here all evening. I'll see you when you get back."

Jude followed his superior into the cavernous dining room, with bowed head and no appetite whatsoever.

BOOK OF THE DEAD

——— *Chapter Six* ———

James parked the Citroen on the grass verge of a narrow, winding country road. It was a stroke of luck that a car had pulled out of the space just in front of him. With crawling traffic still edging its way behind them, James, Geraldine, and Donald emerged from the car as cranky and hot as Irish people ever get when out and about on an Irish summer's day.

"Well that was a bloody long forty-five minutes!" Donald snapped.

"Donald, I never dreamed it would be so crowded. We should have remembered it was Saturday and people would be coming on their day off," Geraldine said sheepishly.

It had taken two hours to reach the far outskirts of the small village. Once they had realized their predicament, they were trapped in a snaking line on a road with no turning. Now, ahead of them, remained a thirty minutes' walk.

"Well, in for a penny, in for a pound," Geraldine said as she shrugged her broad shoulders eloquently.

"Not to worry. Let's just get on with it. Maybe we can get some late lunch . . ." James, as ever, was conscious of his meals, or lack thereof, and together they set off briskly.

As they neared the town itself they met with the first evidence that the events at the grotto in May had taken on real dimension for at least some people. Perched precariously by the side of the road, balanced between the tarmac of the road and the inevitable ditches and hedgerows that defined the Irish countryside, and surrounded by hundreds of parked cars, were a series of purpose-built portable stalls. Each was heavily bedecked, hung with rosary beads of every hue, with small plastic statues of the Virgin in blue and white, with small Celtic crosses, and prayer books, with medals and crosses and leaflets on the miraculous apparitions of other places and their times.

"Would you credit that!" Geraldine exclaimed as they examined the contents of one such stall. She held up a T-shirt, modeling it against her chest, words emblazoned in blue: I'VE SEEN THE LIGHT!

"Lord, how tasteless." Donald grimaced and glanced back at the steady stream of pedestrians following on behind.

"We'd better get on," James said uneasily, but Geraldine's enthusiasm was to the fore.

"God! What a pair of stuffed shirts. Aren't we very sophisticated . . . Hah, if you really were so sophisticated, then none of this would affect you."

"It's not that," James said as he negotiated a puddle and handed her across to Donald. "It's just not what I expected . . ."

"Which was?" She laughed in her teasing way, lightly, warmly.

"Something hushed, I guess. Something more reverent than all this . . ."

The threesome halted as a car approached from the wrong direction at a speed of a half mile an hour. The other pedestrians around them laughed and waved, indicating the driver should turn because his attempt was hopeless. As they waited for the car to pass, James glanced beyond the double line of parked cars, beyond the sheds and stalls, to the undulating fields that stretched to a horizon of low hills. He could see within his range of vision perhaps four active farms, centered by their low farmhouses and outbuildings. Black and white dappled Friesians were grazing lazily on a second growth of spring grass, content and oblivious to the milling throng along the road. James looked up and noted the cumulonimbus clouds massing in the west, the white of their bulging thickness showing magnificent against a clear blue sky. Only their dark blue-gray bottoms warned of the rain that was always a factor in the Irish climate.

As they walked in single-file fashion he caught snatches of the conversations of their fellow pilgrims. One older woman in sturdy walking shoes was murmuring the Rosary, he deduced from the beads in her hand. An older frail-looking man was slowly following behind, smiling at James as he echoed the prayers of the woman James supposed was his wife.

As the three of them strode on, they passed a young family, the woman laden with clear bags of sandwiches and a thermos. A toddler held onto her thin flowered skirt as her young husband balanced a younger child on his shoulders, who periodically called out a loud hello to the cows in the fields.

Eventually the three friends were parted, swept along in a thickening crowd. As James trudged on with no companion to share his thoughts aloud, he mused as to why the whole scene seemed somehow familiar. Scrolling through his memory, he recalled walking along in other crowds when he attended the football matches at Lansdowne Road. There had been the same sense of happy anticipation, the same bags of sandwiches in hand, umbrellas furled. His college scarf wound around his neck, he would meet up with his friends as they neared the gates, lining up, passing through, remarking always on the old-fashioned white-lettered signs above the narrow gates: BOYS read one, and the other, OAP. It was an American friend who had asked what OAP stood for: old age pensioner. How it amused her that these two social groups had their own entrances. It had been of such long standing, it hadn't even struck James. Apparently, girls were of a higher social order—Shirley had commented—since they went in at the wider general gate!

But it wasn't just football matches this spectacle recalled, he mused on. This crowd was mixed: the elderly and the babes in arms, married couples and women of every age all intermingling. Perhaps it was this coalescence that reminded him of the few Masses he'd attended in Dublin, when he had been a curious Protestant high school student wondering about the *mysterium magisterium* of the Church that dominated his country and his culture. Yes, those masses at Mass, as they used to say, had been a cross section of the city of Dublin, and it was the numbers that always impressed him—compared with his own small parish, where everyone knew everyone else for three generations.

Yes, the crowd and the crowd's mood was just like that of a large Mass breaking, pouring out onto the forecourt of one of the big Dublin churches: not noticeably reverent, but lively, full of chat, something comfortable in the mood, something even warm. But this was neither Mass nor a football match . . .

He glanced up, suddenly aware the crowd had fanned out and thinned. Donald and Geraldine waved to him and he ran to catch up.

"It's just up here," Geraldine said, "we take this turn in the road and the shrine will be just up on the right." She stopped suddenly, her eyes widening. "We're really here," she murmured.

They walked on in silence, following Geraldine as she slowed her pace. James looked up to his right, up the small rocky hill now denuded of every blade of grass it might have once borne. He saw, hidden in the shade of leafing trees, the white outline of an oval shrine, and massed below it on a man-made steppe was a group of people kneeling in prayer. Other people were scattered, in smaller groups or singly, around the shrine, some standing, some kneeling. He noted with interest the policemen standing discreetly near the grotto and throughout the crowd. Bits of yellow crime-scene tape littered the ground.

The narrow paved road where they stood was clear, and to their left rose another low hill. Surprisingly, to James, Geraldine climbed up this hill, finally pausing at a point just opposite the grotto. Here people stood in prayer, and others stared through binoculars.

"Is this it?" Donald hissed through clenched teeth.

Geraldine looked at him uncertainly.

"Look, we've spent literally hours getting here. We've done it now . . ." He looked around. "Listen, I spotted a row of portable toilets down the hill. I'm going to use the facilities!" he added sarcastically.

As he veered off, James noted his brother's hunched narrow shoulders and his hands deep in his pockets, a sure sign that Donald was more than a little fed up. He moved to Geraldine's side.

"Do you think they're here?" she whispered.

James glanced around. "Who?"

"The seers? Do you think they're here now?" She strained to see across the little valley. "One was an old farmer," she said when he expressed ignorance. "The other, I think, was an older woman. And a young woman, a young teacher, I think."

She made an impatient gesture, and as James began to speak, they were both loudly shushed by the people standing nearby.

"I'm . . . I'm going closer now." She looked up into James's eyes. "Coming?"

James in answer merely followed behind her as they descended the small hill and crossed the potholed and puddled road. As Geraldine began to walk up to the hill, weaving in between the kneeling and standing pilgrims, James fell behind, finally stopping.

A strange tension had gripped him. He glanced at the statue, ahead and above his level of vision, and as quickly glanced away. He looked instead at the people around him. Yet again anticipation filled him and his eyes were drawn to the statue. Again he glanced away. A swirl of emotions filled his mind, surprising him with their intensity. He wondered, however briefly, how he would feel if he too suddenly saw the statue move, how he would feel if suddenly the now pale sun flared into a fiery ball in the sky. He squeezed his eyes shut against the idea and saw instead on his inner eye a flood of images of saints and madonnas, of Christmas card stable scenes, of the infant Jesus in the arms of His mother. All images familiar from his life in Ireland, pictures he hadn't even realized were registered in his memory. He tried to recall the spartan Protestant church of his childhood, the modest altar, the simple stained glass, and saw instead the white statues against a dark gray church wall which represented the apparition at Knock in County Mayo.

Suddenly, a firm hand grasped his elbow and he expelled his breath along with the images.

"Jaysus!" he whispered hoarsely as he turned to see Donald.

"Wrong . . . I think it's Mary the Virgin we're supposed to be seeing," Donald drawled.

"Oh, shut up, Donald," James said crossly, surprising his brother.

"What's with you?"

In response James waved his hand, indicating the silent devout kneeling near them.

"Where's Ger, then?" Donald whispered. "We've wasted enough time on this whim . . ."

As he spoke, the two men so alike in general build, so different in personality, spotted Geraldine slowly wending her way back down the hill. Her face, at least to James, seemed different; he had a perception that the sharp lines of her jaw and features were somehow softened. Yes, a softness was there. Or rather a sadness, he decided, as she came up to them.

They walked down to the road, where they could converse in normal tones.

"Well?" James heard himself ask anxiously. Geraldine heard the eagerness in his voice and smiled at him intently, an expression he did not remember ever seeing when they had been—once upon a time—more than friends.

Chapter Seven

Geraldine had heard James's question as from a great distance. She shook her head, not in answer, but in an effort to clear it. As a physician, she tried to assess her state, for she thought perhaps she was in a state. But of what? A bit light-headed, perhaps a bit faint? She turned her gaze back towards the grotto, with a longing she could not fathom. Suddenly her knees buckled and she felt two pairs of hands reaching for her, grabbing her arms and waist, strong arms lowering her to the ground.

She could see a pinpoint of light that swiftly widened to a view of the grassy slope she was lying on. Through the buzzing in her ears she could hear voices.

". . . a faint . . ." cried James.

"I know it's a bloody faint," Donald snapped. "I'm a doctor, remember?"

"How could any of us forget?" James snarled.

Geraldine felt him pushing the hair from her eyes. She struggled to sit up, feeling that quick rush of embarrassment all people feel who've lost control of their bodies, if only for seconds.

"Don't sit up yet," James commanded.

"Leave her. She can sit if she feels able. What the hell is the matter, Ger?"

James watched her face, so white beneath the makeup, the eyes wide, the perfect mascara smudged with a glistening of tears. He saw the embarrassment beneath the sophisticated veneer she never let down, and he wanted to punch Donald's stupid angry mouth. But even more than that he wanted to know what powerful emotion had moved her, for that was what he sensed.

"I'm fine, I think," she said, her voice gaining strength.

"What's wrong, Ger?" James knelt by her side. "Did you see . . ." He watched as Ger's face closed over.

"What's wrong is that she had only coffee for breakfast about ten hours ago," Donald blurted angrily. "No nutrition, no lunch, not even a glass of friggin' water in this place."

His baleful stare had kept away the pilgrims who'd moved over near them, concern in their faces.

"Can you walk?" James asked. "There was a stand we passed farther back with mineral waters and packets of crisps. Come on."

Slowly, silently, they walked towards the kiosk, and buying what little was on offer, they walked to the car. The weather had changed, the clouds James had noted earlier now having spread over the sky in a pale gray bordering on the colorless. As the fine drizzle began to fall, they passed ever more pilgrims heading from where they'd just come, huddled in macks and scarves beneath umbrellas that seemed to sprout like extensions from their arms.

They fell damp and cross into James's comfortable car, and still he hadn't had an opportunity to ask Geraldine what she'd experienced. Nor was it forthcoming from her.

"Where now?" James asked, breaking the silence as he

maneuvered a difficult three-point turn and crawled along the narrow road, a now heavy rain having scattered the last of the pedestrians.

"Let's try the town," Donald said in a more conciliatory tone. "Perhaps a café or pub—we could get some 'pub grub' as they say in these places."

"What do you mean, these places? They say that in Dublin!" Geraldine's normal tone if not natural manner had returned.

"I've a better idea . . ." She waited.

"Yes," James said kindly.

"I'm pretty sure, no, I'm certain, that an old friend of mine is the curate in the parish around here. Let's find the rectory. If he is there, then we might have a lovely country tea."

She flung herself girlishly over the back of James's seat, but she whispered seductively in his ear, "And we know how much you enjoy your food, James."

James laughed as the mood lightened. They finally emerged from the narrow road, which veered in a fork and led to the single simple main street of Buncloda. As James cruised along, they peered across the rain-blackened pavement, spotting ever more travelers standing in sodden queues at the entrance to the two pubs and the fish-and-chip stand, sheltering in vain under folded newspapers or white handkerchiefs knotted at all four corners.

"Well, no chance of a quick meal there," Donald reluctantly agreed. "But I'm not too thrilled with this detour to a bloody rectory."

"You're close to blasphemy there, darling." Geraldine laughed, obviously recovered from her previous mood, or so it seemed. "Just think, if Jude is at home, he'll get to meet you two outstanding examples of Dublin Protestantism!"

"Jude?" Donald snapped. "Was his mother a big fan of Thomas Hardy?"

"Hardly Hardy." Geraldine laughed. "His mother prayed

to St. Jude because she'd lost hope of ever having a child. Along came a baby boy, and she named him Jude in gratitude."

"I don't get it," James murmured as he slowed the car at the end of the main street.

"St. Jude is the patron saint of hopeless cases, of lost causes. There, there it is . . ."

The spire of the Roman Catholic church rose beyond the roofs of the small village at the far side. James drove up to the church's forecourt, where they read through the window the small black and white sign standing in its wrought-iron frame: Our Lady of Mercy R.C. Church, and the times of the Masses on Sunday. The church was surrounded by a cobbled yard and a high wrought-iron fence. A few of the devout or curious were just emerging from the open wooden doors.

"Now what?" James asked. He reversed the car and pulled close along the curbing. "Hallo! Pardon me," he called through his now open window, the wind driving a warm rain into his face and eyes. "Can you tell me where the rectory is?"

Following the local man's pointing finger, they spotted the square, dark stone, turn-of-the-century building. They parked on the street and ran quickly to the front door, which was opened after the first ring by a slender, elderly woman dressed in a well-cut tweed skirt and thick, nobbly, gray sweater.

"Come in quickly, dears," she said without hesitation. "Out of this dreadful sea of water . . ."

They stepped into the square entrance enclosed on three sides by wooden panel walls and beveled glass windows. The three shook themselves like wet dogs and then stamped their feet on the woven mat.

"That's better now, dears," she said, looking at James admiringly.

James blushed at her scrutiny. "Let me introduce Dr. Keohane," he said quickly. "She's hoping to see, ah . . ."

"Father Donnelly?" Geraldine broke in. "I think he was curate here at one time, perhaps still is. Am I right?"

"*Doctor* Keohane?" The elderly lady was clearly impressed.

"Yes, indeed," Geraldine replied, smiling. "And this is Dr. Fleming, and his brother James, a solicitor."

"Glory be," she said, putting her hand to her throat. "Is there something wrong?"

Geraldine smiled kindly at the woman's alarm at their combined presence. "No, and we're not a committee. You see, I was a school friend of Jude's, and I thought since we were in town I'd look him up. Is he here?" she repeated.

"You've come to the right place, dear. You're so young to be a doctor." The woman smiled, waving them ahead of her. "This way, please . . ."

Rather than showing them in to one of the small reception rooms where parishioners came seeking counsel or permission to marry, she brought them farther into the dark old building past a wide, balustraded uncarpeted staircase to a comfortable sitting room of large dimensions. Its windows looked out on an expanse of rain-swept garden. Worn but comfortable sturdy sofas and chairs were awkwardly arranged around the room, which was dominated by a large fireplace and overmantel. The mirror, now clouded with age, reflected the room at a peculiar tilt and made their heads seem larger than their curiously foreshortened bodies.

Within seconds a youngish man of average height, slightly paunchy, with a soft white face already inclining to jowls, rushed into the room, glancing quickly at the two men before seeing Geraldine.

"Ger? Geraldine Keohane?" he said, recognizing her and moving at once across the room, his long black soutane swishing with his strong, quick movements. He took her two extended hands in his and gazed at her face. James was caught by the man's decisiveness, which seemed somehow at odds with his appearance.

"It is you. My God, what brings you to these parts at all?"

45

He threw back his head and suddenly roared laughing. "Need I ask? Need I ask!"

"You're right, of course, Jude. It wasn't to see you. I came to see the goin's-on here in this village of Buncloda."

Geraldine had fallen back easily into the speech of their mutual country childhood. "And to think it's yourself who's supervisin' all this excitement."

"Indeed, myself it is," he bantered back, then drawing breath, he said in a more cultivated tone, "Seriously, though, Ger . . ."

James winced at the familiar use of her name. In fact he was wincing at the whole scene, strangely irritated by this contradictory man. Black, curly, unruly hair framed a pallid but lively face. His square, hairless hands were strong and capable. He seemed to James a curious blend of the ethereal and the physical. An attractive, almost seductive charm would flash out from beneath his more clerical demeanor, and James was alternately repelled and drawn by his swift changing moods, the pace of his rapid speech.

"The parish priest, Father Maguire, a wonderful man, you'll have to meet him, he's in charge. I'm just his assistant," he added modestly.

"And an outstanding one, I have no doubt," Geraldine said. As she was supposed to, James observed to himself, and he watched the priest take the compliment with an unseemly acquiescence.

"Sorry, James." Geraldine turned as though he'd spoken. "Jude, Father Donnelly, these are my friends, James Fleming and his brother Donald. Donald is a doctor, like myself. Well, actually fully qualified and in practice now."

"Yes, yes, I'm happy to meet you," Jude said, shaking hands warmly, yet with a glint of curiosity in his cold blue eyes.

"It's marvelous to see Geraldine again after all these years. We were great pals in the old days, roaming the hills and fields of Drogheda. Please, sit, sit down, get comfortable, tell me your news." He turned to Geraldine.

"News, we've no news. It's you who must talk to me . . . to us . . . Tell me," suddenly her voice deepened, "what's it like? What's it really like?"

Donnelly waved his hand in an encompassing gesture. "Our recent events? What can I say but marvelous, marvelous!"

Even Geraldine was startled by his odd choice of words, or was it his manner?

"I imagine it is . . ." she said slowly, but Donnelly was already talking rapidly, his voice strong and carrying, the enthusiasm roiling beneath it like a powerful undertow almost, but not quite, pulling the listener in.

"This great event has done wonders for the parish. I can't begin to tell you . . . in the two months since it happened, our revenues have increased tenfold. Candles, donations for Masses. Attendance at Mass is up, standing room only. We've had to add additional Masses on Sunday. It's more work, mind you, but that's what I'm here for! I'm stretched almost to my limit with the new responsibilities this has brought. I cannot believe something like this could happen so early in my career . . ."

James glanced at Geraldine, but her face was unreadable. When the priest drew breath, she managed to insert a quick question.

"But Jude, have you seen it? Have *you* seen it!"

"It?"

"Have you seen the vision, or the statue moving, or heard her speak, a message, anything . . . at the grotto, at the shrine?" Her voice was anxious.

"Ah, well now . . ." Donnelly hesitated. "No, I haven't. I certainly haven't heard anything. You know, only some famous visions or appearances have had spoken messages. Knock, for example. That was purely a manifestation. Nothing was heard. No message . . ."

He stood up, pacing quickly. "But we don't need a message, really, you know . . ."

His three guests were puzzled by his statement, but he

47

quickly veered off as the door of the study was gently kicked open by Mrs. O'Leary bearing an enormous tray.

"Oh, thank God," Geraldine said heartily, jumping up from her seat.

For the next half hour the three friends made the most of the afternoon repast of scones, ham, butter, jam, thick wheaten brown bread, boiled eggs, and three pots of tea. Geraldine chatted easily about their trip to the Irish music festival at Enniscorthy and their impulsive visit to Buncloda. But she never revealed her own feelings, about which James was so intensely curious. James joined in out of courtesy, describing their long walk into the village of Buncloda, but Donald was painfully silent, restive in his movements and clearly anxious to be gone.

When Mrs. O'Leary returned, Geraldine jumped up to help her clear away, expressing her thanks.

"That was a feast from my childhood," she exclaimed.

"Ah, one look at ye at the door and I knew ye had not got any food in the town."

"Tell me, Mrs. O'Leary, have you seen anything at the grotto?" Donald asked suddenly.

She answered him with a great composure. "Yes, I thank God for that great privilege—"

"Indeed, it is. A privilege, I mean. One which I have not yet been granted . . ." Donnelly interrupted.

Mrs. O'Leary gazed at him with an impressive equanimity.

"Oh, tell us, please, Mrs. O'Leary!" Geraldine blurted, kneeling on the wing chair and gazing at Mrs. O'Leary; with unwonted admiration, James thought, yet he too wanted details.

But the priest had opened the door, and with what seemed to be a dismissive air, nodded his head.

"Another day, dear. Or I should say, Doctor," the woman said as she moved off with the tray.

"You know," Geraldine said as she lit one of the French Gauloises cigarettes she favored, its pungent aroma filling the room, its characteristic blue smoke drifting towards the fireplace.

"Yes . . . ?" Jude said.

"I've spoken to some of the patients at the hospital and a couple of the nurses. The ones who've been down here. And—most of them had seen *something*. But they were so vague . . ." She looked meaningfully at Jude, her tone almost impatient.

"I haven't seen anything, as I said. Not yet." Suddenly Jude's voice was almost intimate. "But it could happen at any time, Ger." He moved towards the window, waving his soft, smooth hands as if opening a curtain. "Today? Tonight? What I do feel is a sense of endless potential, a wonderful sense of immanence . . ."

James too now realized he had felt something of what Donnelly was describing, a sense of something ineffable even as he had stood at a distance from the grotto.

"A brooding presence?" he interjected.

Jude swung around abruptly. "No, to be honest, not that. But you . . . did you?" Anxiously he stared at James, a jealous look passing like a cloud across his face, a look of longing gone as quickly as it had come.

"I felt . . . a presence, I think." James hesitated as Donald snorted.

"Nonsense. Collective hysteria."

"Hardly, Donald, you didn't see one hysterical person," Geraldine snapped.

"Look, Ger. You've heard patients and nurses speak of their experiences. You've read of the so-called visions in the daily papers. You're a Catholic and grew up with stories of miracles and images and statues and pictures since you were in the cradle . . . For God's sake, you're predisposed to come here, see a statue, feel an atmosphere that's a little more restrained than that at a church fête—"

"Please," Jude said, holding up his pale hands.

"No, let me finish." Donald was standing now, obviously prepared to leave. "Geraldine was predisposed by her

49

background to want to see something, to perhaps even believe that she saw something . . . and James? Well, he defies explanation."

"Sorry, Donald, but I felt what I felt. There was an atmosphere at the grotto. Hard to define . . ."

"Perhaps it was the atmosphere one senses in certain churches. Surely you've been in churches where you feel there's a . . . lack of emptiness . . ." Geraldine stumbled in her effort to explain to Donald precisely that sense of presence that she had felt. She looked towards Jude for help.

"Friends, friends, what we have here is a wonderful manifestation of the holy power of God's mother. She has appeared before—at Lourdes, at Fatima—she has brought to those times and places messages of importance. Rejoice that she has deigned to come here to our humble place. Her message is one of humility, and I will do everything in my power to make that message famous, ah, promulgated . . ."

James watched Geraldine's face change ever so subtly, but Donald was at the door. She looked at Donald and back at Father Donnelly with an expression of disappointment.

"I'd like to continue this someday, Jude. I have more questions," she said, "but I guess we have to get going."

"I hate to seem churlish," James interrupted, "but *I* have a question."

"Yes," Donnelly said, obviously startled. He even seemed uneasy, James observed.

"You haven't mentioned the tragic news about the young man's death yesterday morning. As a solicitor—"

"And part-time sleuth," Geraldine added, grimacing. "Go on, admit it, James. He solves cases, Jude," she said. "Some of the time."

"That's very interesting," said a voice from the door.

Jude flushed a deep red as he introduced the parish priest, Father Maguire.

An older priest, tall, ascetic-looking, with fine features and clear, sad blue eyes, entered the room. He was thin to the point of gauntness and his sparse white hair was carefully combed across his high, domed head. As he gently shook hands with each of them, he inclined his head, smiling in a reserved kind of way. He held James's hand briefly, looking into his eyes.

"This has been a terrible tragedy, Mr. Fleming. For the poor young man. And for the Church here in Buncloda. I know it's early days yet, as they say, but my concern is that—"

"Yes, a terrible tragedy," Jude repeated. "But I have faith in the police. In fact, Sergeant Molloy wishes to talk with us, Father, so if you'll excuse us?"

And without further ado, Jude ushered the three of them from the rectory, with a fond farewell for Geraldine only.

Chapter Eight

"Ah, so it's back you are from the country, is it?" said James's tall, redheaded office manager, Maggie by name, as he entered his office early Monday morning.

"And glad I am too," James answered, laughing at her broad mimicking of a country accent.

"Ah rum tiddly ta, tiddly ta, tiddly ta," Maggie trilled in an *a cappella* rendition of one of the many refrains common to Irish songs.

"Well, how was it?" she said at last in her normal tone, as she stacked legal-sized reams of printed paper on James's already cluttered desk, his in-tray long since having been crushed by the weight of endless documents.

"The music was great, just a little too much of it on Saturday night, or should I say, Sunday morning!"

"Too much music or too much Guinness?" She laughed, tossing her rich auburn hair around her shoulders.

"Now, Maggie, you can never have too much Guinness!"

"But how was it, really?"

"I just said—"

"Not that, pilgrim, how was Buncloda?" She plopped uninvited in the leather chair in front of his massive mahogany desk.

"How the hell did you—"

"Language, James," she mockingly admonished. "Especially under the circumstances. How did I know? I know you'd be a fool to be within a stone's throw of Buncloda and not go. After all, detecting is your *raison d'être*. Unless you count train-spotting!"

James bristled as his hobby came under attack. "Right, I went, I saw, I came away."

"You saw!" Maggie leapt to her feet. "So did my ma, saw the statue move her head or her hands in a gesture or a blessing—she was so excited she could hardly tell it straight, but I never thought—"

"Whoa," James said, surprised at the usually cool Maggie's enthusiastic reaction. "Sorry, sorry . . . all I meant was that I did see the grotto. For Christ's sake, Maggie, I didn't have a vision . . ."

Maggie caught up her notepad. "I wouldn't joke about something like that, James." And with a flick of her fashionable suede platform heels she walked out of the office in disgust.

"Maggie, I would never—" But the slamming door cut him off.

Startled at her reaction, James sat for some minutes pondering on the power of the events at Buncloda. And his thoughts drifted inevitably to Geraldine. He'd been surprised by the intensity of her reaction too, on that strange Saturday afternoon. That brief swoon. The glistening tears.

Try as he would, he hadn't been able to get her to talk about it. A quick, brilliant smile, but no details. James suspected she'd experienced something powerful. He was glad for her. Donald's bitter skepticism was much harder to take than Geraldine's emotional response. Donald, what a pompous ass!

The documents Maggie had left behind lay in an uninviting pile before him. He looked out the window. The rain that had begun early on Sunday, when he left Enniscorthy, seemed to have decided to settle, and it had been raining ever since, the same steady wet rain—not mist, not torrents. Just a blanket of rain. Rain on Geraldine's skin. Drifting thoughts of Geraldine's smooth forearms with their sprinkling of freckles, the freckles she so much disliked, held his wandering thoughts, and in his mind an image formed of the curve of her neck as it was lost under her smooth black hair. The glint of gold at her ears and the hollow of her throat. He gave himself to memories of their brief but passionate affair of some years before, obscured for some long time by Sarah's presence.

"Ah, but Sarah isn't here," he said cynically to his pen top as he studied it. *And Geraldine is:* a small voice spoke in his brain.

"Oh, indeed, with Donald." He spoke aloud. He sat up abruptly in his swivel chair.

But try as he might, he couldn't forget their parting at the hotel. It had been late on Saturday night, and Donald was very drunk. As the three had walked wearily upstairs to their rooms, Donald had staggered on ahead. Without a glance he'd fallen through the door of his own room, leaving Geraldine and James alone for the first time. They were both tipsy, he knew that. He wondered, now, how much desire colored his recollections. But he did know she'd kissed him on the lips in that light, infinitely seductive way. Just a little pressure, just enough, he thought, as he imagined what might have happened if he'd kissed her back. Lingering touch, fingertips touching, remembering? What James remembered was Donald ten feet away, and it was he who had pulled away, abruptly, crossly.

Pushing these troubling thoughts from his mind, James finally pulled the first document off the pile and opened the folder. Within seconds he was immersed in his reading.

Some hours later, after a tasteless lunch of muesli eaten at his desk, the monotony was broken by Maggie's urgent buzz.

"Dr. Keohane on line two."

The result of Geraldine's call was an impulsive decision to return to Buncloda.

"I don't understand Father Maguire's haste, Geraldine," James commented as they neared the long, winding approach to the village. On the drive they had, for the most part, been rather silent, keeping, for some reason he could not fathom, to general trivialities. The strain of being alone with her, ever conscious of Donald's absence on this particular venture into the realm of Buncloda, was telling on James. He wondered if it affected her, but was in no position to ask. Now the actual reason and motive for the flying visit, their impulsive trip, was puzzling him. He'd been so caught with the notion of spending time alone with Geraldine, so fired by infectious excitement, and, truth be told, so bored with his current workload at the firm, that he'd agreed without asking this most basic of questions.

"Why do you say haste, James?"

"It seems, well, rather previous—to use an old expression. As though we're ahead of ourselves. The body was found Friday, as we know. And here we are, it's only Tuesday, and we're driving down in a headlong rush to offer aid!"

"The aid was solicited, James."

"You take my meaning. The police have hardly had time to draw breath. On the other hand, perhaps in this interim, they've discovered the truth . . ."

"That would be good, very good. Then it would be already over." Geraldine smiled with a sense of imagined relief.

"No, you missed my point. Why is Father Maguire in such a hurry? Why not give the police some time to do their job!"

"Look, James, I never thought of that. And I don't think I would have asked even if I had. Father Maguire phoned me lateish on Sunday night. He'd got my number from Jude. You met him, James! He's gentle, and so serious. He asked me a few questions about your former cases, and then he asked if I would, as a friend, ring you and ask you to lend a hand in the investigation." Geraldine's voice was a little tense, and James took note of her irritation.

"It's all right, Ger, I'm here, amn't I?" His voice was light.

Geraldine relaxed. "Sorry."

"What else did you learn?"

"Well, more by implication. I think he holds Jude responsible. Not for the murder, of course, but for the whole situation in the parish of Buncloda since May. Father Maguire seems to have kept his distance from it all, but Jude—"

"Embraced it wholeheartedly, yes?"

"Yes, he did. And why not?" Geraldine bristled.

"No, no. Go on, please." James held his tongue.

"I think Father Maguire feels that if the police don't solve this quickly, the scandal will escalate. And I think that Maguire will get increasingly angry with poor Jude. You've seen the papers, I assume?"

"Yes, the death was the lead item. But of course it would be. Murder in Ireland is still rare enough to merit headline status. We're not in New York here."

"Yes, but it wasn't merely the report of a murder, was it? Don't be coy with me, James. You saw how they stressed where the body was found, at the shrine. And that's here in Ireland where the media still use a modicum of taste and discretion. Imagine the papers abroad!"

"Ireland has got bad press abroad for years, Ger. The political strife here captures the world's attention, welcome or not."

"But James, don't you see? This isn't about Ireland." Geraldine's voice rose and surprised James with its intensity. "This is about the Catholic Church, not about Ireland. The Church is larger, wider, universal. Christ! It's a world-wide institution. That's what's getting the attention. The

Catholic Church. It just happens to be in Ireland this time. Attention of this nature ill serves the Church. Surely you can see that."

James was silent, because he had not seen the issue in this light. The murder's consequences grew in magnitude for him, and he began to feel uneasy.

"You know, Ger, maybe I'm not the right man for this job. A straight murder inquiry this is. The police have greater resources obviously than I. And . . ." He hesitated, and not merely because he was overtaking a tractor with an unbalanced load of hay.

"And?" she prodded.

"And, after all, I'm not a Catholic. I'm not sure I have the background to discern, to deduce, to probe."

"But that's just it. You don't have the background. That was Father Maguire's point when he discussed with me the idea of asking you to help. He felt you could be entirely objective, neutral even. That you might see what others might not just because of their predisposition as Catholics to view things as . . ."

"What? As superstitions?"

"No, no, as clouded in mystery." Geraldine suddenly laughed at the seeming contradiction of what she was saying to James.

James laughed with her. "Okay, okay. What you're saying is I'll see things as a dull unimaginative sort, impervious to mystical experience, hard-bitten and objective and without sensitivity to shades of meaning, to the power of myth, to the majesty of ritual, to the force of history."

He whistled through his teeth, and Geraldine looked over at him nervously until he too smiled.

"Something like that," she said hesitantly.

"In that case, you yourself will have to help me." He stressed the last word.

"Of course."

"Then perhaps you'll tell me, or rather describe to me, what happened the other day at the grotto."

"When at the grotto?"

James was surprised at the change in her tone. "Well, at the grotto when you went on alone. And then later when you swooned, as we laymen say." He tried humor but it failed.

"I'd rather not, James."

Stymied, James waited and tried again. "All right, I was not being entirely honest with you. Frankly, I am just curious. As a man. As a friend. I felt that something happened to you there . . . and . . ."

"And you're just plain nosy?"

"Why, yes, I am."

"I can't, I won't."

"For heaven's sake, why not?"

"Because it's too personal, too private right now."

James was suddenly struck. "If I can't coax you to tell me about these experiences, then how the hell will I get anyone to open up to me in Buncloda?"

"Perhaps, James, I feel vulnerable—telling you," she said shyly. "Or perhaps if I experienced something, then it was just for me to experience it. Mind you, I'm not saying I did," she added defensively.

"All right, let me get this straight. For future reference. You might have had some sort of spiritual experience at the grotto. You either cannot share it with me because I know you, or you posit that this experience was intended only for you and you feel you should not share it. Is this the common reaction? Surely religious experience is by its very nature meant to be shared, is a communal experience, is meant to serve a wider purpose than just the edification of one particular soul."

"'Just'! Did you say just one soul? Every day for centuries, individual souls have been touched, reached, uplifted. There is a long history of private spiritual experience . . ."

"How would I know that? Remember, I am the neutral Protestant." James smiled a little.

"I take your point, Mr. Lawyer . . . You trapped me with my own statements."

"Ah, Geraldine, that's not my intention. I'm teasing you a little. I do know of the famous visionary experiences that have been shared with the world. Lourdes. Fatima. And even, in recent years, I've read reports of the pilgrimages to Medjugorje, before the war in Bosnia. And surely that is the point of such visionary experience—such as I have heard of it. Of course I am assuming a lot for the sake of this argument."

"Assuming what?"

"I'm assuming that those experiences are legitimate—the visions which the seers eventually shared with the whole world."

"Well, Mary Dowd has done that. And so, I believe, she will share her experiences with you."

"And now will you?" James pressed his advantage.

Abruptly, she turned to face him. "You're doing it again! You are tricking me into revealing something I already said I don't want to reveal. And then you wonder why I don't trust you!"

"Oh, please, Ger, I apologize," James said, realizing his mistake too late.

He was deeply disturbed. He hadn't, more than anything, wanted to raise this issue of trust with Geraldine. They had shared a passionate past, but that ended when she saw she could not trust him when he was acting in the course of what he perceived as his duty. He had used her to solve a case, and with the conclusion of that case, their friendship, their romance, had ended. If Donald had not entered the picture, James doubted whether he would ever have seen her again. Yet here they were, brought together again at her request, or at least in her acknowledgment of another's need for his particular skills. The same skills that had parted them some years before. She had chosen to overlook the past hurts and remember only his ability. She had made a bigger leap than he had realized, and now he'd jeopardized their fragile new relationship, even before they had stepped out of the car.

He sighed unconsciously, but she noticed it.

"Yes?" she asked.

"I apologize again, Geraldine. From the bottom of my heart. I want to help Maguire. And Jude too, but only on your account. You want to help Jude on his account. We need to be allies at least for a few days. Shall we start again?"

"Yes, but there is one thing . . ."

"Anything, just say it."

"Why do you say you'll help Jude through me? Surely he merits it on his own account?"

James tread carefully over this one. This was not the time, nor might it ever be, to tell her that he had not taken to Jude, that he suspected Jude was self-serving, that he'd spotted Jude for a careerist, albeit on an unusual career path, an ambitious man who wanted to make his name. But he said none of this.

"All I meant, Ger, was that he is your childhood friend, companion of your girlhood days in the country, sharer in precious memories. You are responding to him in memory of those days. I don't know Jude, but I know you. What I am doing, if I can indeed help him and Father Maguire, is with the memory of what you and I have shared—happy memories for me at least."

James's voice had grown thick with emotion, and the air in the car was heavy with a sweet nostalgia and an intensity of feeling. Both were intensely uncomfortable.

Geraldine straightened in her seat as James cleared his throat.

"Buncloda is just ahead," she said lightly, as though he'd not spoken.

Thank God, James said, but only to himself.

James visited eight so-called bed-and-breakfast establishments before he got lucky. Two had been hostelries for years, as was obvious from their signs and expertise, but the others had been, until recently, private homes now thrown open to house, for a small price, the many pilgrims descending daily on Buncloda. Tidy handwritten signs appeared in the front windows of the many bungalows, old and new, scattered around the village and its environs. It was in the small neat hallway of one of these newer houses that James now stood, being inspected by his erstwhile landlady.

Mrs. Kehoe eyed his hand-sewn alligator shoes, the battered Louis Vuitton bag he'd had for years, the cut of his suit, the fine cut of his hair, and finally the absence of a wedding band. Shrewdly she asked why he'd come to Buncloda, but in a most indirect manner.

"If you're staying, you're in luck. A poor old soul just left with her bags and her aluminium walker. Stayed almost a full week and was a joy to have in the house. I took her up to the shrine," here she blessed herself, "every day in the car. A most devout old lady and full of good stories. She passed a good few pleasant evenings here at the fire. I light a fire in the sitting room," she added gratuitously. "Some of the guests sit in with me and the da. Their stories, now, they're very important."

She was in the Irish tradition, observed James to himself. Hospitality offered in return for storytelling.

He met the question in her eyes.

"Firstly, I don't know how long I'll be staying. I may be here for a few days, or up and down to Dublin. How say you to that?"

"That won't do," she said simply. "Even paying me up front, as they like to say on the telly. In conscience I could not hold a room empty while there are so many unhoused."

"All right, let's say for now I'll stay three days and nights. I'll be in and out—"

"So you won't be needing the sitting room?"

"Let me say I don't know yet." She frowned at this. And after his debacle with Geraldine, he knew he needed allies wherever he could find them.

"Listen, Mrs. . . . Kehoe, is it?"

She nodded.

61

"I am a solicitor, working privately on a case. I can't of course confide in you the nature of my work, you understand." His voice was low and confidential.

She nodded, beaming now.

"But I know I can trust you. And of course while I am here I would like to visit the shrine."

"But of course." She smiled knowingly. Here was surely a Dubliner, too rich for his own good, and too proud to admit—yet—that he'd come like any other pilgrim to kneel at the feet of the Virgin. She would collude in his small story, for it would make a bigger story in the retelling, when the opportunity arose.

"This way, then, Mr. Fleming."

"James, please."

"James it is."

She escorted him up the narrow pink carpeted stairs and opened the first of four doors off the narrow landing. This revealed a small bathroom and toilet all done in pale pink. She closed the door again, shyly.

"My husband rises early for work and is out of the house at seven, so he'll not be in your way, James." She used his name with authority now.

She opened the next door, revealing a small square room, decorated with a bright satin-finish wallpaper set out in pink stripes alternating with brilliant pink cabbage roses. The bed too had a pink comforter. James was nearly blinded as the afternoon sun streamed in, lending brilliance to the pink, but no warmth. She handed him a single key.

"Breakfast is at eight, but I'll serve you until ten."

He nodded. "And the phone?"

She indicated over the banister the phone table in the tiny hall below. "There's a glass jar there beside it. You're on your honor to put in the cost of your calls, especially to Dublin." She lifted an eyebrow, a gesture that hardened her round face, framed by short, coarse, salt and pepper hair neatly styled.

She mentioned in passing down the stairs her ludicrously

low rates and told him to be at his ease. As he shut the door she called out one final instruction.

"And James?"

"Yes?"

"No visitors in the room."

"No what?" he fairly squawked, thinking illogically of Geraldine.

"No female visitors, James. Cheerio for now."

Feeling like a chided adolescent discovered arranging a "dirty weekend" as they used to call it, he closed the door rather too loudly and surveyed the room.

It must have been a girl's room, he concluded as he hung his clothes in the narrow wardrobe. Perhaps a daughter now moved away or married. Only this could explain the overwhelming abundance of pink. He set out his few toilet articles on the tiny washbasin in one corner and then sat heavily on the only chair in the room. He looked across the single bed, straight into a mirror fixed in an indentation in the room's wall. And he laughed out loud at the sight of himself in this bower of roses. Despite all of his travels, this particular accommodation was unique in his experience.

He felt cold and weary. A quick afternoon nap might be in order, he decided, before he met with Geraldine at the rectory at eight. He stood up and took off his suit jacket, hanging it carefully in the wardrobe. He drew the drapes across the double-width curtained windows and was amazed again to see more cabbage roses bursting out at him. Glancing away from the crucifix hung prominently over the bed, he pulled back the comforter, lay down, and pulled it up again over his long body. As he waited, in vain as he thought, for sleep to come, his eyes traveled over the room.

He spotted a row of religious statuettes lining the wooden ledge above the curtain rail, statues now revealed by his closing the drapes. From this high vantage point the Sacred Heart glanced benignly into space, flanked by what James dimly recalled to be the Infant of Prague in satin robes, and two different versions of Mary, one as Madonna, one as

Virgin in blue. These cheap plastic replications, the simple cross over his bed, and a framed picture of the Sacred Heart which balanced the room on its fourth wall, ensured, he observed, that no one would even think an impure thought in this particular room. Let alone have a "female visitor"!

And despite his uneasiness at being guarded in his sleep by this echelon of saints, he quickly fell into a slumber a baby would have envied.

Refreshed by his rest, a change into more casual clothes, and a welcome cup of tea from the increasingly friendly Mrs. Kehoe, James set off on foot for the grotto, which was on the other side of the low hill that separated the group of bungalows from the side road where stood the shrine.

Even as he approached, James noticed the significant increase in the crowds of visitors compared to the previous weekend. The death of the nameless man, he assumed, had drawn hoardes of the curious if not the devout.

Luckily, for James that is, he'd arrived at the hill in time to see a cluster of uniformed gardai taking down the remaining tape that marked off the murder scene for the forensic team. Pushing through the dense crowd of people, some kneeling oblivious to their surroundings and the now damp ground, he got close enough to assess the policemen and their activities. Concluding rightly that the older, slightly grizzled-looking man with a demeanor of authority was in charge, he approached Sergeant Molloy.

Having found often enough in the past that honesty with the police was inevitably the best policy, he shoved himself forward until he was at Molloy's elbow.

He introduced himself as a solictor from Dublin and saw the instant hostility in Molloy's eyes.

"I'm acting in the interests of the Church, I assure you, and I have just a few questions. If you have a moment?"

Molloy murmured final instructions to the young garda nearest him and then, nodding his head, moved slowly through the ever thickening crowd. James followed. When they reached a small clearing, he spoke softly.

"How is it you are involved?" he asked neutrally.

"In a private capacity, of course." James smiled pleasantly. "In an advisory capacity really. My client would like to employ what the Yanks call 'damage control.'"

Molloy eyed him doubtfully. "Your client . . ." he mused.

"I assure you my client's concern is the welfare of the Church as a whole, as well as individually."

James had given Molloy enough for him to go on. "I see," he said at last. "What do you need from me, then?" he said fairly cordially. "Whatever I tell you, of course, is a matter of record. The inquest was held earlier today and the verdict was held open."

"I see. Well, then, perhaps you can tell me how far the investigation has progressed."

"The key fact is that the medical examiner has determined, in his preliminary report, that the poor lad was struck a fierce blow to the jaw followed by another to the side of the head. He died as a result of massive bleeding in the brain caused by the blows. There is some suspicion he had what they used to call a 'glass jaw.' For a strong young brawny lad in good health, it seemed the bones of the jaw and head were weaker than most."

"Are you saying he died of blows another man might have sustained and survived?"

Molloy shrugged eloquently.

"Anything else, about the injuries, about the body, that would be of interest?" James was reacting to Molloy's calm and diffident manner with studied diffidence of his own.

"Let me see now. The blood, it showed high levels of alcohol. The hands and arms showed the signs typical of a fistfight . . ."

"Rather than a struggle?"

"Indeed, that distinction is being made. Oh, yes, and the poor lad's money was still on him."

"So it's looking like a fight, then, maybe a drunken brawl?" James mused aloud.

Molloy nodded. "The layman could see it that way."

"A drunken brawl at the foot of the statue of the Blessed Mother?" James glanced back at the grotto, having struck the right note of wonderment, of dismay at the blasphemy such an act implied.

"That, thank God, wasn't the case," Molloy said simply.

"No? How is that?"

"The medical man tells me that the poor lad's blood had pooled in his body."

"Ah, lividity," James said with some knowledge and a little authority.

"Indeed. He can say conclusively the lad died elsewhere and the body was moved after death. Was at rest somewhere, and then moved, unfortunately, to this holy ground."

"They said in the papers that he was clutching something. A crucifix?" James asked.

"So they reported. But in fact it was a rosary, intertwined on the fingers of one hand."

"But why?" James said uneasily.

"I think . . . I think that the beads were placed there when the body was . . . But why? Only God knows that right now."

The two men turned as one and gazed up the hill to the shrine. The faithful, for it seemed indeed that's what they were, had crowded in as close as possible to the base of the statue, and the majority were now kneeling. A nun dressed in a modern habit was standing before them, fingering a rosary, and the monotonous rhythm of the third century prayer began to be carried on the air to James's ears, strangely soothing to him. Whether it was the repetition, or the simplicity of the murmured words, or the earnestness of the voices—he could not decide which—it was to him there and then as moving as a mother's lullaby at this dropping time of the day.

Chapter Nine

"I must say I was surprised," James said, settling back in his chair.

The remains of a fine meal of roast beef and roast potatoes had been cleared away by Mrs. O'Leary, and now Father Maguire was pouring Geraldine another glass from a very good bottle of port.

"Surprised?" Jude said, nervous as a cat, as he had been throughout the meal, warily eyeing the morosely silent Maguire.

"When I first arrived at the grotto today, I really did think the increased crowds were a result of morbid curiosity. But during the time that I spent there, I realized that the crowd was not only increasing in number, but increasingly devout. I admit I am puzzled."

"Oh, my God, yes." Maguire spoke quite suddenly. "The numbers are up since the death, and I agree there is a different mood to the crowd. As I moved among the people myself and later, when I spoke to people here in the church itself, I noted a more than subtle change coming over them. Somehow the people have twisted this tragic event to suit their own needs . . ."

"Father Maguire, I protest." Jude blushed deeply at his own audacity. "I too spoke with the faithful today. They are viewing the death of this young man as some kind of sign . . ."

"Precisely. As I said, Jude, they are doing so merely to serve their own ends. They wish to turn everything into something mystical, something unreal. But there's nothing more real than death, my boy, because there is nothing more final." Maguire glanced pointedly at James with a look James could not read.

Jude intervened. "Yes, there is a groundswell of emotion, and although I can't agree with you, I admit I can't define it. Yet."

"It's wishful thinking," Maguire said, drinking slowly from his glass. "The people are overly eager for drama. Any kind, Jude, any kind. First there was their embracing of the so-called apparition in May. And now this. This death, we can be sure, was the waste of a young life. Yet the people want to tie them together. Drama, all drama, I tell you! The people are craving excitement, bah!"

"No, Father, again I ask you to see this differently. They don't want drama or excitement. They want signs, even miracles!" Jude cried.

"Assurances are what they want. And they can't have them. I'm sorry, Jude, Dr. Keohane, James." He looked at each in turn. "This topic makes me more heated than I would normally be."

"I'm interested that you speak of miracles," James interjected in a neutral voice.

"Yes?" Jude and Maguire answered simultaneously.

"It occurred to me after I spoke with Sergeant Molloy that perhaps, assuming the young man died as the result of a brawl—accidentally, in other words—that the man or men involved took grave fright. Perhaps, given recent events here in Buncloda," James chose his words carefully, "these men, young men I think we can safely assume, brought the body to the grotto in the hopes of a miracle occurring."

The others shifted uneasily in their chairs.

"I could see that," Geraldine added with a sudden enthusiasm. "They fall out of a pub somewhere, perhaps locally. Have some silly drunken male type of argument, the lad gets hit and dies on them. They're overcome with fear and horror at what's happened and bring him to the statue. Perhaps he'll revive. And if not, at least he's in a holy place."

"Aye," Maguire answered sardonically. "Instead of getting help, instead of finding a doctor—such as yourself, or driving the poor lad to the hospital over in Wexford town? Is that it? Instead of being men, facing the consequences of their actions, they are instead just sniveling cowards hiding behind the skirts of the Blessed Mother herself. You see, you have illustrated my point admirably, if unintentionally. If our parishioners had not claimed to see the Virgin, if the people had not taken this up in an unthinking frenzy of devotion and emotion, those men would not have even given a thought to Buncloda, or the small private shrine here on a side road in the middle of nowhere. You choose to see their actions, if such they were, as some sort of twisted form of faith in miracles, of a childlike trust in the power of our Blessed Mother. What power! I ask you. Power to raise the dead? I think not. The shrine and its notoriety merely gave them an easy way out. Perhaps leaving the body here eased their consciences, if they have any. That shows great devotion, doesn't it, Doctor?"

His tone was such that Geraldine knew he expected no answer. Maguire finished his wine. "If you'll excuse me, I am very tired. Mr. Fleming, James, I appreciate your coming here to help us, and I wish you Godspeed in getting to the bottom of this crime. Molloy's a good man. When he phoned," Maguire added as he stood in the open doorway, a knowing sort of look on his expressive, thin face, "he said you seemed a fine young lad. Oh, and that any help was welcome. The Church's welfare is his concern as well as ours." He smiled wanly.

Amused at Molloy's description of him as a young man, James stood out of respect for the priest and bid him a good night as he left the room.

Jude heaved a sigh of relief and poured himself his first glass of port.

"I can talk more freely now, you understand?" He looked first at Geraldine and then at James, who had sat again at the table. He noted that Jude's diffidence had been replaced by a sudden energy.

He continued, "I do believe Father Maguire has missed the point. I can't persuade him otherwise. But that is a function of his age, don't you think?" Again he didn't wait for an answer, which in any case was not forthcoming, from James at least.

"His age and the limitations of working in a rural setting such as this—"

"That hardly seems fair, Jude," Geraldine interjected. "You and I both grew up in a place much like this. And obviously you've been living right here a few years now."

"Of course, of course, Geraldine. But look at you. Hardly the country girl now, are you?" His laugh was unpleasant to James's ears. "Well, the same applies to myself. You can be from a place but not of it, surely?" Jude was directing most of his conversation towards Geraldine, and James wondered at this. He was, in fact, annoyed.

"Perhaps Father Maguire is merely taking a well-founded philosophically or theologically supported approach?" James snapped.

"Perhaps." Jude was pointedly noncommittal.

"Perhaps," James continued, "he means what he says. He seems to favor a muscular, active Church, in the here and now. Perhaps he posits that Church against what he sees as a transcendental Church such as is represented by the visionaries here in Buncloda . . . ."

"And elsewhere! There is room in Holy Mother Church for both, you know." Jude was obstreperous. "The Church, if you do not know—how could you, being Protestant?—the Church represents the mystical union of the world with Christ."

James had bristled at Jude's presumptions, but held his tongue.

Jude went on unheeding. "I think that is just what we need. A strengthening of the mystical aspect of our faith. Divine manifestations serve just that purpose. Perhaps that *is* their purpose."

James looked archly at Geraldine, as if to remind her of her unwillingness to share her own experience. That is, if she'd had one.

"So you believe that an individual who has experienced such a manifestation should share it with the community at large?" James prodded Jude.

"Most definitely. I cannot understand why anyone so privileged would not crow it from the rooftops. Fortunately, Mary Dowd had no such hesitation, after we first talked."

"Perhaps not everyone can talk so freely about something that has touched them deeply," Geraldine added softly. But Jude was not listening.

"James, what is your plan?" Jude poured another glass of port and handed the bottle around.

"Well, what you were just saying now was very much to the point. I want to interview all three of the people involved . . ."

"I see. Well, I imagine you could interview Miss Dowd and Miss Garrotty. But the third woman who found the body, young Mrs. Duggan, is very depressed. She very recently lost her baby in a cot death. Discovering the body at the grotto with the other two women has deeply upset her. She told me when I rang her that she's decided to go to her sister in Birmingham for a rest. Sergeant Molloy has given her the go-ahead. You know, Fleming, Mrs. Duggan couldn't tell you any more than she already told the police. Nor for that matter can the others . . ."

"Well, I work in my own mysterious way," James said sarcastically, not liking to be told his business.

Geraldine turned to look at him, and he moderated his tone. "I need to get a feeling for the visionaries, and for this town, if I am to form any insights. If this young man's death is connected to Buncloda, I need to learn what I can from the inside, while, I might add, the police are doing everything to be expected from the procedural point of view. You know, Jude, they're very good at what they do."

"And I have no doubt you are very good at what you do," Jude said, placating James. "I shall arrange for you to meet Mary Dowd as soon as possible."

"And the others?"

"I'll try."

When Jude left to make his phone calls, Geraldine stood up restlessly.

"Will you see them tonight?" she asked finally, lighting one of her French Gauloises cigarettes and inhaling deeply.

"If possible."

"I'm not sure why I've come," she said, turning to him.

"Well, I imagine you wanted to smooth the path with Jude. After all, he doesn't know me—except through you. Or perhaps you wanted to visit the shrine?"

Geraldine answered simply, not rising to James's teasing and he felt embarrassed. "No, I didn't go up there today. I thought I might, if Jude was going. But Jude was occupied all afternoon. His workload has increased with the endless callers, with the visitors and letters. And now further calls from the media. A small group of women here in the town have begun a little 'cottage industry.' They put out a newsletter about the vision in May and about the parish of Buncloda. He meets with them fairly often, or so he said, and he met with them today."

"Maguire must be thrilled with that."

"Well, Jude didn't say, but they certainly made it clear

tonight at dinner how diametrically opposed they are. I must admit I was very uncomfortable."

"Are you staying here as planned?" James asked, noting her uneasiness.

"Oh, yes. That's arranged. They have buckets of room in this old barn." She wrinkled her nose. "It's seemly, as they say. In other words I can stay because Mrs. Thing, the housekeeper, you know, lives in and sleeps in. My staying will cause no scandal."

"If anyone even knew you were staying here in the rectory!"

"Oh, please, James! In a small town like this?" She smiled.

"You're right, of course," James said, relieved that she had smiled at last.

"I can't in all conscience ask you to join me in these interviews, Ger, at least not in these preliminary ones. But you know I'll be relying on you for your insights."

"It's all right, James. It's just that I'm at loose ends, I guess." She paced restlessly again, stopping to leaf through some religious magazines on a side table.

"Believe me, I'd much rather be spending the evening with you at some cozy little local pub." He'd said it before he even realized it.

Geraldine's head snapped up, but she didn't speak.

Fortunately, the sudden awkward silence was broken by Jude's return.

"Right, James. I've spoken to Miss Dowd. She's at home, as I expected, but she may be going over to the shrine later. If you'll excuse us, Geraldine, I think if Fleming wishes to see her tonight, we should leave now."

As they drove in silence the short two miles from the rectory to Mary Dowd's neat bungalow, James was filled with anticipation, his mind full of myriad images of saints and remembered fragments of stories and superstitions. At last he would get to meet this intriguing young woman, at last be able to put a face, a personality, on the visionary whose experiences had fired the imagination of an entire country.

When Mary Dowd opened her front door to them, James took note, first of all, of her unexpected blend of shyness and assertion. Her demeanor was quiet, almost self-effacing, yet her handshake was as firm and hard as a strong man's. As he followed her into the sitting room, he observed her straight posture, the firm set of the broad shoulders, the athletic build. He briefly imagined her in her school uniform, green no doubt, playing an energetic game of camogie, the girls' version of Irish hurling.

She didn't ask him to sit, but when she and Jude placed themselves on the sofa at the low coffee table, he too sat down. There was, he realized, no standing on ceremony here.

As she sat studying her fingernails, avoiding eye contact, James watched as her short, thick, black hair fell in tight curls around her extremely pale white face. Blue eyes finally glanced up under heavy, determined brows. A straight nose and small mouth made her look at times childlike and at others shrewish. Her jeans were fashionable and new, and the crisp shirt of white and pink neither flattered nor detracted from her appearance of extreme youth.

Finally she looked at Jude, who'd been unusually silent. James let the tension in the room play itself out, remaining silent himself.

"Well, now," Jude said at last, "this is Miss Mary Dowd, James. Mary, this is the fellow I spoke to you about, James Fleming. He's a solicitor from Dublin, highly recommended by a friend of mine there, and he's going to look into the murder, as I guess we must call it."

Mary studied James, two faint pink spots appearing in her cheeks.

"What can I tell you I haven't already told the police?" she said; fairly aggressively, James thought, considering he was there to help.

"Quite a lot, Mary, if I may call you that?"

She nodded.

"For instance, I'd just like you to talk in your own time about the events of last May and since. We can't cover it all in an hour, of course. But, you see, what I'm looking for is anything strange that might have occurred. Any chance meetings you had or . . . a stranger approaching you perhaps?"

"Surely you don't imagine Mary was connected with this in any way?" Jude burst in.

James glared at him. "If I may continue? Mary, was there anything odd at all, anything out of the ordinary?"

"Anything odd? Mr. Fleming, my whole life has been odd since that day in May." She glanced quickly away out the window, as if to restrain some anger. She resumed more quietly.

"I've tried to live as normally as possible since then, under the circumstances." She smiled as Jude placed a hand over her clasped ones, her knuckles showing white.

"Tell me about that, then . . ." James encouraged.

"I don't know how to begin . . ."

"All right," James said softly, "tell me about your life before . . ."

"Before the . . ." She didn't fill in the word either.

James merely nodded.

"I'm a teacher in the local national school here in Buncloda. I teach the infant class and have done for three years . . . since I left the college."

"And very well too," Jude interjected.

Mary smiled at the praise. "I don't know about that," she said shyly. "This is my third year." She stopped.

"Tell me about your friends," James prompted.

"After teacher training college in Limerick, I returned home here. I was lucky to get a job in my hometown. Or so I thought . . ." She again glanced quickly at Jude.

"What I meant was: it was great to get a job. But I'm last in, as they say. Most of the teachers are a bit older than I am.

75

All the girls are married, with families of their own. And the lads, well . . ." She threw up her hands in a comical gesture.

"Hopeless?" James said, smiling.

"Absolutely. There's just the two. Well, I don't call the principal a lad, really." She blushed.

"I know what you mean," James added, realizing just how young Mary really was. "So it's a bit lonely, then?"

"I suppose so. My parents died when I was still in Limerick, within a year of each other. My father had been sickly for months. He couldn't walk at the end, and it was difficult for my mother. I think all that worry and strain might have brought on her stroke. It was very quick . . ." She looked around the room almost vacantly. "So here I am," she said at last.

"I'm very sorry about your parents," James said.

"I've heard they were wonderful parishioners," Jude joined in.

"So you're a bit on your own, then, Mary?"

"Oh, I've friends from college," she said quickly, almost defensively. "We try to get off on a sun holiday each summer. They're teachers too; we're all scattered around the country. We'd a great time last year in Greece. And I've gone out with a local lad a few times. He lives up in Dublin, but I see him on weekends."

"I don't want this to seem like a job interview, Mary. Why don't you just fill me in on recent events?"

He'd so many questions to ask her, but James was patience itself, not wanting to alienate this complex young woman.

She seemed to relax. "All right," she said, and she began in a narrative tone of voice. "One morning in May, this May just gone out, when I was with Rita, Miss Garrotty, saying the Rosary, the Virgin Mary appeared to me."

James was stunned. Not at her words, but more at his own reaction at hearing the girl herself say the words. Despite all he'd heard and read, he hadn't expected this very simple statement issuing from her own lips. No preamble. No explanation. Just fact.

The two men were mesmerized as Mary stood up and moved slowly towards the picture window, not so much looking through it, but through the distance that intervened between her and the shrine. Unconsciously she lifted her hands in a prayerful gesture. She spoke again, but in a hoarse whisper.

"I had my eyes closed, praying, and then suddenly I opened them. I sensed something different. I thought someone else had joined us. But it wasn't that at all. It wasn't another person who'd joined us. It was Herself . . ." Mary closed her eyes and kept them closed as she resumed talking.

"There she was, shimmering, just in front of the statue. It was as though I could see the statue through a thin curtainy film. But Our Holy Mother Mary was in front of it, in front of the statue, I mean. The light was brilliant white and yet it didn't hurt my eyes at all. Holy Mother bent her head, almost leaning down towards me, and then she opened her hands to me. It was as if I had been handing her something, and she was going to accept it from me. Then . . . oh, then . . ." Mary's voice dropped even lower, and the hairs on the back of James's neck rose up. He waited, holding his breath. "And then she smiled at me . . ." Mary paused, clearly remembering this smile.

"I lifted up my head, I stretched up on my toes, and it was then she began to fade . . ."

Mary Dowd crossed her hands on her breast and turned around, tears shining in her eyes and rolling singly down her cheeks. Her pale, closed face had been transformed into an expression of love.

Silently Jude crossed himself and then stood up, walking near to Mary but not touching her. "You are blessed, Mary," he said softly.

She turned suddenly, unaware he'd been standing beside her, and she gave a little start. "What? Pardon me, Father?"

"You are blessed, Mary, and so are we, hearing this from your lips. And so is all of Buncloda."

Mary Dowd hung her head, and then shook it as though clearing her thoughts. She looked up again, first at Jude and then at James, blushing a deep motley red. "Oh, I don't know," she mumbled. She sat down as if exhausted.

"Tell me, Mary," Jude said, "do you really feel up to going to the shrine tonight?" He said it so gently, as if to a small sick child, that James regretted his earlier harsh opinion of Jude. Everything happening in this room was turning his many opinions on their multiple heads.

"Oh, Father Donnelly," she cried out, immediately startling them both. "I must! I must. I'm being drawn there. Since last night, and all day today. I've felt this sort of pressure, here." She touched her breast and then her temple. "Oh, I'm not hearing voices, don't worry." She laughed deprecatingly, with a self-awareness James was glad to observe.

"It's not a voice, but . . . it's like, oh, it's like something calling to me silently, to come, to come. Can you understand?" She threw up her hands again, girlishly. "*I* can't . . . so how could you? But I have such a longing to go there. Now. Come quickly. It's time!"

Energized, she grabbed a cardigan off the back of her chair and was out the door. With a sense of haste arising from whatever complex source, all three of them piled into the priest's Volvo and Jude raced the old engine.

In minutes the car was on the fringe of the crowd. As it was recognized by the local people, they herded their fellow pilgrims aside to allow the priest to pass, to come as close as possible to the shrine. James watched through the small rear windows of the car. He felt, for a moment, frightened by the surge of people, of peering faces and the rising voices. When Mary got out of the car, Jude and James moved to stand on either side of her.

Cries went up throughout the crowd that had swelled since late that afternoon. He guessed it to be upward of two thousand people, and the realization of that made him shiver. He felt Mary's arm, hooked in his own, begin to tremble like a young animal being held for the first time. She shrank back against the car for a moment, mumbling what he imagined to be a prayer. Slowly, the crowd opening before them, the threesome edged their way up the incline towards the stone grotto.

Filled with an ill-defined tension, James glanced over his shoulder. He could see the crowd closing behind them, like the Red Sea behind the Israelites, remembering fleetingly images from old movies. Behind them the Volvo was swallowed up and the late evening sky, clear blue till then, began to intensify and darken.

James moved forward watching, when he could, Jude's face, as pale as Mary's, and he questioned the wisdom of this whole situation. But Mary pressed on slowly, determinedly, staring straight ahead. Voices called out her name and the names of God and His mother, separately and in unison. Individual cries rang out, calling on Mary Dowd to bless them.

Some people crowded quite near her, reaching forth their hands, wanting to touch her, but she shrank back, touching none of the pilgrims. James and Jude stayed close against her.

"A sign, a sign!" This was the cry of the crowd—whether they wanted it from Mary Dowd or from God, James couldn't determine. The three were close to the statue now. Even more tokens, rosaries, and scraps of paper with written petitions were adorning the ledge and its pedestal. Some papers had been taped to the cold stone folds of the Virgin's faded blue skirts, to the bare toes, to the stone sandals.

"They want a sign, Mary," James heard Jude whisper to Mary as she suddenly shook their arms free of her own, falling to her knees, face uplifted, oblivious to the surging throng behind her.

In the growing darkness Jude turned to face the crowd. He raised his two hands, palms outward. This seemed to still the people nearest them. As they fell to their knees, those behind them followed suit, and in a ripple effect, row after row of pilgrims bent their knees to the ground and folded their hands. All that James could see left standing or sitting were those poor souls in wheelchairs and the police, four of them, posted on the distant perimeter of the crowd. When Jude knelt, James knew he had no choice but to kneel also. He did so, feeling self-conscious, feeling somehow hypocritical.

From the surrounding area of the grotto women of all ages suddenly appeared with candles—tapers, votive candles, stubs from the mantelpieces and candlesticks from a hundred local homes. They dropped melted wax on the ledge and the stone surround and stuck the candles deep into the softened wax. The flames flickered and burned bright against the navy-blue night.

James watched Mary for the twenty minutes while she knelt, face uplifted, hands pressed against her breast, eyes open and staring. Then he too began to watch the statue, then he too was caught by the intensity of Mary Dowd's gazing at the statue, caught up in the mood of the place, in the solemn recital of the Rosary that hummed in the air behind him, around him, above him.

Suddenly Mary's head dropped, her eyes closed briefly, and she shook herself. As she stood up slowly, so did the two men. Jude took her right arm. A hush crept over the crowd, spreading again like ripples from a stone tossed into a still pool.

"We must try harder," she said hoarsely to Jude, who repeated the words to the people nearest them. The simple words spread, and on their slow progress back to the car, James heard it repeated several hundred times.

When they reached the Volvo, Mary got in first, leaning her head on the back of the seat in complete exhaustion.

"James," she said through the open window.

He bent down.

"I must be alone now . . ."

"Oh. Yes, of course," he said, but he felt suddenly cut off, bereft, excluded.

Jude called to him from the other side of the car, "You'll be all right, then?"

Without waiting for James to reply, he got in and started the engine. James stared after the car as it made its way slowly through the crowd and out of sight. He was at a loss, and not merely for a means of transportation.

Chapter Ten

Mary Dowd let herself into her house, and switching on the
hall light, turned to wave to Jude that she was safe inside.
She watched as the old Volvo chugged up the road, and then
she sighed. It had been a long, long day, but she was
well-pleased.

Stepping into the sitting room, she realized her kitchen
light was on, and only this prescience, coming immediately
before a deep male voice spoke, prevented her from fainting
with fright.

"Is it you, Mary?"

"Glory be to God, are you trying to kill me with fright!"
she called out. "Tim, Tim!" She shouted out now in anger,
standing where she was.

She watched him as he lounged out around the wide
doorway of the kitchen.

"You've got some bloody cheek, Tim. I didn't know you
were coming. Why didn't you phone? It's not even the
weekend."

"And hello to you too, Mary." She was stung by the coldness of his tone.

"All right, hello, then." She flung herself angrily in the chair by the fire. "You know, Tim, when I gave you the house key, it was for emergencies only."

"Sorry, but I didn't feel like waiting on the doorstep till your boyfriend dropped you home."

"Don't be daft. Father Jude brought me home, from the shrine," she added.

"That's what I said." Tim came into the sitting room and stood looking down at her.

Mary glared at him. "What's this all about then?" she said, rubbing her lower legs and her hands to get some warmth into them, for she was chilled to the bone from the night air.

"I got a lift from Dublin. From another one of these pilgrims." He nodded his head in the direction of the shrine. "Couldn't believe I was a local. Thought she was blessed just to have me in her car. She's staying with family friends down here but she drove herself—and me—straight to the grotto."

Mary Dowd said, "Oh," in a small voice.

"'Oh' is right, Mary. I saw you there tonight. I couldn't get near to you, if I'd cared to. What with the crowds and Donnelly and some other fellow, a tall dark man."

"James Fleming. He's come down from Dublin."

"No matter, you seemed well taken care of . . ."

"Actually, I was," she said sharply, implying more than her words said. "How is it you got back here ahead of me, then?"

"Och, I didn't stay, Mary. I couldn't stay and watch that performance."

"How dare you!" she shouted, jumping to her feet. "How dare you say that was a performance."

Tim shrugged as he moved towards the window, closing the heavier curtains over the light net ones. He switched on the table lamp near the sofa and sat down heavily.

"Maybe I shouldn't have said that, Mary," he said softly, and waited as she sat down on her chair, keeping a distance between them.

"Look, Tim. First you scare me half to death, and then you insult me."

"Sorry," he said again, his youthful face, under unkempt reddish-brown hair, looking pained and less arrogant than before. He shrugged again, dropping his hands on his knees. "I came to talk. Really I did."

"It's too late," she said.

"I think so too."

A shiver of fear ran through her and she started to tremble. "I meant, it's too late tonight to talk . . ."

"Oh, sorry again. I spoke out of turn. Perhaps you're right. I guess you're tired. I should go. I'll ring my brother to collect me."

"No, no, wait. I can drive you, or . . . here, I could make tea or—"

"No thanks, really. This was a mistake." Yet Tim didn't stand up. Mary was encouraged.

"Here, wait, I have some sherry. I'm so chilled it will warm me."

She rushed to get the glasses, and poured out double measures for each and set them on the coffee table, trying vainly to steady her hands.

"There's no easy way to say this, Mary."

"Then don't say it, please, Tim. I'm . . . I'm sorry that I was cross just now. I'm tired. I was frightened. There are media people always around. When the kitchen light was on, I thought one of them got in, or even worse, some poor crazy person. They want to touch me, Tim. They reach out their hands. It frightens me. I hate it." Her tone was vehement and she checked it. "Let's start again," she said more softly.

"I've thought of that, too," Tim said. "But there's no going back, Mary."

"No, no . . ." She felt each time she spoke, she set herself up for a fall. "Let's start this night over. I am really glad to see you. I've missed you, you know." Her face and tone were so sweet, so endearing, that Tim looked away.

"Listen, Mary, it's best said quickly. We can't go on—"

"We can! Just as before," she implored.

"No, no, no. It can never be like it was before May. You're like a different person, someone I don't know. You know, I've read articles in my sister's magazines in the flat. About how some men can't be with their partner after she's been raped. I used to think what bastards they must be. But now, I can't be with you. It's as though you've been violated."

"Stop it, stop it!" Mary cried out, covering her ears with her hands. "That's blasphemy!"

"You're not the same person, Mary!" Tim shouted, half crying.

"How could I be? This is a miracle, don't you understand?"

"No, I bloody don't."

"You've never let me talk about it to you, Tim. Right from the beginning, you put me off. But I can explain it to you. Well, I can't explain it to you, you must realize that," she faltered. "I am still the same person, but I've been granted this great grace. That's how Jude has explained it to me . . ."

"Jude! Bah!" Tim turned his face away.

"No, Tim. He's been so helpful. He's given me prayers to say, and told me about other visionaries. In the past—"

"Aye, I'm sure. He's encouraged you from day one!"

"Of course he's encouraged me. He's a priest. Who else could help me? Who else could I turn to that first day? You weren't even here that day. And when I rang you in Dublin, you thought I was drunk." Mary's voice was rising again.

"Ringing me in the middle of the night with that wild story? Of course I thought something. Better drunk than daft. Let me tell you something, then. How do you think I felt up in Dublin? Going along thinking how we're getting on nicely, how I'd be seeing you on the weekend, how maybe we'd get a weekend away in the west. Did you . . . Have you ever stopped to think how all this has affected me? I doubt it, Mary Dowd."

"And you haven't considered how this affects me. Right now my life is not my own. I didn't choose this, Tim!"

"Somehow I don't believe that, Mary."

"If only you'd listen, Tim. Or read something. Or pray with me." Mary's voice was hard now, and he turned to face her. "It isn't my fault that you've given up your faith. How could I ever marry you in a church when you don't even bother with Mass from one end of the year to the next?"

"Who said anything about marriage?" Tim shouted.

Mary stopped, flushing red. "Sorry," she said. "It was just something that used to come into my head. But—But . . ." She tried to recover her anger as her stomach began to churn with fear. "Tim, I'm not saying I took anything for granted. But sometimes when I thought about us, I wondered how your lack of faith would . . . you know, might affect us in the future."

"Uh-uh." Tim shook his head. "It's not my lack of faith that's the problem here, Mary. It's this crazy business you've got yourself into."

"Crazy business! What are you saying! Go to Knock and look at the shrine there. You know the Pope himself came to visit it when we were children! Is that some crazy business?"

"I've been to Knock, Mary, like the rest of the bloody country at one time or another. Is that what you have to say to me? Am I to be going out with some plaster saint! Am I going to be the man who dated the saint of Buncloda? Isn't that what they call you here, if only behind your back? Donnelly might be mightily pleased to be connected with you. I can see he is. Has been from the very start. Well, I tell you, I'm not going down as the man who dated the little saint, the little virgin from Buncloda!"

"I am a virgin!" Mary shouted.

"Exactly!"

"You're horrible, Tim," she cried, covering her face.

"All I know is that you belong to them!" he replied,

standing up and waving his arms angrily, shouting towards the curtained window. "You belong to those people crowding around out there in the dark, milling around like mindless, stupid sheep. You belong to them, Mary, and to Donnelly, to that bloody grotto I wish I'd never set eyes on. Damn and blast it, Mary . . . but you don't belong to me!"

"You're right." She too stood up, speaking quietly. "I don't belong to you. I never did. I'm sorry if you ever thought I might! I don't belong to you. I belong to . . . I belong to . . . to God!"

Tim stared at her for a long minute. "Christ, I need a drink," he said, at last turning away.

Too late she realized she had gone too far. In an instant he was gone from the room, the bang of the front door sending shudders through the solid little house, through her.

She did not move. She did not cry out. She merely stood and suffered the ice cold tremor to take her over, to invade her, reaching deep into every particle of her body and soul.

After Jude and Mary Dowd had left the scene at the grotto, James glanced around him. Unwilling to remain with the crowd in its now heightened mood, he shouldered his way past the people and turned at last down the side road that led to his bed-and-breakfast accommodation. Mrs. Kehoe was happier to see him than he her.

"A cup of tea, Mr. Fleming, before bed? You're looking a little pale. An early night will do you good. Here, I've just brewed a fresh pot."

Nothing would do, but she herded him to her kitchen, where he morosely took tea with herself and the da. Just this side of rude, James managed to gulp his tea and convey very little of his reaction to events of the last few hours. Or so he thought. Mrs. Kehoe had, shrewdly she thought, concluded that he was feeling some disaffection with events at the grotto. Composing her own fiction that James was, despite all, seeking some personal boon from the Virgin, she missed the fact that he was now feeling oppressed by the presence, by the actions of the faithful—one and all. He longed for privacy, and with a mumbled apology he fled to his upstairs room.

Drained, seemingly tired from the long day, he threw himself, still fully dressed, across the bed. He closed his eyes against the tropical lushness of the floral wallpaper and tried to sort out his reactions.

Convoluted, wandering thoughts and images filled his mind: Mary Dowd kneeling, her face transfixed; the eerie silence of the crowd. Yet was it silent? He only remembered silence. He tossed and turned, seeking mental rest in sleep, but virginal Mary Dowd intruded, her face merging with the stylized young painted face of the statue. He tried to block out her face; tried instead to think of Sarah, so far away in the States. But Geraldine's face, Geraldine's figure, came unbidden.

James sat up abruptly on the side of the soft pink bed. There was only one respite for him, he knew, when he was in this sort of mood. Swapping his jacket for a woolly pullover, he left the house, banging the door behind him as a message for the endlessly curious Mrs. Kehoe.

The short main street of the village was a strange sight for someone used to the ordinary dead-quiet Irish village at midnight on a weekday.

Many of the shops and two-storey flat-fronted houses were shrouded in darkness, as one would expect. But the chip shop and the small café were as full as at lunchtime, with crowds on the pavements and seated inside. People were either walking to or from these food emporiums, seeking food in the middle of the night.

James, hopeful, walked on. Passing one barred and shuttered pub, just for form's sake, he went to the farthest end of the main street, about two hundred yards, and stopped near but not in front of another elderly pub, called Reardon's. In the silence here away from the shops, he heard the unmistakable sound of talk drifting through the shutters.

He tapped the window sharply with a pebble from the

road and waited hopefully. Alert to any action, he saw the narrow door open almost imperceptibly.

"Any chance of a pint?" he whispered with a mixture of confidence and supplication. His unseen interlocutor merely widened the door, and he slipped in with bowed head beneath the old and very low lintel.

Mirabile dictu! It was his favorite sort of pub. Wood from another era darkened to the color of ditch water by generations of smokers. Dim lighting filtering from some unlocatable source behind the bar. The bar itself, high and short of span. No music. No telly. No radio even. Blessed silence and a few companionable souls all bent on the same purpose. He sat at the bar, shrinking his height onto a bockety stool, and a pint of Guinness stout appeared as if by magic before him. He smiled, just a small smile, and paid up the wizened old barman.

Head bent, he sipped mightily and realized just how tense he had been, how drained by the challenge presented to his own beliefs in the previous few hours. He felt it all slipping away now. What a night, he said to himself as he drank contentedly, feeling he was in touch once again with at least one of the realities of his life. He let his thoughts drift.

He heard, rather than saw, another person enter the small room, which now held about a dozen men of varying ages. He felt, rather than saw, that person slip onto the stool beside him. More pints appeared.

James's attention was finally caught by the motion of the man's browned hand as it rolled a pound coin between his fingers, and across the knuckles in a smooth, practiced motion—back and forth, back and forth. The rhythm first irritated James and then lulled him.

On his third pint, James turned his face towards the man, younger than himself, ruddy and open-faced. He smiled at James.

"You're ready, then?"

"Ready for what?" James asked.

"For talk, for adventure, for whatever comes your way?"

"I suppose I am," James said, intrigued.

"Had to let you get it off your mind."

"What?"

"What it was that was troubling you. Time and Guinness. They do the trick."

"Is that so? Perhaps I was merely enjoying a quiet drink."

The younger man laughed. "And perhaps I'm the Lord Mayor of Cork."

"But I was," James protested.

"Indeed, and I could see that. But I wanted your full attention, not to be shared with phantoms and ghosts out of your mind or your heart."

"All right, then, and why do you want it?" James asked, wondering if he was to be hit on by a rather unique panhandler.

"I've something to show you," said the man, tossing the coin into the air and catching it.

James glanced around him. "Why not one of the others?"

"Because you're a jackeen, and I'd lay money that you've not seen what I've to show you. Och, I thought I smelled adventure off you."

"You might." James bristled. He was annoyed at the interruption. Then he reconsidered. If, after all, it was a setup, what did he have to lose?

"All right," he said at last, "you've piqued my curiosity."

"Come on then."

James followed the man, who had introduced himself merely as Tim, through a narrow passage at the rear of the pub and into the virtually open field behind the terraced row of houses and shops. Tim started off at a brisk pace, and James, although fit, had a job to keep up. And as they walked, the young man talked. He told James that he was a local, had grown up on a farm not ten miles out. Then he stopped in his tracks and looked around him. "Do you know what night this is at all?" he asked.

"Tuesday, now Wednesday morning," James said, laughing. "I'm not as far gone as all that."

"Aye, but do you know it's the summer solstice, that most famous of all nights, midsummer's eve? There's magic in the air, a summer madness, all around us. Permeates everything. Look, look over there, *there's* some fine magic going on." James caught the slightest hint of sarcasm in Tim's voice.

James looked up. The ground had been rising so gently that he hadn't noticed they'd been climbing a long slope. Now in the distance he could see the small hill, across the shallow valley, where the shrine stood. Drawing level with it, they could see the flickering of the candle flames and torches, flashlights and car lights, all seemingly centered, circling in the optical illusion that light creates over a distance.

"You call that magic!" James said admonishingly.

"I said 'of a sort.' More like smoke and mirrors . . . but come on, there's something else to see."

He led James off to the left, swerving down another slope. In the dark James felt the ground grow marshy underfoot. The air was thicker, heavier, and as he glanced up from watching his fine shoes sinking with each step in the muddy ground, he gasped.

Before him lay some indeterminate place, shrouded as if with a fog or mist that shimmered here and there and then suddenly conjoined into some sort of strange fire, a fire that didn't burn bright, but hung and moved diaphanously.

"Midsummer's eve!" Tim crowed as he let James enjoy his first sight of the eerie fire known in modern times to be caused by marsh gas.

"Think, man! If you didn't know, wouldn't that for all the world make you see faeries or centaurs or leprechauns or gods—depending of course on where you hailed from down the centuries?"

"I admit it," James said softly. "It's truly a sight to see. I've traveled a bit, but this is new to me." He stared for a long time at the strange light, grateful he had a companion as the scene pressed in on his imagination.

They turned back regretfully as a heavier mist drew in upon them, thoroughly drenching their hair and skin and quenching the faery fires.

In answer to Tim's question about his travels, James described, briefly, his passion for steam trains and his memorable trips to Russia and, more recently, Peru.

"I'm impressed," Tim said, as somehow James hoped he would be.

As they retraced their steps to the rear door of the pub, Tim described how as a boy he'd longed to travel the world. But thus far he'd only managed hop-picking in England one summer, a job that had helped pay for his education in Dublin during the year.

"Amazing where a knowledge of farming can get you." Tim laughed ironically as they settled back on their stools, hardly missed, but a lot wetter for their expedition. James mopped his hair with a damp handkerchief.

"Hot whiskies, I think," Tim said.

"Right you are."

"So, you're here in town to find out about the murther!" he stressed the last word in a humorous way, but James nonetheless jumped.

"Who says so?"

"The town, I guess you could say. So, you are?"

"Well, in a sense, yes."

"What are you looking for, then?"

"Deep background, as the journalists like to say. I don't suppose *you* can tell me anything." James was challenging. "Perhaps about the principals involved?"

"In the murder!"

"No, in the vision, the vision here in Buncloda in May. This is all pretty new to me, religious experience of that kind, and I'm looking for an insight into it, and into the people who took part. You see, my feeling is that this murder is linked to the events at the grotto in May. After all, the body was found there. And the man was clutching a rosary . . ." James deliberately let his sentence hang.

92

"I see . . . I see . . . Well . . ." Tim hesitated, but the missed beat caught James's attention. "I can tell you that my old man knows Devane pretty well, from years here as farmers. But you know Devane has dropped out of sight."

"Do you mean he's not here in Buncloda?"

"Oh no, he's here all right, but he doesn't come out anymore, to the auctions or the grange. Even for a pint, although he was not what you'd call a drinker."

"Was he, I mean, is he a religious man?"

"Not that I ever noticed. Mass on Sunday. The usual thing. Holy days. After his wife died he kept to himself. But then after a year or so, I heard he came back around to Sunday Mass and a drink after." Tim tilted his head in the direction of the church a mere hundred yards from the pub, around the small bend in the road.

"It was like that until May gone out. Since then, well, he's been among the missing," Tim added conspiratorially.

"But you know," James said, considering Tim's description of Devane, "he must have been a bit more religious than you say he appeared."

"How so? Because he's all cosy with Miss Garrotty? I'd say it's more than the Virgin Mary that's on their minds."

"Oh," James said with interest. "So you're suggesting it was more than spiritual devotion that brought Devane to the grotto every morning with Rita Garrotty?"

"What are you talking about? When did Devane go to the grotto?"

"Before the apparition." James stumbled over the word.

"Ah, you've got the wrong end of the stick there, man. He didn't go near the shrine as far as I know, in the way you mean. But his farm is beyond the grotto, down that windy road. He passed that shrine every day for twenty years, ever since old Mr. O'Rourke put it up. On the tractor, or driving the cattle from one field to another."

"And he'd stop to pray?"

"Perhaps he tipped his cap. But he was no mama's boy running to be with the women."

"Then I don't understand. How was it he was there at all with the others the day of the . . . the big day?"

"Oh, I see what you're getting at."

James waited as Tim ordered more hot whiskies with a lift of his eyebrow. The smoke was thickening and there was no movement among the sedentary little group of men, puffing on their pipes and contemplating God-knows-what.

Tim resumed. "He was only passing in his lorry. It was very early and he was going up to the dairy to get some milk cans he'd left there in an oversight. He'd seen the women on the hill, as he often did. It'd become part of the daily Buncloda scene. You know small towns. Or maybe you don't," he said, again ironically. "You can't move a muscle in this town and someone doesn't know it." His eyes clouded and he fell silent.

James too let his thoughts drift as the blue smoke moved in large swirls before his eyes, backlit like dramatic scenes in old movies. There was something soothing, more soporific than the whiskey, in the mood of the room, something timelessly Irish. The dimness, the shushing sound of low voices murmuring, the warmth and dryness within, the dampness and rising wind without. He felt he could stay always, amusing himself with solving the mysteries of the world, or the human heart. He faintly heard Tim's voice.

"Sorry, what did you say?"

"I was saying—if you're still interested, that is—that Devane was only passing when he heard Miss Mary Dowd calling to him. She'd come down the hill a little and was waving, beckoning, as he said at the time. So naturally he stopped and went up to her. She'd seen her vision by then. According to Devane, she was nearly incoherent. Miss Garrotty from the hardware was still on her knees." Tim finished off his whiskey in a gulp.

"So . . . Devane didn't really see anything?" James was genuinely surprised to hear himself say this.

"Now I didn't say that either. Devane saw something all right." Tim's tone was suddenly bitter.

94

James was about to speak when Tim checked his watch. "I best be going," he said abruptly. "Good night, then." Before James could reply, the young man was gone.

James realized it was time for him to go as well. Regretfully, he pocketed his change and stepped out into the drizzle. The street was, at last, truly deserted. The drinkers and the devout alike had finally gone home to their beds.

——— *Chapter Eleven* ———

At breakfast the next morning Mrs. Kehoe was eager to tell
James that crowds had been assembling at the grotto ever
since dawn. What startled him more was that she'd been up
there already and was able to report that Mary Dowd and
Miss Garrotty had spent nearly three hours there on their
knees.

"It was only when Father Donnelly finally arrived that
they allowed themselves to be led away through the
crowds," she added with immense satisfaction.

James was genuinely puzzled by this seemingly sudden
increase in the momentum of events. He wondered now, as
he walked towards the Garrottys' hardware shop, if in fact
Miss Garrotty would be available to see him. As he neared
the shop he was in for yet another surprise. A long, loose
queue of pilgrims clutching prayer books and rosaries had
formed at the door. James observed they were clearly not
eager to buy nails or screws or wrenches from the sizable
shop. He dawdled around the fringes of the crowd, debating
what to do. Although he had an appointment fixed by Father

Donnelly himself, he feared that if he pushed through to the head of the queue, the crowd could turn a titch ugly. But after ten minutes of standing idly by, he advanced in a roundabout fashion until he was beside the people standing just at the entrance to the shop.

"Sorry," he said affably. "Sorry. It's just . . . I do have an appointment, sorry . . ."

He began to elbow his way in, repeating his apology in a soft tone. Perhaps it was his expensive, dark three-piece suit, or his imposing height. Perhaps it was his commanding manner, but the people made room for him, with only one man shouting out that the bloody press were everywhere. Assuring them he was not a reporter, he moved slowly forward through the crowd within the shop until he reached the counter, where a balding, burly man stood serving some legitimate customers.

"And who are you?" the man shouted into James's face as he acknowledged his presence at last.

James explained and the man stared hard at him. "Wait here," he said at last, and went through a curtained door to the rear of the shop. He just as quickly returned.

"My sister says she'll see you, all right, if you're the fellow Father Donnelly told her about?"

"Yes, I am. He rang her. I'm really sorry for the inconvenience," he said humbly.

Satisfied, the unfriendly man lifted the hinged countertop and let him pass. Turning back to his sales, he let James find his own way.

Through a narrow hallway James found what was the kitchen of the house cum shop. Here sat Miss Garrotty, he assumed, clutching a mug of steaming tea in both hands. When she looked up, James saw a great weariness in her face, mingled with apprehension.

After a quick introduction of himself and his intentions, James sat down.

"This seems to be a bit of bad timing," he said matter-of-factly.

97

"Ah, God, this is an awful day!" Miss Garrotty exclaimed. "I'd no idea it could ever get like this." Again a look of fear passed over her plain face.

"It hasn't been like this up until today?" James queried, leaning back into the ladder-backed wooden chair and feeling every inch of his spine against it.

"No, no, not even in May." Miss Garrotty looked around the room as though seeing the crowds in front of her eyes. "Somehow people then had the sense to leave us alone, you know, me and Devane and Mary Dowd. They might see us at the grotto or whatever, but they didn't approach us like." She sipped her tea, and James saw her hands trembling.

"Can you tell me about this morning, then? All of this is so new to me."

"Surely, but I'm not certain it will help your murder investigation." She seemed to regain a sense of herself and she looked closely at him for the first time.

"I don't know yet, Miss Garrotty, but I can see you've been through an ordeal today, and I am sympathetic to your situation . . ."

Rita seemed to appreciate this attention. She appeared to warm to James.

"Mary Dowd rang me very late last night. She said she'd had a feeling, I don't know, a premonition or whatever she calls it . . ."

"Had this happened before?"

"Not like this. No, she's never called me so late at night. And I felt I couldn't let her down, you know. I don't think she'd any idea about the crowds being there today and all that. She was telling me over the phone that there was a force like, driving her to the grotto. Not callin' to her, but drivin' her. I remember she said that now . . . And I didn't like to let her down, as I said, so agreed to meet up with her before first light. She was cryin' and sayin' she was frightened by the force of it. And she didn't want to go alone. What could I say?"

James wondered why she was so defensive about her own

role in this morning's events, but could hardly yet ask. "Did you feel this force too?" he asked instead.

"Well, now, I can't say that I felt it. But when Mary Dowd was talking about it, I sort of felt compelled to go with her because of the strength of what she was saying. And when I rose this morning in the dark, it felt, you know, familiar—like it did before."

"Before?"

"Before, in the spring. In April when we first started going to say the Rosary at the grotto . . . like that. I got dressed and in my mind I just saw myself going to meet up with her on the deserted road. You know, I liked it back then. It was peaceful and it was time to myself. I felt, you know, healthy getting up so early, even though I'd pay for it during the day. Used to have to have a quick nap here, sometimes close the shop for an hour or so after the lunchtime rush. It felt like old times this morning. Simple and straightforward. Funny how your mind works, slipping back like that . . . to before . . ." She trailed off. James was puzzled by her tone of regret. It was as if she'd relished those early days more than what had since transpired: her seeing a vision of the Blessed Virgin herself. James sought for a thread of conversation that would get Miss Garrotty to tell him more.

"So you had no expectation that the grotto would be so crowded today? This morning?"

"Ah, no," she said wearily. "Certainly not that crowded at that hour. At first the people were quiet, letting us pass, silent like in church, maybe silent because of the dark morning, the quiet air. But when we were kneeling I had this sense they were crowding in upon us. People were praying aloud and it was hard to concentrate. But Mary Dowd, och, she was oblivious. I got tired bein' on my knees after just one hour. I put my cardigan beneath me knees, and I'd look over at her now and then, but she'd not move. Just staring and staring up at the Blessed Mother." Here Rita blessed herself. "I couldn't get her attention in the normal way, and I didn't like to poke her, you know, touch her to speak with her. God knows what she might be seeing or hearing, and it wasn't for me to interfere on account of my tired legs! But I tell you it was a real sacrifice. I was grateful when Father Donnelly arrived. Three hours and my poor back! And my legs! They were stiff as can be."

She stretched them out for him to see the swollen ankles and the reddish purple dents in her round, plump knees.

"He came and put his arms about us, and lifted Mary Dowd to her feet. Stiff as I was, she was worse, I think, swaying against him. He had to hold her up, and I made my own way behind them down to his old car." She sighed at the thought. "If it hadn't been for the car, I'd never have made it back here."

"You know, Miss Garrotty, I went up to the grotto last evening with Mary Dowd and Father Donnelly."

Rita looked at James with suspicion, but he continued trying to gain her confidence, saying, "We were only there twenty minutes or so, but I think I can share your feelings. I too felt the pressure of the numbers even last night. And when Mary prayed, I was riveted to her face."

"So you can guess how it would be hard to disturb her then. Three hours!" She shook her head at the thought of it and unconsciously rubbed her knees.

"Did Mary Dowd say anything when Father Donnelly came?"

"I doubt it. But if she did, I couldn't hear it with the cries around us. And she was in a faint in the car, I tell you. It was the crowd and their calling out! Bah!"

"Calling out? Her name? What?"

"Well, mixed in with all the prayers was their foolish cry for a sign. I ask you!" She looked up at James as if startled, as if disgusted. "What kind of a sign? What do they want from Mary Dowd? No more, no more . . ." She shook her head.

"I don't understand," James said with affecting humility.

"Why do they want more than what she has already given

them? She saw the Virgin in the holy month of May. What more do those people want from her? And why?"

She stood up stiffly and put the kettle on the gas.

"A cup?" she said tiredly.

"That would be welcome." James wanted to press on, struck with his realization that Miss Garrotty had described only Mary Dowd as seeing the apparition in May, not herself. Was this true humility, he wondered, or some kind of acknowledgment of fact?

"It must have been awe-inspiring for all of you . . ." he hazarded.

"What? The crowds this morning?" she squawked impatiently, her fatigue showing. She sloshed water into the mugs to heat them.

"No, not that. I was referring to the three of you seeing the apparition in May."

James watched carefully as Rita stiffened her back in a self-conscious manner.

"Indeed it was," she said at last as she placed the tea in front of him and sat down again. "It was the greatest thing that has happened to me. I remember clearly coming home here that morning, hugging that great secret to myself. I told no one, you see, but held it inside me. I cooked the breakfast for the brothers and watched them as they sat right here, and all the while I knew I had my great secret."

"But surely you wanted to tell them, tell everyone?"

"In time. But not at first. Looking back, I think I didn't want my secret tarnished. And knowing it—just knowing it—made me feel different, I guess." She sighed a huge sigh.

"But you did tell, I assume?"

"Oh, yes, in time. Mary Dowd told, of course, and so she should. And then I was drawn into it all. Those early days were hectic. There was a fine excitement about it all back then." She smiled, and brushed back her faded brown and gray hair from her forehead.

"People who came into the shop treated me with reverence. As though I were Mother Superior herself up at the convent . . ." She laughed heartily for the first time. "I wonder still what she makes of all this?"

"Who?" James said, all at sea.

"There's a convent here, outside the town. But of course you wouldn't know that. Years ago there was a school attached to it. But that closed before even my time. It's what they call a mother house. When we were kids we called it the henhouse, God forgive me." She laughed again.

"Is it cloistered or what?"

"Ah no, there was the school they ran, a boarding school. But times changed. There was an orphanage too there once, but again times have changed. For the better as we all say, but I never know if that is true. But it's still a mother house for the order of Mary of Nazareth. Young postulants, if there are any left in this terrible world, come there to study and learn, and in time take their vows. They keep to themselves. Have their own chapel and all. As in the old days. And they offer retreats throughout the year. Marital retreats, and retreats for schoolgirls, and young working women, that sort of thing."

"But the nuns are not involved in all this . . . this . . ." James hunted for the right word.

"In the apparition. By no means—" Rita was interrupted by one of her brothers calling from the other room.

"Ah God," she said, wearily standing up, "it's time for their dinner and I've nothing ready. Same thing every day, year in, year out." She faced James, leaning her knuckles on the table and bending slightly forward. "I thought as how things would change . . . I thought, you know, that my prayers were to be answered . . ."

As she looked at him, it was as if James were seeing her for the first time. She wasn't that much older than himself, yet it seemed that she was from another generation. He saw her regarding him as a man, and guessed in an instant that what she wanted was a man, love and marriage and children. That would have been her prayer at the grotto on those early mornings. Perhaps it had been Mary Dowd's as well. He wanted to ask, but knew that he couldn't, not now or ever.

Sympathetic to her narrow life dominated by her unfeeling brothers, as he imagined them to be, James said softly: "Perhaps your prayers have not been answered outwardly, Miss Garrotty, as one would hope. But surely inside, for you, I mean . . . to have had this experience, to have had your secret . . ." He stumbled in his clumsy efforts to console.

"Och," she cried. "If it was ever that!" She waved him off. "I'll support Mary Dowd and that's an end of it. Go, go now. Talk to her, if you will. It's herself that has all the secrets now."

Rita turned away to drag out a bag of potatoes from beneath the sink. He stood up dissatisfied but clearly dismissed for now.

James passed back through the crowd at the door. It had lessened, but still people stood there sheeplike. Compelled by his own sympathy for Rita, he said in a voice loud enough to be heard by those nearest the door that Miss Garrotty was otherwise occupied and wouldn't be seeing anybody. As some pilgrims began to drift away, the Garrotty brother came to the door, angrily calling to him.

"And what business is it of yours, to be speaking for me sister?"

James wanted to tell him it was obvious to all that he was using his sister's notoriety to draw in custom to his shop. The man called to him again, and the crowd murmured angrily.

James stared at them blankly for a full minute, wondering again what manner of people these were, and, as Rita herself had said, what in God's name did they want?

James drove with all possible speed to the rectory, to be met by a grim-faced Geraldine at the door.

"Do you have any idea what the time is?" she snapped as he entered hurriedly.

"Actually, I think I'm late, but my interview with Miss Garrotty went on a bit longer than I'd anticipated. I'd like to tell you . . . run it by you. I don't . . . let me say, I thought they would be different."

"Who? What?" she snapped again, and he finally noticed how pale she was beneath her perfect makeup.

"The visionaries. I've learned so much since I've seen you."

"I'm so happy for you." Geraldine rudely walked away into the priest's sitting room, where she lit a cigarette, one of many, judging from the blue haze in the room.

"What's the matter, Geraldine?" James said kindly.

"Oh, nothing, except I've been cooped up in this barn since teatime last night. An endless boring night in my room while you're out in a pub!"

"How did you know?"

"Oh, James, you stick out like a sore thumb here. I never did know what that was supposed to mean. Anyway, Joe Soap told Jim Soap who told whoever, who told Jude. How else!"

"Well it's true, but—"

"And then this morning," she interrupted. "I've read the papers three times over. I want to leave, James."

"Of course, of course, I . . . you know we didn't really plan this out. I thought we could talk about the investigation. But here," James saw her luggage by the door, "let me take your things to the car."

"I can do that, James. Just tell Jude you're leaving—"

"Oh, but Geraldine, I'm not. I can't. I've only begun the investigation. You know that. I need to talk to the principals again. And I've got nowhere yet on the murder. I should speak to Molloy about that, something may have turned up . . ."

"All right, all right," she answered despondently. "I get the picture. It's just that—"

"Ger, you're the one who got me into this, remember? To help Maguire and Donnelly. I can hardly pull out now, can

I?" He said this lightly, drawing near to her, trying to tease her a bit.

"All right!" she said, pulling away.

"Listen," James changed tack, "let me run you up to Dublin. I can call into my office when I'm there and I can be back down here tomorrow or even late tonight."

"I guess I didn't anticipate such enthusiasm, James," she said dryly. "After all, religious visions aren't your thing."

"What the hell did you expect, then?" James was losing patience at this assault on his integrity.

"I'd forgotten, that's all."

"Forgotten what?"

"How preoccupied you get. How, oh, immersed. You forget everything else."

James shrugged the implied criticism off. The last thing he wanted was a rehash of the unresolved and thorny issues that still remained between them. His conscience pricked him.

He quickly made his phone calls and as quickly got them into the Citroen and onto the main Dublin road.

They drove, for the most part in silence, with Geraldine dozing or listening with distracted attention to James's collection of jazz tapes. As he left her off at St. James's Hospital, she spoke at last.

"Look, James, I'm sorry I've been so rude. You know, I don't like my own company much—"

"Ger!"

"Don't interrupt. It's true. It gives me too much time to think. It's as though when I'm alone I can see clearly how hollow my life is."

"Ger, you're a medical doctor. You're in life and death situations on a daily basis. So how can you say that?"

"I'm saying it, aren't I?" she snapped. "And on that point, Donald is a doctor too. It doesn't seem to alter your obvious low opinion of him!"

"That's a completely different issue," James said, none too sure why it was so, but still knowing it was.

"Donald's not what you—"

"If you want Donald, Geraldine, what the hell are you doing here with me!" James exploded at last.

"Sometimes you are so bloody thick, James Fleming!"

Geraldine slammed the car door with a shattering bang, and James knew better than to follow her. Hopelessly, he sat staring after her tall slim figure as she walked away from him, as she had so many other times in their troubled past.

——— *Chapter Twelve* ———

"Oh, is it Lazarus back from the dead, then?" was Maggie's acerbic greeting as James rushed in the door to his law firm just at closing time.

"What kind of a greeting is that?" James snapped, worn-out from a day of dealing with so many different women's various moods.

"It's just that we've had no word from you at all. You never rang with your number or where we could reach you. Assuming you were dead, we held a wake. You'd have been disappointed at the turnout . . ." Maggie clicked the cover over her computer screen and turned the key in her desk drawer with finality.

"Sorry, Maggie, I could have sworn I told—" He stopped, knowing that if he had left his number, she would have noted it in her infinitely efficient way. He didn't want to lose this one constant in his life. "Sorry," he said again, with his easy charm.

"You'll be more than sorry if you don't get over to your mother's by six," Maggie said more jovially as she took off her low court shoes and put on a pair of her habitual three-inch high heels, which she wore regardless of the changes in fashion.

"How so?" James said as he flipped through the opened post on her desk.

In answer, Maggie handed him a stack of yellow phone messages.

"I took care of your other messages, they're on your own desk. These are from your *mater familiaris*."

James cringed at reading the contents. He honestly couldn't recall this particular proposed dinner date with his widowed mother. But then this had happened countless times before. Yet lurking in the back of his mind all these years was the thought that perhaps he hadn't in fact agreed to these various dates, not to all of them at least, and yet in her convincing and accusatory fashion his mother made him feel guilty for forgetting what perhaps he'd never known.

"Well, it's inevitable I suppose," he mumbled to himself.

Maggied laughed. "At least there's one woman pursuing you, James," she said. "Good night to you . . ." She was at the door.

"Wait, Maggie! Look, I'll be off again tomorrow. I'll—"

"Be sure to write," was all she said as she shut the door.

With no time to return to his flat and still read through the material on his desk, James quickly changed into the suit he kept at the office for sudden court appearances and the like. A wash, a shave, and a flick of the comb through his curly, well-groomed black hair made him more than presentable, he thought as he eventually finished his work and went to get his car.

From the dark green Citroen he phoned his mother on his cellular phone, the latest of the many gadgets he'd accumulated in his acquisitive fashion.

That there was no reply puzzled him. On his third try the phone engaged and he was to hear a rather garbled taped message of his mother's voice. She was referring to the fact she didn't know how to run the tape, as if talking to a third party. This bit of speech was followed by a screech rather than a beep. He sighed to himself. Yet another of his Christmas presents that was not a success.

As he pulled the car in front of the substantial, well-proportioned detached house—now with the new addition of his brother's surgery at the side—he mused for the thousandth time on how little he remembered of the years he'd spent there as a child growing up with Donald. When he returned home, it was always as a stranger. He was so used to this sensation that he'd come to accept it without question.

He glanced at his watch, wondering what new events might be at that moment transpiring back in Buncloda. But presently there were filial matters to attend to. As he reached to press the front doorbell, the door flew open.

"Stop him, Stop him!" he heard his mother shrieking from the long entrance hall on which the heavy door opened.

Chilled by her tone of panic, he stood ready to brace himself against the onset of a thief, a burglar, a serial killer. Muscles tensed and poised for confrontation, James looked wildly about him.

"You've missed him," his mother yelled as she approached down the hall, her short and bulky frame pushing past him. "Such a dope you are, James!"

Confused, James looked to see the object of his mother's frantic but nonetheless hobbling pursuit.

A small beige animal, presumably a dog, was running in ever decreasing circles in the hedged front garden of the house. Fortunately for James's self-respect, he'd latched the gate as he entered and the dog was trapped in the rectangle formed by the front yard.

"Here boy, now, stop! Stop that, you foolish thing!" More high-pitched commands followed at random as the dog ignored Mrs. Fleming's flapping apron. With a lunge that spread a deep green grass stain onto James's trousered knees, he grasped the dog around the throat. As he knelt and calmed the wriggling animal, he realized it was a great deal smaller than its speed and bark had at first indicated.

"Gracious," said his mother, throwing a hand to her forehead in her best Victorian mode, "this calls for a sherry." She disappeared into the house, leaving James to follow, carrying the now docile animal in his arms.

It was a strange-looking thing, he observed, thinking that it was perhaps a bulldog pup. But the flat face and dark markings caused it to resemble a monkey more than anything else. It had a tawny, gleaming coat, and multiple folds of skin at the neck. A vivid pink tongue lolled from its mouth as the dog panted, regaining its breath. The dog was a mere eight pounds, if that, but it was a tyro nonetheless.

"And what is this?" James asked pleasantly as he entered the dining room where his mother stood fanning herself with a small Chinese fan in one hand, her other holding her sherry glass.

"I must revive, James," she gasped, and then sipped. "Come into the African room, it's cooler there." James duly followed her into the large room, which opened through French doors onto the spacious back garden. Carefully avoiding the small wooden tables carved in the shape of elephants which came barely to his knees, he sat hesitantly on a rattan chair that felt poised to give way. His formidable mother threw herself on the chaise longue positioned beneath the wall hanging of an African lioness. She rested her head briefly before lifting it to stare at him.

"You didn't ring!"

"Indeed I did, not more than half an hour ago. Did you check the tape?"

"Of course not. If you'd rung, I would have heard it and answered."

"But that's what the tape machine is for. Haven't you got any messages as yet?" Exasperation crept into his voice.

"Not at all," she snapped. "If my lady friends wish to speak with me, they wish to speak with me, not a machine.

No one leaves messages except tiresome tradespeople, and I ignore those."

James suppressed a sigh. His mother, as he well knew, referred to all people other than her personal friends as tradespeople. No matter that it may be the bank, or the garage about her car, or the repairman scheduled to fix her central heating. He realized the pointlessness of her having the machine at all, since her friends refused to take advantage of it and all others went unattended.

"Do you want me to disconnect it, then?" he said resignedly. It was the wrong tone, he realized too late.

"How can you give me a gift and then take it back, James! That's so like you. Donald now, gave me that lovely new calculator so as to help me with my finances. You don't see him rushing here to repossess it."

"He hardly needs to rush here when he works next door. Anyway—what finances?" James squawked, easily distracted when it came to his mother. "Your accountant does all that."

"Donald is so thoughtful. He doesn't disappear for weeks and not let me know . . ." She finished fanning herself and looked suddenly at the sleeping dog on James's lap. "He likes you, it seems. How strange."

James felt himself go rigid, but he didn't rise to the bait. "To whom does he belong?" he said instead.

"Why, James! Don't be ridiculous. He's mine, of course. He's a pug and his name is Mack, after my dead friend Mackintosh. Poor sweet man, wanted to marry me, you know, but I was spoken for." She lowered her eyes demurely as she sipped her sherry.

"He's yours," said James flatly, discouraged already.

"Yes, James. And he's worse than having two sons about the house, although thus far he's broken no windows. You were a terror for that."

"Not I, Mother, that was Donald."

"Donald, Donald, stop about Donald. He tells me you had a lovely weekend in the country."

"Did he, now?"

"Yes, musical evenings, long walks, fresh air . . . the kind of country weekend I always enjoyed at your age."

"Mother, at my age you were married with two children."

"Indeed, child bride, that's what I told everyone. Your father was so insistent."

James thought sadly of his father long since dead, a quiet man, a solicitor who'd never, it seemed to James, said more than two words together. He tried to imagine his father overpowering his mother's wishes, and failed.

"I suppose this is definite, then?"

"What?" She finished her sherry in a gulp and stood up, sitting down again as suddenly.

"This—This dog, Mack." Mack opened his eyes slightly at the sound of his name.

"But of course. A fine dog, a lapdog, affectionate, loyal, brave, not very intelligent I'm afraid. I got him from a shop, two hundred pounds he cost me. A breeder called by to see me. Said the dog is not quite show quality, with that tongue of his." They both turned to study the long pink tongue that lolled through the dog's mouth even in sleep.

"It's called an 'awry tongue,' it's a flaw apparently," Mrs. Fleming tutted as she studied the animal.

"Well, Mother," James said, knowing in his heart his mother could never organize herself to the extent of keeping a dog for show purposes, "not to worry. It gives him a comical expression that's rather endearing." So it did. Mack moved in against James's stomach and stretched his short, bowed legs in a monkeylike clasp around his thigh.

Strange, he thought, the relaxing effect the warmth and weight of a dog's body had on one's nervous system. James looked more kindly on Mack and hoped this soporific effect would quickly extend to his mother—for many years to come.

James deposited the limp, sleeping dog on the chaise longue and went dutifully around the house locking up doors and windows. His mother changed into yet another of her flowered summer frocks and she carried yet another capacious—this time embroidered—handbag.

As he gallantly armed her to his car, he could not but notice the enormous opal ring she sported on her right hand.

"Is that new?" he asked as he lowered her into the low-slung front seat.

"It was dear Mummy's," she said, dropping her eyes again in that old flirtatiously demure manner that so drove him mad.

As he started the engine he could not suppress a comment. "I'm surprised, that's all."

"By its size? But you know my father always bought—"

"No, no," he said as he deliberately roared the engine—awakening the somnolent birds in the cherry trees that lined the gracious cul-de-sac, and letting the neighbors know he was back. "No . . . it's just that opals are meant to be bad luck."

This was met by a long silence. His mother, despite her Protestant upbringing, was nonetheless as susceptible as all Irish people to the powers of superstition.

"I didn't know that," she said at last. He saw her from the corner of his eye as she studied the ring, slowly twisting it. Finally she quietly slipped it off her finger and put it in her bag. "It's a wonder Mummy didn't know of this," she said, and James as usual was riddled with guilt.

"I didn't mean you . . ."

"Well, you'd know a deal about these things after your visit to Buncloda," she interjected most pointedly.

"So Donald did tell you!" His guilt was replaced by irritation.

"He said it was all stuff and nonsense, but that you were most influenced." She stressed the last two words. "Apparitions indeed!"

"Jaysus!" James said through clenched teeth.

"No, really, James. It's as I would expect. He's a man of science, unlike yourself. Objective, logical, not easily swayed . . ."

James saw the traffic slow suddenly ahead of him and slammed on his brakes.

"And a better driver, even though you're older."

"This will be a long evening," he mumbled under his breath.

Their preprandial cocktail in the restaurant was fraught with tension. His mother was as tenacious as a ferret, and he felt like a schoolboy justifying a visit to an X-rated movie.

"Mother," he said at last, "the whole country has been interested in the events in Buncloda since May! You can't just ignore what's going on around you! The three of us were curious . . . well, Geraldine and I were. It was a lark, but then having been there, and now having stayed on, I can say it's more than that."

"But that's what I don't understand, James. Why have you returned to that place?"

"If you must know, I am on a case . . ." he said hesitantly.

"A legal case?" she asked with suspicion.

"No, actually." He tried to slough it off. "A private case, a private arrangement . . ."

"An investigation, is it? You know my feelings on this, James. These mysteries of yours are nearly as bad as your preoccupation with trains. Although I must say I am happy to see that has faded."

"Look, Mother, it's time to order . . ." James said it pleasantly. He chose a fine Haute Medoc, and while waiting for their meal, they both got slightly tipsy. Mrs. Fleming was amusing when it came to telling him about her ventures into the upper-class society of pug enthusiasts.

"Do you know, James, they are replacing corgis as the dog of choice? And on Sunday I had an especially pleasant excursion, out in the Phoenix Park . . ."

"Mother, I'm surprised. I thought you never crossed the Liffey to the north side," James teased, referring to her snobbery.

Her cheeks were flushed from the wine and she laughed at

herself. "Only on special occasions. This was the outdoor meeting, James, of the pug society. It was lovely weather. All the owners of pugs meet of a Sunday once a month, so that the dogs can mingle and run free. They need socialization, you see. Although I couldn't let Mack off the lead, since he won't come when I call his name. Most worrying, that . . . Some charming people, though. I've already two invitations for get-togethers. A Mrs. Brennan for afternoon tea next week. And a handsome man, trés suave, a widower actually. Mentioned tickets to a play at the Gate."

James's ears pricked up. Although his mother's social life was very full, it had never occurred to him before this that she might start seeing a man.

"A date?" he blurted, letting the wine loosen his tongue.

"We shall see. I have the idea he was in trade. Maybe a plumber?" She made a little moue of distaste. "No future there then, James."

James didn't know whether to be relieved in some adolescent fashion that his mother wouldn't be dating, or courting, as she would call it. Or annoyed that she was yet again revealing her genteel snobbery.

"Honestly, Mother, it shouldn't matter what he did for a living. We're all one under the skin."

"Of course you would say that now, since you are in thrall to these people in Buncloda."

"Wait a minute. I am not under any thrall. But I admit I find it fascinating to observe an event such as this at firsthand."

"Observe what? It's just nerves. I'd expect that in the Mediterranean countries. Italians, now, they are so highstrung. They seem to go in for that kind of thing, don't they?" James groaned but stopped himself as the waiter served their soup.

"I imagine it's the heat there, and all that hot blood," she resumed, and then paused as if struck by an idea. "But you know what the papers say?"

"No . . ." James said, expecting the worst.

"That the spring and summer weather have been so bad in Ireland this year that the people are restless, depressed, to use that foolish word the papers are so fond of. That's it! The people are looking for excitement." She looked at him triumphantly.

"It's not excitement, Mother, or hysteria," James said patiently. "Nor mob psychology, as Donald no doubt described it to you. It's a large number of people, a crowd, yes—that has some kind of common will. And there is a certain atmosphere. There is at times a great sense of awe, even of reverence. Then times of great silence, a sense of devotion that is palpable. And almost always there is a feeling of potential energy."

He wisely chose not to speak of the visionaries themselves, or of Geraldine, but he felt compelled as ever to try to make his mother understand.

"Listen," he continued. "Do you remember Mrs. Leahy?"

"No, I don't think so."

"Of course you do," he started to snap. "She was the local woman who minded me at times when I was a young boy. When you had your golf lessons or whatever . . ."

"Was that her name?" she said absently. James grew irritated, for he had strong, fond memories of the kindly maternal woman.

"Yes, and when she minded me, sometimes she'd bring me into her church—"

"Oh dear! Had I but known . . ."

James ignored the interruption. "She'd take me sometimes, and sprinkle me with holy water." He smiled inadvertently at the memory. "And we'd light candles in the small side chapels, and pray for all the dead people she knew. She seemed to know a great many. At first I was uneasy, it was so strange. The church itself always seemed dark, but the candles shimmered, and the gold on the altar, and the painted statues seemed rich and darkly warm. She showed me the little red light, the sacristy light, that always burns near the altar. I remember sensing then more of a presence in that Catholic church, and the others we visited, than I ever sensed in our own."

"James! Please. I am shocked."

"No, you're not. And I'm making a point. The atmosphere in Buncloda is sometimes like that."

"No, James. I think it exists in your own mind. Somehow a faint childhood memory was triggered off. As I say—if I had but known about this Mrs. Leahy's activities . . ." She drifted off as the main course of duck à l'orange was served before her. Her eyes lit up.

"Well you might have, but you never asked me about her, or anything else, for that matter."

"James, such whining. Eat your food. Or else next you'll be telling me you've seen an apparition or a ghost or whatever it is supposed to be."

"No," James said slowly, "I don't honestly think that will happen."

His mind had drifted as they finished their meal and ordered coffee and brandies. But why, he mused, was he so sure he would not see a vision? Why had he answered with such certainty when caught off guard, when asked like that, so suddenly? But it was true. He had no sense of anything remotely happening to himself in that regard. And yet he was almost convinced that Geraldine had experienced something. Why did he believe that, accept that? Did he believe in any of it, and if he did, why did he not believe that he too might experience a spiritual manifestation?

Such was the theme of his thinking that night as he drove slowly back to Buncloda. He'd rung up Mrs. Kehoe to say he would be returning very late and not to be alarmed if she heard him coming in. She wouldn't mind waiting up herself, as she said. He knew this was true since he had himself observed that the demarcations of day and night had blurred in Buncloda. Ordinary life, ordinary time—they had been fractured by the intervention of the divine into daily life.

James's thoughts turned to the principals in the rural drama. His interview with Tim had suggested that Devane had not been an actual seer. Yet he'd been portrayed as such in the early reports in the papers. Devane himself had never contradicted those reports. Perhaps, like Geraldine, he was shy of speaking of it, played down his experience with the hard-headed farmers and scoffing youth of his acquaintance.

And Miss Garrotty? She hadn't made her role, her experience, as clear as he would have expected. He'd wanted details. But then she had obviously been drained by her ordeal of the morning. And she didn't really know him from Adam. Perhaps for her, it too was immensely personal, too large, to somehow betray by talking about it. At least to him.

After all, Mary Dowd was younger, full of life, a young woman with a boyfriend, a fulfilling job, a fine little house. She could afford to speak out. Miss Garrotty, she was a sad case, really, stuck with her unfeeling brothers in a sterile kind of lifestyle. How much more, then, would she cling to the great secret? Hadn't she used the word "tarnished"? He could see her point now. Miss Garrotty would want to keep that thrilling larger-than-life experience unsullied, pressed close to her unfulfilled bosom.

Actually, he observed, as his mind cleared from the wine and the mixed emotions his mother always called forth from him, Mary Dowd was the best possible witness for this event. How much more dubious people would have been if it had been Miss Garrotty or another like her: alone, and lonely, embittered, wanting to make her mark. Her testimony alone would have been suspect. Fulfilling too many stereotypes, it would never carry as much weight as the testimony of a young girl with her head clearly screwed on like Mary Dowd.

There was, he speculated as he neared Buncloda, a larger pattern to be discerned in all of this, a wise design.

It was just three when he drove down the main street to where it branched off into the little road he now called his temporary home. How familiar it seemed, so quickly he'd come to know it. Yet something was different, something amiss. Lights were still on throughout the village, and far out in the countryside in the farmhouses. He noted more cars parked on the main road, on the verges. More caravans too. Perhaps he just hadn't noticed before, he thought, remembering the night he'd walked home from the pub full of hot whiskies. Now, thoughts of his soft bed and a very large fry in the morning impelled him to his destination.

Chapter Thirteen

James might have slept longer than the lunch hour if Mrs. Kehoe had not pounded on his door.

Calling out a muffled greeting to silence her, he was more than surprised when she entered the room with a small tray.

"I knew better than to wake you for breakfast, Mr. Fleming," she said, disapproval in her voice. "You know, I did hear you arrive in the wee small hours. Took your lady friend back to Dublin I imagine."

He shook his head in wonder at her nosiness. But he noted with enthusiasm the glass of orange juice and the steaming mug of coffee. "I must say this is very thoughtful of you, Mrs. Kehoe," he said as he settled on his pillows, feeling for once like a well-loved child home from school with the measles.

"Ah, don't go coddin' yourself like that," Mrs. Kehoe said wryly. "It's just that Sergeant Molloy called by here at breakfast and he's downstairs now, wanting to see you. I hadn't the heart to tell that hardworking man that the young

solicitor was still in his bed! You'll be wanting to get dressed,
I imagine." She said this quite pointedly.

"Molloy? Did he say what he wanted?" James was surprised the man would call at his lodgings.

"No, but I can guess. It's Rita. Miss Garrotty. No one's
seen her this day."

"Surely she's at the grotto, if anywhere," James said,
falling back on the pillows and wondering how he was to
dress quickly if she didn't take herself off.

"Seemingly not, but the sergeant is waiting." She planted
herself in his open door, and James realized that, like any
mother, she wasn't leaving until she saw he was out of the
bed.

"Right, right!" he said, getting out from under the pink
cloud of coverings. Even the sight of him in his underwear
didn't cause her to blush. "I'm up," he said challengingly.

"Good enough. I'll tell him you're on your way."

In moments James was down in the small, sunless sitting
room. The day was overcast. Everything in the room,
including Molloy, appeared drab and worn.

"Sergeant," James said heartily, "what can I do for you?"

"Mr. Fleming. We are all of us a little alarmed. Miss
Garrotty hasn't been seen about these last few hours . . ."

"But how can I help you? I only returned last night, or
rather this morning, after a strenuous trip to Dublin." James
felt obliged to justify his late rising.

"Aye, yes, so I've been told."

Mrs. Kehoe again, James thought. "Well, what can I do?
How long is she missing?"

"That's just it. We cannot pin it down. The brothers
didn't see her at breakfast. Now strange as this might sound
to you, they have their own fixed routine. Rita has made
them a full breakfast every day of their lives, or close enough
to it."

"But recent events at the grotto, surely . . ."

"No, even then. And they know her ways well, natural

enough. She would go out in the dawn, and return in good time to have the rashers and sausages and eggs all on the table. She'd be servin' them in the back kitchen while they went around, opening up for the day, putting on lights, taking deliveries. Naturally, when the breakfast wasn't there, and she wasn't either, they were alarmed. They checked her room and she wasn't there asleep, as they thought she might have been."

"Then surely she's at the grotto," James said, stubbornly repeating himself for the third time. "You must have heard yourself she was there yesterday morning with Mary Dowd." If Molloy knew he was up in Dublin last night, James thought, then he sure as hell knew that. But he refrained from saying so.

"We've been up there."

"Those are large crowds, Sergeant."

"Aye, but she's never to anyone's knowledge gone there without Mary Dowd."

"And where is Mary?"

"She's at home. She hasn't spoken to Rita. Not since the whole thing last evening . . ."

"What whole thing?"

"I'll get to that . . ."

"What's been going on?" James asked again.

"When exactly did you leave yesterday, Fleming?" Molloy demanded, taking his notebook out.

"Let me see, I saw Miss Garrotty at the shop at about half-ten. Stayed an hour. I think I was at the rectory by noon or thereabouts. I honestly didn't check my watch. I left then to drive my medical friend back to her hospital in Dublin. Why do you ask?" he said, suddenly aware that Molloy was actually questioning him.

"Just tell me now, how did Miss Garrotty seem to you?"

"She was clearly tired, weary in fact. Her hours at the grotto on her knees, she told me, had worn her out."

"Anything else? Anything more telling than that?" Molloy seemed impatient.

"Well, she seemed a little fearful when we were talking first . . ."

"Of you?" Molloy said harshly.

"Of course not," James replied, taken aback. "She said the crowd that morning, yesterday morning, had frightened her. She felt threatened in some way."

"She used that word 'threatened'?"

"No, no, no. She was describing the change she'd sensed in the people's mood. She felt they were more demanding, that they pressed in close on herself and Mary Dowd. She was bothered too, she said, by their calling out for a sign. I hadn't been up at the grotto so I couldn't gauge for myself how much of what she was saying was her own reaction and how much was perhaps genuinely threatening."

"Nor I, Fleming, but I've been there since and . . . Listen, Fleming, you do realize that you are the last person to have spoken to her—"

"She's been missing since then!" James was stunned at this piece of news, but at least it explained Molloy's demeanor.

"No, no. She was *seen* after that, the brothers ate lunch with her. And Mary Dowd spoke with her too . . . last night."

"Then what in the name of God are you getting at?" James was annoyed at being misled, however briefly.

"You were the last, how shall I say it, the last neutral person to see her, to actually talk with her about things. Everyone else is involved. Everyone else, let me say, has been . . . a part of the events here."

"Why don't you just say I am the outsider here and be done with it!"

"That's it, Fleming, as you say. But you've taken me up wrong. You are the outsider, and as such your insights are valuable to me."

James looked at the man's impassive, long face. He'd underestimated Molloy.

"Right. I'll help you in whatever way I can."

"It's that conversation you had with her. Think again. Did she seem all right to you? You said she seemed fearful. Could she have been fearful of one person rather than of the crowd as a whole?"

"I definitely did not have that sense. It was much more that events here in Buncloda seemed to be overtaking her. She seemed a little depressed, but again that might have been fatigue. Remember, I don't know this woman. I have no basis for comparison. She was recalling how she used to pray at the grotto before the apparition. She seemed nostalgic. And she described how after the apparition in May the people who came were devout and reverent. I tell you, Molloy, I think she just seemed frightened by the crowd yesterday morning."

"Right, then come with me and you'll see why."

Together they walked until they rounded the bend of the small hill and the panorama came into view. The little valley formed by the two hills was a moving sea of people. As far as the eye could see there were people, a seething, colorful mass of indistinct faces and limbs, of blurred hues of clothing and baggage. As the crowd moved forward, the sea became a living wall, enjambed, immovable.

James, increasingly uneasy, inched forward with Molloy, elbowing their way. If Molloy hadn't been in uniform, James doubted they would have made any progress at all. Slowly, slowly, sweating profusely now from exertion and the heat around them of hundreds of bodies, they edged ahead until suddenly they came upon a ribbon of a space.

James glanced to his left and right and saw that the path, for so it was, wound its way up from the actual tarred road, crossed in front of the statue, and presumably descended back to the tarred road on the far side. Rope looped through iron fencing stakes demarcated this path from the crowds. James marveled at the fact the people respected even that feeble attempt at order, and he said so.

"Ah, they've not lost their reason entirely. Although when

they surge forward, pressed from behind, the path does get obscured. But they right it themselves. They're respectful still."

James heard the first note of apprehension in the phlegmatic Molloy's voice.

"This path is Father Donnelly's doing. He saw the necessity of it yesterday. Even poor Father Maguire had to cave in and come over to help out. He addressed the people. And then they got a team of young ones to work out the path and put in the stakes. I've a few men of my own posted on the perimeters too."

"But why? What is this all about?" James was puzzled.

"Look, look now, here's another one." Molloy pointed his finger down the path, focusing James's attention.

Coming up the path towards where they were standing, nearly at midpoint of the first leg of the triangle, was an older woman painfully edging her way with the support of an aluminium walker. She was accompanied by three other people, her family presumably. James could see that others were following in her wake. Looking up the hill, now that his attention was caught, James observed even more pilgrims, some on crutches, some using canes, and two, to his astonishment, climbing the hardened path on their knees.

"I can't believe this," he cried. "I was here in town yesterday! What happened to bring all this to a head?"

"It's hard to say exactly. I do know that Mary Dowd spoke with Father Donnelly yesterday morning. At about the time you would have been talking to Miss Garrotty. Donnelly told me that Mary Dowd said there was to be a great sign given here." Molloy's serious face scanned the crowd as he spoke.

"She didn't say this sign would be to herself. She did say the people should pray and have great faith. It's my guess, knowing him, that Father Donnelly spread the word here in Buncloda. And then it was just word of mouth. But I can hardly believe the numbers myself, or this, this . . ." He waved his bony hands at the pilgrims on the path. "It seems every cripple from here to Cork has arrived."

The two men stood in dumbfounded silence for some minutes. James acknowledged to himself that he was secretly excited, caught up in the events unfolding around him, wondering what the great sign could be. He drew himself back to matters at hand.

"With a crowd this size, Miss Garrotty would easily be lost in it."

"That's true. The question is why. She always prayed near the statue, and always went with Mary Dowd. We know her habits. Why would she suddenly choose to lose herself here in the midst of this mass when only yesterday she told you she was afraid of the crowd?"

"Perhaps she was so overwhelmed that she has taken herself off somewhere, hoping to avoid further attention from the crowd, further attention from the media."

"I hope that's it, Fleming, out of character as it would be for her. But perhaps we're all a little bit out of kilter here in Buncloda, hmm?" He looked at James and, for the first time, his eyes crinkled in the hint of a smile.

"Listen, I've got to get back. The Garrotty brothers said they'd cousins in Cork city. They're to ring them to see just in case she went there, unlikely as it seems. Fleming, I'll be in and around the shop if you think of anything else that might be of help. Anything at all." Molloy despondently shook his head.

"Molloy, before you go. Has there been any progress on the boy's murder itself?"

"Aye, a bit. We got a sketch artist from Dublin to draw the dead lad's face. People, you know, they don't like to look at a photo of a dead man. We're circulating the drawing now around the outlying villages. You know, we can't just fax these things to the rural places. And so it all takes time. Of course we're sending it to the big cities too, but my gut feeling is that he was a country lad." He shook his head again. "I can't tell you, Fleming, how simple a place this used to be." He looked up to catch James's expression and smiled. "Then again, maybe it wasn't. But it surely wasn't as crowded," he said over his shoulder as he began to push his way off into the crowd.

James remained where he was for some long time, mesmerized by the scene in front of him, like a curious child at some strange parade. The next person on the path who caught his eye was a stocky woman in her fifties, moving painfully forward on her knees. Her hair bound up in a kerchief, her lips were moving and her forehead was knotted in concentration. She was grasping a long pair of rosary beads as she moved slowly, pausing every few seconds to balance herself on the rough, inclined ground. About twenty feet behind her was a painfully thin teenage girl in a wheelchair. As the old man who pushed it stopped to gasp for breath, James saw the nearly vacant expression of the girl, whom he guessed to be anorexic. Suddenly aware of his stares, she looked up, pulling a thin blanket around her before looking away. James stood stock-still, horrified by what to him was so unfamiliar. He glanced around him and realized no one else thought this scene was strange.

A strong young man approached on crutches. Surely a mere broken ankle, James assumed, until he saw the peculiar twist of the lower left leg, the unnatural angle of the misshapen foot. Still, the young man's face was smiling as he looked straight ahead at the statue in the distance, sweat rolling off his brow. Behind him James saw a family group praying aloud, a father carrying a spastic child of ten in his arms. James was overwhelmed by a powerful rush of pity and wonder. He turned his face from the sight of so much pain. But as he shut his eyes against it, he knew it wasn't the pain he could not abide, but the naked expressions of hope.

Drawing breath, James moved deeper into the crowd, away from the petitioners' painful queue. Their numbers so great, there was no way the people could pray as a group.

Prayers were being said of all manners and kinds. A sound that must have resembled that of the biblical Babel rose to the heavens.

He scanned the crowd from his single vantage point, hoping to spot Miss Garrotty and put Molloy's mind at rest. After twenty minutes or so he realized how very difficult a task this would prove. Already his eyes were tired from straining to distinguish one plain face from the many before him, female forms in summer dresses, blouses, skirts, and cardigans. Miss Garrotty, he realized, would be indistinguishable from many of her countrywomen at a distance. James gave up in despair at the numbers and, increasingly uneasy, left the scene to gain a sense of relief, a bit of fresh air in some open space. Turning away from the direction of the town, he took the road on the far side.

This road, leading as it did into the countryside, was less well-traveled by the pilgrims flooding in from around the county. There were still some cars parked by the roadside for at least a mile, and some pilgrims walking. Even the vendors had abandoned this road as a good site for impulse buyers. James walked on past the last car parked on the verge, finally gaining a stretch of road that resembled the others in Ireland: lonely, deserted, bounded by large tracts of grazing land, bordered by hedgerows still intact, untrampled by pilgrim feet.

The day had brightened, and James breathed in deeply, clearing his mind from thoughts of Miss Garrotty. He made his mind a blank. He'd walked, with his long loping stride, about five miles when he noticed a farmhouse across a field to his left. As he walked, he saw Keep Out signs posted on two cow gates he passed. More were nailed to the occasional sycamore trees that rose from the drainage ditches. As he approached the driveway or entrance to the farm itself, he noted also a newly built gate reinforcing the narrower cow gate and stone pillars. As he stood, he counted at least ten of the unwelcoming signs, all roughly hand printed, around this entrance way.

The location of the farm and the fairly new and numerous signs gave James the idea that this farm might belong to the now-reclusive Devane.

Hopping over the two fences, James strode up the drive with determination. If he was being observed, he wished to show confidence and purpose. As he neared the house a man with a shotgun stepped from the blue-painted front door, waving wildly, shouting.

James made a show of holding his hand to his ear in a gesture of not hearing. He walked on, his heart pounding, but the man did not seem to be terribly threatening, hugging his doorway and waving as he was.

"Get out, I tell you!" James could decipher the words at last.

"What, what is that you say!" he shouted, waving one arm in a friendly greeting.

"Get out, get out!" The man's voice seemed to be cracking.

James stopped within shouting distance.

"I'm a friend of Father Donnelly's," he shouted as loud as he could.

The man paused abruptly in his frantic waving. "What do you want?"

"Just a chat, that's all, I assure you. I mean you no harm." James's voice was growing hoarse.

"Are you a reporter?" screamed the man.

"No, no. I'm a friend of Father Donnelly's. I'm trying to help him . . ." James's voice gave out. Fortunately, the man waved him on, still hugging his shelter.

"How do you do," James said as he drew near and held out his hand. "Mr. Devane," for so he assumed it was. "My name is James Fleming. I'm a solicitor and I've been helping Father Donnelly sort out some issues since the murder of the poor young lad."

The man's face relaxed a little, but he didn't stir or invite James inside. He kept his shotgun open-breeched.

James thought him to be in his early sixties perhaps, or

even late fifties. He was small, and hardened from years of outdoor work. His face was hard to read except for the initial fear that James had seen there. Now it was nearly impassive. Yet James thought he could see something there: either great fatigue or else signs of some illness unaddressed.

"And what would you be wantin'?" the man said.

"I've been talking with Mary Dowd and with Miss Garrotty, and I wish to talk with you, if I may?"

"So they've found her, then," the man said with a sigh of relief.

"No, I'm afraid not, but I've no doubt they will," James replied.

"Oh, that's bad. Tell me your name again?" he asked, suddenly suspicious.

"James Fleming."

"Hold on, then. I've no wish to offend, but I've been tricked by reporters before. I'm going to ring Father Donnelly now." The man watched James's face for a reaction and saw only that James was agreeable.

The man went inside, not inviting James to come with him, but James took this with good grace.

Moments later he returned. "You are who you say you are."

"I'm glad to hear it!" James laughed, and Devane joined in. They began to stroll companionably through the grassy field that surrounded the house. In the distance James could see five or six young heifers frolicking and rubbing themselves along the dry stone wall.

"You have a fine farm here, Mr. Devane."

"Not bad, not bad, but a lot of blood, sweat, and tears, as they say. And for what in the end?" The man sighed.

"It's a credit to yourself, surely," James said.

"Aye, but I've no one to leave it after me. My wife and I had no children, you see, and now she's gone too."

"Was she a religious woman, would you say?"

"She was indeed, Mr. Fleming. That's what made me a bit

130

bitter after she passed away. She was a good and holy woman. Never missed Mass of a Sunday or holy day. Went to her devotions regular. Said the Rosary in the bed every night . . . you know the way." He said this rhetorically, nudging some small stones out of the ground with the toe of his muddy boot.

"A fine woman and a good wife. She was so sad she never had family. It takes the stuffing out of you after a while. And then she upped and died on me. Ah . . ." He exhaled with some level of bitterness or loneliness, James thought, or a mixture of both.

"And yourself?" James prodded, knowing time was short with this laconic farmer.

"Oh, the usual. Never religious like the wife."

"But now you've taken part in this great event here in Buncloda . . ." James said, continuing to lead, but straining not to put words into Devane's mouth.

"Well, now," Devane sighed, "like I told that Father Donnelly at the time, how much a part of it I was, I'm not sure."

"Tell me about it. It won't go any further, I assure you."

"And this is a help to you?" The man looked skeptically at him.

"Yes, in a way."

"All right, then. I was passing that morning as usual, and Miss Garrotty came down the hill waving wildly at me. I left the truck and hustled up to her, thinking maybe one of them was taken sick.

"She was wild-eyed, nearly stuttering. Waving back towards the grotto. She said she'd seen a bright white light, or a globe of light, something of that nature. I could see Miss Dowd staring up at the statue, standing like a statue herself.

"We walked up the hill and I stared too, and after a few minutes I could see a light sort of shining all around the statue. Mary Dowd was calling out the Hail Mary and the Memorare and God-knows-what-else holy prayers. Then suddenly she dropped down on her knees and hung her head. You know, Fleming, all this was only taking seconds. It's taken me longer to tell it than it took to happen . . ."

"Go on, please, I'm very interested."

"I bent over her to see was she all right, and she let out a great sigh and said it's over, oh, it's over. Tears were streaming down her face. I helped her up and only then looked at Miss Garrotty, and she looked so frightened I got a bit alarmed myself."

"What was it that frightened you?"

"I can't put it into words, sir. It was as though we'd seen something fearful. A ghost perhaps, only not a ghost. This was a holy place after all."

"What did you do then?"

"Mary stood up and was leaning on me and crying out: 'Did you see it, oh God, did you see it?' Miss Garrotty came near and asked her what she'd seen.

"Mary Dowd said as clear as day: 'The Blessed Virgin, didn't you see her?'

"Miss Garrotty nodded her head as though struck dumb, and then they turned to me, Mary Dowd screamin' at me did I see it, and I told them how as I'd seen the glowing bright light that was gone.

"We were all shaking with the cold by then, and I walked them to the truck. Mary sat into it and said, 'Oh thanks be to God all three of us saw it.' She kept repeating to herself that it was a miracle. Over and over again.

"I drove them to Mary Dowd's house and they both got out, Mary still trembling and weeping, and Miss Garrotty, I thought for a strong woman she looked like she'd faint herself. They asked me in but I'd got to get to the dairy . . . and so I went."

The man fell silent. James pondered the discrepancies between the story he'd just heard and the version of that story Tim had given him in the pub. He tried to get Devane to open up again. But the farmer preempted him.

"I've to get to the bottom field now, Mr. Fleming."

"Of course. I won't keep you any longer from your work, Mr. Devane, but I thank you for talking with me."

"Aye, talk to Mary Dowd—she'll tell you all. Or Father Donnelly, if he hasn't told you already."

"Told me what?" James said puzzled.

"All of what happened next. I'll tell you this for nothin', though," Devane said. "I'm not sure if my own wife would have taken to all of this."

James retreated to town, analyzing, as he walked, all of what he'd heard, trying for the first time to fit the pieces of the various stories together. By the time he reached the grotto, the road was nearly impassable. The weather had brightened considerably, and there was a warmth in the air that seemed to have lifted everyone's spirits. Although the crowd and its activities were exactly the same, there seemed a more festive atmosphere, a different tone to the voices. As he passed, he heard people chatting pleasantly, some sitting on the far hill spreading out towels and rugs, eating their sandwiches as though at a picnic or on the strand on the fine summer's afternoon that it in fact was.

James marveled at the power that the weather in Ireland had in influencing the population. In a matter of two hours the crowd, which had seemed earlier to have become a threatening beast, had transformed itself into something comfortingly familiar and pleasant. The crowd's mood lifted his own. He looked to the statue as he stood with the people on the tarred road. From this distance, it looked very small, its outline fuzzy and indistinct. No features could be made out, just the familiar tilt of the head, the shades of white and blue of the robes. The slanting sun was catching what little gold and pink paint still adhered to the trim of the robes and the sandaled feet, and it seemed to glint and gleam. There was nothing frightening or threatening here, he thought. Nor was there anything divine or mystical. A familiar statue in a familiar setting—common to rural Ireland, common to the front yards of New York, common to seaside villages in Italy, common to Catholic communities throughout the world! So . . . why here, he wondered, and why now? Why—if he chose to believe for the sake of the argument—would the Mother of Christ manifest herself in this place, this small village in Ireland, in the month of May? And allowing that she chose this place and this time, then why appear to Mary Dowd, to Rita Garrotty, to Joseph Devane? As he headed for the nearest public telephone kiosk, he had formed these and many other questions to pose to Jude Donnelly.

—— *Chapter Fourteen* ——

It had been difficult to pin Father Donnelly down to an appointment time. James appreciated his concern over Miss Garrotty and for the growing crowds at the grotto. What James did not appreciate was the priest's dismissive attitude towards himself over the phone, and his implication that James had large amounts of disposable time. Billable time, were it not for Geraldine's personal request!

He resented being shuffled around in Jude's life, primarily because he didn't like Jude Donnelly. There was something that didn't ring true about the man. As James strode along the now balmy main street, past women and children in light summer clothes, he neglected to consider that perhaps he resented Jude's proprietary attitude towards Geraldine's childhood years.

James met Father Maguire in the front hallway of the rectory, and together they entered the dining room, chatting cordially. James caught the irritation in Jude's eye as he stood to greet them.

"Has there been any word, Father Donnelly, on Miss Garrotty?" James asked after they all sat down.

"No, I'm afraid not. I've been up and down to the grotto all day. In fact this will be a very quick meal, since Mary Dowd is waiting for me to bring her there." He paused slightly. "She's distressed about Rita Garrotty and wants to pray for her."

"Humph," Father Maguire said as he spooned potatoes onto his plate. "And who's to say she's in need of prayers?"

"Father Maguire, I think all of us need prayers, especially the prayers of someone as close to God as Mary Dowd obviously is . . ."

"Who of us can know another's heart?" Maguire commented.

"Surely that she's been, ah, *chosen,* is proof of that?" James asked.

"Fleming?" Maguire looked at James closely from rheumy eyes. "I had hoped you would be a neutral observer."

"I think I remain neutral, Father, but at the same time I cannot but be aware of a certain religious atmosphere here in Buncloda," James said sincerely.

"Ah ha," Jude broke in. "Something in you is responding to the truth embedded in these events . . ."

"What truth?" Maguire snapped.

"That the eternal intervenes in our temporal world . . ."

"Indeed, Jude, what you say is true. *Has* been true for two thousand years! Christ was born into this world and changed human history forever . . ."

"You deliberately misunderstand me, Father. I'm saying that Mary, Christ's mother, has appeared here, just as she appeared at Knock and Fatima and Lourdes and Guadalupe and other less well-known sites . . ."

"That's the nub of my question," James interrupted. The two men looked at him. "Assuming Mary has manifested herself here in Buncloda, my question to you is: why? Why do these events always seem to take place in rural places?

Why not in Dublin, for example? And for that matter, why does she appear to peasants and children?"

"Fleming, Mary Dowd is hardly a child. But I assume you are thinking of the seers at Fatima and Lourdes. They were children. But there have been many others: documented history of such things has shown that there have been more adult visionaries than children, and more men than women!"

"All right, but still these have not been people of power and influence—why?"

Jude finished his meal and stood to leave. "Firstly, Fleming, you must remember she only appears to us as an intermediary, not as a power in her own right. Secondly, imagine if a head of state claimed to have experienced an apparition, and announced this to the world? How would that news be received? With ridicule, or suspicion. And if the public did not think he was deranged, then they'd say he'd concocted the divine message to serve his own ends. Such a person's credibility would be questioned."

Jude continued, now waving his hands in excitement. "But when it's this way, people accept the miraculous with simple faith. Because the visionaries who bring the message have nothing to gain—not wealth nor power—no suspicion attaches to them."

"I have to interrupt here, Father Donnelly," Maguire said, leaning back in his chair and pushing away his plate. "What you describe sounds so straightforward. But a lot intervenes between the time the so-called visionary has the vision and the point at which the news is disseminated to the faithful."

"What are you getting at?" Jude said crossly.

"I'm suggesting that other people can influence the visionary and thereby the situation." Maguire looked pointedly at Jude but his expression was impassive.

"Father Maguire is a skeptic, I'm afraid," Jude said at last, shrugging at James.

"But skeptics are infinitely valuable," James said. "I

know from my practice of law. To convince a skeptic of the truth of an issue is going to be your greatest triumph, in fact not your own, but the triumph of objective fact."

Father Maguire had gone to his desk, and from a locked drawer withdrew some papers. "Perhaps I am a skeptic, perhaps I am objective, Jude. But my point is that these statements which I took down from Miss Dowd, Miss Garrotty, and Mr. Devane tell me something." He turned to James. "Miss Dowd came to the rectory. She spoke with Jude and then with me in Jude's presence. He came to me already completely convinced."

"Yes, I admit that. But please remember, Father, I *was* the first person she had told of this. The rush of her words, her animation, her very demeanor was as convincing as her story . . ."

"But surely she had already spoken with Miss Garrotty and Mr. Devane—at the grotto?" James interjected.

"Oh, yes, I was forgetting. I should say . . ." Jude paused, almost stumbling, "that I was the first nonparticipant in the vision whom she spoke to."

"Jude, you must see that your quick acquiescence, your haste to believe, might have only served to encourage her?" Maguire was very serious.

"Why wouldn't I encourage her! She shared the miracle with me! And I realized that I was privileged to be part of this experience. This would be the unique moment in my life . . . and of course important for the parish, for the village as well," he added hastily.

Maguire sighed. "I just want you to see that you contaminated the evidence of Mary Dowd with your unthinking enthusiasm and acceptance. By the time I spoke with her, she was convinced that what she thought had happened, had actually happened."

"Is there a difference?" Jude said loudly.

"Of course there is, man! She was virtually unshakable . . ."

"You know, even eyewitnesses to accidents, for example,

have doubts, second thoughts, get confused." James interrupted as he saw the standoff developing between the two men. "May I look over the statements?"

James read the papers as the housekeeper discreetly served the coffee to the three silent men.

"At a quick glance," James said finally, "I can see an obvious difference in the three statements. Mary Dowd's seems more coherent, with a real narrative flow. Miss Garrotty's actually adds very little. Her statement confirms Mary's, but it seems more concerned with describing Mary Dowd's behavior rather than her own reactions or interpretations of events. Yet she is obviously fully in awe of what has happened. Devane's is the shortest. He seems at pains to describe how he happened to be at the grotto at all. But then we get more description in his statement than in the others about the great white light, as he calls it."

"Let me see those again," Donnelly said rudely. Feigning diffidence, James handed them over and watched as Jude flipped through the pages.

"Look here, Fleming, in Mary's statement she says: 'I saw at first a shimmering light, formless and like a mist really. Then it brightened, it seemed to surround the statue, and then I realized it was in the form of the statue. Then I realized it was not the statue glowing, but a figure of a woman in front of it. A beautiful young woman.' See, she does speak of the bright light!"

"But only initially, Jude," Maguire said. "She very quickly moves on to describe the figure. Read on. The next line is more important. I remember, because I was taking down her words as she spoke."

Jude read: "'I know now that it was the Blessed Virgin who appeared to me . . .'"

"Right. Listen, Jude, where does it say that in the two other statements? Hmmm? They both describe Mary Dowd, and Devane describes the light. Why aren't they also saying they 'know now it was the Blessed Virgin'?"

Jude opened his mouth but nothing came out.

Maguire continued, firmly but more kindly than James had seen him. "They don't, because they hadn't personally talked to you before they talked to me. I got their unadulterated versions, Jude. Whereas I got Mary Dowd's only after she spoke with you. I've asked you this before. Did you suggest to her that it was the Virgin whom she had seen?"

"No, no, she said it to me herself. I perhaps confirmed it in my own immediate reaction. But my God, who else could it have been?"

"That's not the question: 'Who else could it have been'!" Maguire shouted, his impatience showing. "The real question is, did this happen at all?"

"Yes," Jude said simply. "Mary Dowd wouldn't lie. You know that for yourself, Father Maguire." This was said with such conviction and honest strength of feeling that it silenced all of them.

The simple statement was persuasive for James, who pondered on the idea that for Jude not to believe the seers was to challenge the veracity of three adults, three parishioners, who had no reason to lie.

"Father Maguire?" James was on the point of asking if he could make copies of the statements, but he was interrupted by the housekeeper ushering in Sergeant Molloy in an excited state.

"Sorry to rush in upon you like this," Molloy said, taking off his hat. "But I've some news.

"A fella in Tipperary has made an initial identification of the dead lad from the sketch and description we sent out. He knew him in Tipperary. It seems his mother's dead and the father's in England. The lad had been in the States with his two brothers, and came back when his visa didn't work out. He'd been working as a laborer on a big Tipperary farm. When he went missing, they thought he'd gone off to England on a lark. He'd been paid that day. But they thought he'd be back. Apparently he was a good lad, nothing strange or startling yet . . ."

"Except he's dead and murdered," said Mrs. O'Leary, who'd been hanging on Molloy's every word.

"I know, I know, but it's a start. The body's still at the morgue in Wexford, and the witness is being run up to view it. If it is this lad, well, we've got a place to focus on."

"Tipperary?" James said.

"Aye. I know it's a longish way, but at night in a car or truck—it's what? Perhaps a two hours' drive?"

"But why bring him here if he was killed in Tipperary?"

"Well, now, Mr. Fleming, there's nothing to say he was killed there, merely that he was of that place. I'm leaving now for the morgue."

He put his hat back on his unruly gray hair. "It's a breakthrough, surely."

"Indeed," James said. "Perhaps we'll talk later?"

Molloy nodded and rushed from the room, followed by the housekeeper. The three men stood restlessly, the thread of the conversation now broken.

"Father Maguire," Jude said casually, "I'm taking Mary Dowd up to the grotto."

"Yes, I know you said that. I'm on duty tonight, so you're free to go, but use sense, man, use caution. The people are agitated enough. Moderation in all things, right?" Maguire struck James as a parent admonishing a headstrong adolescent . . . as usual, to no effect.

"Jude, would you mind if I tagged along?" James asked.

"By all means," Jude said, then he hesitated. "That is, if Mary Dowd doesn't mind?"

"Right, if she objects, I'll make my own way. I am going to the grotto." He stated this baldly.

The mood in the car was tense as they sped over to Mary's bungalow.

James was shocked when he saw Mary Dowd appear at her door. Although neat as a pin in her anorak and jeans, her face was drawn, sickly in its grayness.

She let them in the front door with no sense of formality. "Oh, Jude, any word?"

"No, not yet. I'd hoped perhaps you'd heard from her."

"Oh. God, that's bad, Jude, that's bad." Mary walked into the cool, spare sitting room. "She's not with the relatives in Cork, then?"

"Not as of six o'clock this evening. I just saw Molloy—he would have mentioned it to me if he had further news."

"I'm worried, Jude, and frightened. Why would she leave without a word to me . . ." Mary was plaintive.

"But you did speak with her," James said.

Mary cocked her head and looked at James, confused. "When—When do you mean?"

"The other morning, at the grotto, when you stayed three hours on your knees—praying. She told me about it."

"Oh, yes, yes, of course. I was so exhausted. She told me only afterward we'd been there for hours. It had been like a trance to me. I could have been there hours or minutes, I'd no sense of time passing. The message came in on me that there would be a great sign. I can't tell you the feeling, Mr. Fleming. Jude, I think, understands. It's like a weight. I don't know if I hear the words or if I feel them. Whether it's in my ears or in my mind. Rita came back here with me after, for a few minutes, and I was so grateful . . . she understands, she has from the beginning." Mary sighed and smiled slightly at Jude, who nodded.

"Well, of course she would," James said.

"How is that, Fleming," Jude said, "obviously not everyone can or does!"

"As Mary just said, Rita has been a part of all this from the first," James said pointedly. Turning to Mary, he looked at her closely. "Tell me, Mary, did Rita also 'feel' this message?" Jude glared at him, but he ignored him.

"I don't know, but she *was* overwhelmed. That was what she told me. We drank some coffee, I think." Mary swung around to face him, her hands loose at her sides, like a helpless child.

"Would you say that she seemed uneasy?" James asked.

"Uneasy? Not quite that. But she wasn't herself. I'd not

142

seen her nervous before. But then we've only become friends in recent months."

"Did she seem to want to pull out?"

"Pull out?"

"Get away from all this, back to a simpler life perhaps?"

"Well, perhaps."

"Or perhaps she wished it hadn't happened."

"Oh, God, no!" said Mary with passion. "And why would she? How could she not want to be touched by God?" She looked at James as if he were mad himself.

"I only meant that she is an older woman who has led a quiet life. I'm trying to get at her psychological state, if you will. My theory is that she's retreated from the pressure."

"I wouldn't blame her one bit. But I do miss her. I'm used to going with her to the grotto. It frightens me going there alone." She looked suddenly small, shrinking in on herself. He watched as she righted this impression, pulling herself together, zipping her light jacket.

"But I will go alone now. I must pray for her. Wherever she is, I believe she's in distress. You see, I'm sure she'd contact me. We've shared so much. And she never ever let me down. Prayer is the answer, at the grotto. Perhaps my prayers will draw her back to the grotto." Her face was worried and her level of concern communicated itself to the two men.

As before, they traveled in Jude's old Volvo. As before, they elbowed their way to the statue, the crowds opening when they saw Jude in his soutane.

The long summer evening was drawing in, the blue sky fading to palest mint, clouds massing and bundling in the west. A chill was in the air, a dampness that everyone felt as they put up collars and tugged on their cardigans. The numbers had lessened, and there were fewer pilgrims struggling on the path.

At last at the feet of the statue, James and Jude stood to one side, Jude obviously engaged in prayer. James again watched as Mary knelt, a young girl in her light summer jeans and jacket, head bare and bowed, her shoulders hunched in concentration, eyes tightly closed. If physical effort were a part of prayer, he observed, then surely this prayer would pull Rita Garrotty from whatever hole she had retreated to.

No thought of praying passed through James's mind, and he wondered about this. Not once, not yet, had he been moved to pray. He had been moved by awe, by curiosity, by uneasiness, but not by a need to pray. Am I so dead inside, he thought, startling himself. Seldom given to self-analysis, he pushed the thought aside. Instead, he looked at the statue above him, straining to see a light, a movement, struggling to gain a sense of another presence.

James had been standing about twenty minutes when he began to wonder how he could gracefully leave. The dampness was deepening, as was the dark. He hadn't thought of the consequences when he'd come along with Jude. He'd acted on an impulse, wanting again to see, to watch Mary in action. Like any thrill-seeker, he acknowledged to himself self-critically. He looked at Mary, head bent low, hands clenched, and he was moved finally to a deep pity and a growing sense of guilt.

Suddenly the clouds opened just above them, letting down torrents of rain. Unprepared in their light clothes, having trusted the weather for once, people looked around almost dumbfounded. Without umbrellas, they were naked. The crowd began to disperse in an orderly fashion, moving from the fringes, lessening, widening before forming again into straggling lines.

People put papers and tote bags and cardigans over their heads for protection. Others just withstood it. No one here was unfamiliar with such sudden downpours. James turned up the collar of his suit jacket and despaired of the thin material weathering the storm. He waited in vain for Mary Dowd to move, catching Jude's eye as they both looked upward, not to the statue, but to the sky above. And still she knelt and prayed. The crowd had thinned dramatically, with merely two dozen people still kneeling in the rain, some others sheltering under trees farther away from the bare little hill.

James scanned the area, curious as to who would remain, pitying those who did, imagining to himself that their petitions must be truly desperate to keep them in the rain. Even the hardy pilgrims who'd mounted the hill on their knees had retreated to cars and vans and houses. But James saw one poor soul in a wheelchair, still praying, her head and face sheltering in a wide scarf. This wasn't right, surely, he thought to himself, and he was relieved when a youngish man approached her, bending over to speak with her. James glanced back at Mary, willing Jude to do something. He moved closer to him.

"You think we should leave?" James said.

"I'm as wet as you," Jude said grimly, "but look at her. She doesn't even seem to know that she's getting wet." His voice was incredulous, but James agreed.

Mary indeed seemed unaware of the rain as it rolled down her flattened hair and down her face. Her expression, her stance, and posture hadn't changed in the forty-five minutes they'd been there.

The two stood flummoxed until Jude edged towards her very hesitantly, as though hoping to get her attention by accident. But he was interrupted by the approach of the young man in the navy windbreaker whom James had noted earlier. He was running towards them from the far side of the grotto, shouting into the rain.

"Father! Father! Help!" James heard the anxiety in his voice, and looking beyond him, saw the woman in the wheelchair still sitting immobile, her face protected by a scarf. A chill ran through James as he too moved towards the young man, leaving Jude with Mary.

"What's wrong?" He called.

"I think she might be dead! Come, please!"

"Is it your mother or grandmother?" James said as he sprinted ahead of the priest to the wheelchair.

"Not at all," said the young man, slowing down as he approached the woman. "I noticed her there when the crowd thinned out. The wife had gone ahead, and I noticed this woman alone here. I thought that in the confusion maybe her family left her behind by accident, like Jesus in the Temple."

He stood back as James reached for the woman's wrist. It seemed cold and damp and he felt no pulse, but then he was no expert. James called to her, leaning down.

"I thought she was asleep, or maybe unconscious. Is she?" The young man's voice was strained. James gently moved the scarf from around the bent head, and as he did so, it rolled to the side.

"Oh, God!" he cried out to the approaching Father Donnelly. "It's Rita Garrotty!"

Chapter Fifteen

James was surrounded by people at the now familiar Reardon's Pub on Main Street, yet he sat alone and unaware of the steady hum of gossip and speculation regarding Rita Garrotty's death the evening before.

He stared into the ivory froth of his pint of Guinness as it rested halfway down his glass. God, how he would like to talk to someone, someone he knew well. He hadn't felt this alone in some time. Melancholy crept into his being, and the Guinness was not doing its usual soothing trick. Where was Matt now, he thought irritably, when I want him? Thousands of miles away at his new job in Australia! He missed his old friend's pragmatic approach to problems, his common sense regarding human behavior, his ability to stay rooted in reality. Matt's viewpoint was an antidote, James knew, to his own bleaker view of human nature.

And Sarah was thousands of miles away in the States on her six-city concert tour. Not a word from her. James did not count the faxes of her reviews which came into the office periodically with little notes across the top. "See ya" was one he recalled with particular distaste. It seemed so unlike Sarah. Used to her formal ways, her reserve and rigidity, he wondered at the source of this new casualness, this use of slang. He wanted to send her a sharp, witty, pointed little note of his own, but nothing had come to mind! Irritated still, he downed his pint and ordered another.

His mother, now, was not someone he'd choose to discuss his feelings with. He never had. He wondered did any man his age talk to his mother beyond the ordinary level of meaningless pleasantries or sincere inquiries after her health or well-being? Donald too was out of the question— at least on this issue.

James didn't like this feeling of being alone. These black moods were infrequent, he reminded himself, and they invariably passed. He was anxious that this one pass quickly so he could deal with his present responsibilities. He shook his head, but the picture of Miss Garrotty in the wheelchair remained fixed.

Perhaps her death had affected him so strongly because he had discovered her body. It struck him even now—the next day—as infinitely sad: the hopeless attitude of the body. Hands limp on the worn tweed skirt, the bruised knees she'd shown him purple and mottled, the graying hair falling forward from beneath the scarf. Yet no signs of violence. Even now the medical examiner would be working at the morgue. And if it were natural causes, was there not some consolation that she had died at the site of the most important event of her lonely life? James was answering his own question when a small movement, a tap on his arm, startled him mightily. He jumped, spilling his Guinness on the bar.

"Sorry! Sorry, I didn't mean to surprise you like that, Fleming. It's me, Tim Kerrigan."

James looked into the face of his former cicerone. The blue eyes, deep-set under strong eyebrows, showed a tension that made James curious. The young man leaned forward, his posture indicating his intensity.

"I saw you on the road outside and I debated about coming in to you . . ."

"Yes, go on."

"You see," Tim hesitated. "I'm . . . I'm a close friend of Mary Dowd."

"What!" James exclaimed sharply.

"I know, I know . . ."

"What do you know? That you sat here the other night rabbiting on about Devane, and you never mentioned one word about Mary Dowd."

"I know what it looks like, Fleming, but let me explain—"

"Tell me first, are you the fellow she mentioned to me, the 'friend' she dated occasionally, the 'friend' who lives in Dublin?" James was irritated and it showed.

"Yes, yes. There's no other. I live in Dublin. I'm on a course there in Bolton Street. But that's all beside the point. The night I met you I'd an almighty row with Mary Dowd. I was in a temper when I left her and needed a drink. I sure as hell didn't want to talk about her. But you seemed decent enough, and half smushed at that. When you asked, I thought at least I could tell what I knew about Devane . . ."

"So what is it you want now? To tell me more midsummer fairy tales!"

"No, please listen, Mr. Fleming. I'm very worried about Mary. I'm down here again to see the ma since the old man isn't so well. Of course they'd all heard about Rita Garrotty and were telling me. My God, I got a fright. So I thought I'd call on Mary and—"

"I don't understand. Surely you're also here to visit with her too?"

"Ah, well . . . that's all off . . . since the other night."

"Off?"

"I broke off with her the night I was in here with you."

"I'm sorry to hear it," James said genuinely.

A faint color rose in Tim's face. "I'd got fed up, you know, with this new lifestyle of hers, this religious mania or

149

whatever. But that's beside the point too. I'm telling you I've just come from her, and she's in a terrible state, Mr. Fleming. She's got this daft idea that she's going to die."

"What!"

"I know, I know it's daft. But it's Rita, you see! Mary thinks maybe God called her home. That it was the great sign she's been expecting . . ."

"Oh, God." James shook his head at this twist.

"You do see how it is? I'm afraid Mary is losing her reason. That all this has been too much. But she's so convinced of it, she nearly had me convinced—against my better judgment, I tell you!"

"You obviously don't hold with any of this?" James was remembering Tim's ironic comments from their previous conversation and trying to align what he'd learned about Tim then with the Tim before him now.

"Not at all. For me it's the same as if Mary told me she was hearing voices in the back garden. Only it's not," he added bitterly. "It's as though the whole world knew that she was hearing voices in the back garden. How did that make me feel?"

"Perhaps this is the very time for her friends to stand by her," James said. "Especially since she has no family left?"

Tim was silent, a deeper flush creeping up his neck. A young man who didn't like to be told, James thought, but then who did?

"Have a drink since you're here?" James said neutrally.

"Yes, I will," the lad said, relaxing.

Some minutes passed. James, still suspicious as to why Tim had concealed his relationship with Mary Dowd earlier, was keen to find out more. He wondered if perhaps Tim's friendship with Mary could be salvaged.

"Have you known Mary long?" he said conversationally.

"Oh, I'd seen her around the town all our lives, but I only got to know her maybe two years ago. One of her college friends did rally car driving and so did one of mine. We met up at a rally. Listen, you've seen her . . ." he said abruptly.

James nodded.

"Well I tell you, the girl you see is not the girl I met at the rally. She was a bit shy all right, but full of life. We went beagling a few times and she was great fun, very fit. We tramped for miles after those bloody dogs, but it was the day out that was great, eating our lunch under a tree. What happened to her? I ask you. She liked doing things out of doors . . ." Tim stopped and took a drink of his lager, staring at James as though he had an answer.

"I'm not sure I'm the one to ask. Perhaps we have to put ourselves in her place. If she was all you say she was, then she probably still is. But this event in May would surely affect her profoundly, and for a while she may seem different to you . . ."

"But that's just it. She started acting different long—well, not long before, but certainly before the vision, as she calls it."

"How long before?" James asked.

"Around the time she started to go to the grotto. This is a small town. I was up in Dublin, and maybe she thought I wouldn't know about it, but of course the ma knew. The town knew. I asked her about it . . ." His tone again was bitter.

"What did she say?"

"Oh, I dunno. She had some idea that a special prayer would be answered. You know women . . ."

James ignored this remark, urging Tim to talk more. "You seem annoyed by that . . ."

"Look, in a small town you don't want people talking. She never said what she was praying about, but people could guess, couldn't they?"

"I'm not a Catholic, so maybe you could enlighten me."

"I see. Well, it isn't even something to do with religion per se. What did it look like? Mary and I go out with each other off and on for a year. Then I get a chance to go up to Dublin to continue studying. I'm away. She's here. She starts praying at the grotto. I mean, that's not the same as going to light a candle in the church in private. Everybody in town knew she was at the grotto. And of course then there was talk."

"From whom?"

"Well, mainly from my ma. She said to watch out as Mary Dowd was up at the grotto praying that we'd get engaged."

James suppressed a laugh as he watched the young man's face darken.

"I tell you, Mr. Fleming, it's me and only me who will decide if I'm gettin' married, and it won't be because of some novena of prayers!" He finished his drink and nearly slammed the glass on the bar.

"You *and* the girl, presumably," James added wryly, but it was lost on Tim, so James changed tack. "You know, Tim, this is going to be stressful for Mary. Perhaps you'd reconsider sticking by her, if only as a friend?"

"Yeah, my conscience pricks me, and I'd do it if she saw me as a friend only, but I don't know. I guess I will. She seemed so frightened and lost when I called to her house."

"You seem to want me to do something, but I'm not sure what it is," James said as he ordered another round.

"Just call on her and help her somehow, will you? Or solve these murders and then it will all be over!"

James considered Tim's words carefully, noting that he had used the plural. "Perhaps I will call on her and offer my help," he said at last. "But surely there are others who are much closer to her who can do that, including yourself, including Father Donnelly."

Tim reacted to this violently. "The best thing *he* could do for Mary is to stay away from her and let her get back to normal, let her be herself and not some little virginal plaster saint." He glared into his second pint of lager. "If you ask me, he's behind this whole thing!"

"What?" James said, truly shocked, but he quickly realized that Tim meant the events at the grotto and not the deaths.

"Without him feeding her lines, and whisperin' in her ear

152

every minute, and flattering her and making a pet of her, she'd be herself again."

James wasn't sure how to continue. Tim's anger against Donnelly was more than anger: it was jealousy.

Tim took no notice of James's silence. "I've been up to the grotto today, and you know, Mr. Fleming, they've all gone mad there entirely."

A shiver ran down James's spine. "How so?"

"Instead of fleeing that place, they're glued to it. Two deaths there so far. What do they want? More deaths! More signs! More disgraceful displays by Mary falling on her face at the statue!" Tim drank up and ordered yet another.

"I haven't been up there since Miss Garrotty . . ." James said, trailing off.

"Because you've sense. I tell you. They have decided—"

"Who?"

"The people. The mob. They've decided that Miss Garrotty's death was the great sign that Mary Dowd said was coming. If she said that at all. I think Donnelly started that rumor . . ."

James held his tongue, knowing more than Tim, yet not wanting to frustrate him.

"How can a death be seen as a positive sign, Fleming? I'll tell you. Because they turn everything around to suit them. Even Mary was saying as much, that is, when she talked to me at all. God, I've never seen such carrying on. My sisters don't cry the way she does."

James dragged him back to the point. "Are you sure of what you're saying . . . I mean about the great sign?"

"Yes, yes, go see for yourself. They're saying Miss Garrotty was called back to God, that she was a chosen one, that God plucked her from the grotto and took her to his bosom . . . Och, I ask you!"

He drained his glass and stood up. "Thanks, Fleming, for talkin' with me. You're the only one with a grain of sense in this whole bloody town, and that's because you're from Dublin and no doubt!"

James smiled neutrally in a silent farewell. Tim's style was such that he tended to force agreement from his interlocutor. James felt sorry for Mary Dowd. Tim Kerrigan was not an easy lad to deal with if things weren't going his way. Sooner or later, James decided, Mary and Tim would have broken up over any number of issues.

James's mood had altered and, although not as black as it had been, it was rather edgy. So much of what Tim had told him had gone against the grain. He put his change in his pocket and wandered out into the street. Although he didn't much care for Jude Donnelly, he'd been shocked by Tim's description of the man. James knew some things to the contrary, he believed, at least in this instance. He'd rarely seen a man so shaken by a death. Jude had nearly swooned on discovering it was indeed Miss Garrotty. He'd recovered, however, and had dealt with the police and the Garrotty brothers with sincerity and authority. No, there had been no suggestion that Jude Donnelly thought of Rita's death as a great sign of anything. When James had finally left the shop after giving the police his statement, Jude Donnelly had still been in deep conversation with Rita's brothers.

What a strange life—the life of a priest, James thought as he turned his steps towards the rectory, hoping to catch Jude in at lunch hour. The pedestrians on the street were subdued, and the heavy, humid weather contributed to the dullness of sound and action.

Surely their celibacy removed them from the commonality, James observed, but perhaps because of that, they could devote themselves completely to the needs of their people, their parish. Available to them at all times, but most especially in times of need.

As he approached the rectory he was stunned to see a familiar car parked in front up on the path. So stunned, he stopped in his tracks and fleetingly considered turning away. But that would solve nothing, he realized, telling himself he was Tim's age no longer.

The door opened abruptly at his knock to reveal Geraldine in the hall. Their mutually startled expressions dissolved into laughter as James and Geraldine greeted each other as though all was forgotten.

"Geraldine!" James kissed her on the cheek.

She smiled warmly and turned to introduce him to two people beside her. Jude stood behind them. "James, these are friends from Dublin, Nurse Hagan from the hospital, and our friend, Mrs. Farley."

They shook hands all around as Jude excused himself to answer the ringing phone in the office. James scrutinized the two women: Nurse Hagan, a brusque, stocky, businesslike woman; and Mrs. Farley, a frail woman in her fifties who seemed to be suffering with some severe pain.

A sneaking suspicion formed at the back of his mind, a sense of something familiar, some fragment of Geraldine's conversation when she'd been in Buncloda last. He tried to catch her eye as the three women chatted excitedly. But as she seemed to avoid him, his suspicion grew.

"Why have you come down?" he asked pointedly.

Three pairs of eyes turned on him and he was rendered speechless, realizing he was upsetting Mrs. Farley most of all.

"To flirt with you, of course," Geraldine said, recovering the situation gracefully and then flirting with him outrageously.

What an actress, he thought as he flirted back.

"And a fine couple you'd make," Nurse Hagan said matter-of-factly.

Jude's return saved them both from further embarrassment.

"Time is short," he said, looking at Geraldine. "Are we all going, then?"

"Yes, I think so," she answered.

"Right, well perhaps Nurse Hagan and Mrs. Farley could come with me, and you and James could go in your car?"

James was delighted to get a few moments alone with Geraldine.

"Where are we going?" he whispered as they hurried to the cars.

"The grotto, of course," she answered, tight-lipped.

"Ger, what's going on?"

"I'll tell you, James, if you keep your thoughts to yourself!"

James nodded as he buckled himself into the passenger seat of Geraldine's Mini.

"Nurse Hagan has been down here a number of times and she has had some very spiritual experiences at the grotto. Mrs. Farley has been in and out of hospital for the last year with problems with her right arm. She's not my patient, but Nurse Hagan introduced us. She's had operations and physical therapy, but nothing has helped her. She's in great pain, as I'm sure you could see. She's a very devout woman, James. So the three of us decided to come down for the day."

"For the day only?" James didn't hide his disappointment.

"I'm afraid both of them have to get back. But James, just think of it, what if Mrs. Farley is cured?"

James, true to his word, did not reproach her for what he perceived to be this folly, and the last thing he wanted was a fight with her. Instead he asked if she'd heard of Miss Garrotty's death, and Ger informed him it was the talk of Dublin, and everywhere else apparently. But all conversation ceased as they made their way as a group along the road to the grotto.

The crowd, as Tim had described, was large. Eventually Nurse Hagan and Mrs. Farley took their places in the dense queue that was moving slowly up the narrow path to the statue. James watched with pity and dismay as Mrs. Farley knelt and began to make her way on her knees with Nurse Hagan beside her, aiding her when she could. As they passed out of sight, Father Donnelly turned to face James and Geraldine, his eyes glistening.

"Every hour of every day now, I see these demonstrations

of faith and hope. It is overwhelming to me at times," he said.

James, speechless at Donnelly's reaction, watched as Geraldine wiped her eyes and nodded in agreement.

"Geraldine," Jude said in a confidential tone, "I have a favor to ask of you. Mary Dowd has been under great pressure in recent weeks, and now with Miss Garrotty's death, she is very distressed. Our local G.P. is a man, and rather elderly at that. I was wondering if I brought you to meet her, if perhaps you could assess her health in a discreet and tactful way?"

A rush of emotions flooded across Geraldine's face: excitement, curiosity, apprehension. After some thought, she glanced at James. "Will you be coming?" she said.

"I'd like to," he said, looking at Jude, who merely nodded.

"Yes, then, I'll do it, but I'm not sure without a physical if I can be of much help."

"We can but try," Jude said. He glanced up the hill.

"I can see them," Geraldine said. "They'll be ages getting up to the statue. I'll have plenty of time to visit Mary Dowd and get back here before they've finished their devotions."

James watched her as she looked longingly up the hill, her eye resting with desire, with an ardor James could not but envy, on the statue overlooking the complex scene. Silently he followed Geraldine and Jude to their cars.

Chapter Sixteen

Mary Dowd took so long to answer their ring at her bell that they were alarmed and began discussing where she might be and where they might find her.

But at last, after some rustling at the lock, Mary opened the door a crack, smiling wanly at Jude as he and the others stepped into the hall.

Preceding them into the sitting room, Mary threw herself into the chair by the fire. Although the day had been heavy and humid, she had both bars of the electric fire lighting, and immediately covered herself with a heavy blanket. Her face was drawn and ashen and her voice low.

The silence was awkward, and finally Jude made the introductions between Geraldine and Mary. Mary merely smiled weakly and then closed her eyes as though overcome with sleep. Geraldine raised an eyebrow at James.

"Miss Dowd, would you mind if I made us all some tea?"

Mary opened her eyes as if seeing Geraldine for the first time. She shifted slowly in her chair. "Please, Doctor, I'll do it."

"That's good, Miss Dowd, and I'll give you a hand."
Geraldine was professional and firm, a different Geraldine
than the one James knew.

Geraldine followed as Mary walked slowly, stiffly, towards the kitchen, clutching her heavy cardigan tightly
around her. James was surprised to see how haggard she
appeared. He looked at Jude in alarm.

"I know, I know," Jude said in answer to James's silent
comment. "I'm worried. She's changing before our eyes."

The two men sat down and a heavy silence fell between
them. They continued to sit as first anticipation and then
anxiety began to fill the room like a fog. Minutes went by.
Then more. They could hear low voices, whispers, but no
sounds of tea being prepared. As the tension grew, James
stood up and switched on Mary Dowd's CD player, and soft
strains of light classical music effectively drowned out the
murmuring in the kitchen.

James and Jude relaxed enough to talk as Jude acknowledged the purpose of James's gesture. They had been torn
between eavesdropping and ignoring the conversation in the
other room.

"They seem to be getting along?" Jude looked at James
questioningly.

"It sounds that way," James said encouragingly. "It
strikes me that Mary is very isolated now. And that can't be
good for her."

"You mean with Rita gone, God rest her soul." Jude
crossed himself with bent head.

"Yes, of course that has to have had a fantastic impact on
her. My sense is that although they were not close personally, they were bound together in an extraordinary, a very
powerful way . . ." James hesitated to reveal what else he
knew.

"Tell me, Father Donnelly," he said carefully, "do you
know Tim Kerrigan?"

"I've seen him around town but I don't know him. I
understand from his mother, a lovely woman, that he's

wandered from the Church. Full of his own opinions. Might even be an atheist, for that matter. Seems to me that he's known as a right boyo!" He paused, looking sharply at James. "Why do you ask?"

"Well, I daresay all you say may be true. But I was wondering if you knew that he and Mary were friends? More than friends?"

"What do you mean, more than friends?" Jude demanded.

"I've talked to the lad. He and Mary were boyfriend and girlfriend. I have the sense that perhaps Mary might have wanted to marry him . . ."

"I don't think so . . ." Jude cut in.

"Why do you say that?" James was harsh in return.

"She would have told me. Since her vision, I have been her confessor."

"Perhaps there was nothing to confess, Father Donnelly," James said wryly, annoyed at Jude. "Let me say that Tim had a sense that perhaps Mary Dowd was praying at the grotto for a very young woman's wish, to fall in love, to get married . . ."

"He told you this?"

"What he said was that his mother thought Mary might have been doing this. Apparently the whole town was aware of Mary's daily morning prayer at the grotto. Tim, of course, was embarrassed by this notion. But I'm getting off the point. It's my understanding that they were a couple until a few days ago, when Tim broke it off with Mary Dowd."

"So what *is* your point, Fleming? She surely has been fully occupied with her vision, her mystical experience, and her growing prayer life. I imagine that her present experience has transcended some fleeting girlish romance."

James stopped in his tracks, his breath taken away by Jude's view of the situation. He debated briefly with himself but then continued.

"Look, Jude, as you acknowledge, you are close to Mary. I'm suggesting that you take into account a number of factors: the loss of her parents, leaving her alone in the world; the mysterious death of Miss Garrotty; and now she's lost what might have been—for all *we* know—a significant relationship with a young man. Whether it was real or fantasy, if Mary had hopes of marrying Tim, then this breakup must be yet another loss for her."

"All right, all right. But I keep to my own view: that things of the flesh and the devil would surely fall away in the face of a vision of the Blessed Mother." Jude's face lit up as he talked. "I know they would for me. What could stand in comparison to having been called, to be a chosen one of God? What's a boyfriend compared to that? A fleeting physical relationship that would wear out over time or with age. How can that rival the transcendental love of the seer, the visionary, for the divine, and the divine for the human? As the saint has said, the seer has the thumbprint of God on her forehead. Look, Fleming, look at the biographies of the other visionaries." Jude suddenly stopped talking.

"Go on." James was suspicious.

"Well, ah, actually, many of the seers died at an early age. But I think that can be explained by the diseases that were rampant then, and for which we have treatments now . . ."

"Listen, Jude, Tim tells me Mary is afraid of dying—like Miss Garrotty. Has she confided this in you?"

"No, she hasn't, and I don't believe hearsay, Fleming."

"I thought it was to the point, Donnelly. So . . . what of the others, the visionaries who survived?" James tried to keep his voice level, but his anger at Jude's insensitivity was increasing.

"Surprisingly, many of them fell into obscurity over time. But I know that some entered religious life. Lucia, who spoke with the Virgin at Fatima, for example; she entered a cloistered order."

"A convent?"

"Yes, the convent would seem to be the logical answer . . ." Jude lost himself in his own thoughts.

Both men jumped when Geraldine's strained voice called Jude to come help her with Mary.

Jude glanced at him rather smugly, James thought. "Yes —she should be in a convent even now," he said with finality.

James and Geraldine seated themselves on the tall stools in the back snug of Reardon's Pub. There seemed to be nowhere else to meet. James's bed-and-breakfast? Geraldine's car? They felt like adolescents looking for a place to be alone together.

James ordered two large brandies and waited until they were served to ask Geraldine about the strange events of the previous two hours.

Geraldine shivered. "I tried to get Miss Dowd to chat, to tell me how she was feeling. I knew she was ill just by the look of her. Then when she lifted the kettle to fill it for the tea, I saw a reddish-brown stain on her blouse. Her cardigan had fallen open, you see. As she lifted the full kettle away from the tap, she winced in pain. Still, I didn't know how to question her without being rude." She took a sip of her brandy and paused.

"And then?"

"I was setting out the mugs, chatting about my friend who'd come down to pray at the grotto, and she suddenly shook her head, saying 'No, no, no.' I was so startled, James. I turned to look at her and saw a fresh red stain on her blouse. I wasn't very professional . . ." Geraldine smiled wryly.

"I'm sure you were," James murmured.

"No, I cried out, I'm afraid. I pointed to the stain and just asked what it was straight out. I was fairly near to her, and I put my hand over her own to reassure her. I couldn't believe I was actually touching someone who had seen a vision of the Blessed Mother—"

"It was blood, I assume," James cut in.

"Indeed it was. It was fresh. At first she tried to conceal it, but that wasn't possible. Then she allowed me to examine her. James, I have never been so shocked in all my medical career."

"Well, your career hasn't been that long," said James, trying to lighten the mood.

"I suppose that's true, but I hope I never see the like of this again. Mary Dowd has been mortifying herself, James! She finally admitted it when I asked her. Honestly, I thought she'd been attacked. My God!"

"Are you sure it was self-inflicted, Geraldine?" James asked, seriously shocked, and concerned to think of this young woman in such pain and distress.

"Are you asking me if it was supernaturally inflicted, like the stigmata?" Geraldine stared at him.

"No, no. I hadn't even thought of any of that, frankly. What I meant was, is it possible you were right the first time? Perhaps she was attacked? Perhaps she was attacked and is in shock, not dealing with the reality of it?"

"Oh James, you'd have to have seen it. Then you'd know. She told me about her little whip. That's when I called Jude in. Of course he didn't examine the wounds, but I got her to tell him about the whip. And then, my God, she took off this piece of rope she'd been wearing around her waist. Just ordinary rope, but she'd been tightening it and it had left deep red grooves on her skin at her waist. There was blood on the rope, James. I tell you, I went cold." Geraldine's face grew even whiter, and James urged her to sip the brandy.

He was glad she'd filled in the blanks for him. When the threesome had emerged from the kitchen, Geraldine and Jude explained they were bringing Mary Dowd to the convent outside the town. Without further explanation, they left in Jude's car, leaving James to walk back to town completely mystified.

"But why the convent? Why not a hospital?" he asked as Geraldine seemed to relax, the color returning to her face.

"Oh, James, I'm not sure myself. I of course mentioned running over to see the local G.P. to get the wounds dressed, and both of them said no to that. She's never been sick in her life, so there was no one else I could urge her to see. Jude himself mentioned the hospital, but she was afraid of the publicity, the media attention. I had to agree that was a risk. If she were seen arriving, if anyone on staff or in the casualty ward saw her and gossiped! This is not something she wants known."

"No, I can see that. But why the convent?"

Geraldine looked at him. "Why not?" she inquired.

"It's just something Jude said earlier, but I'm interrupting. Please tell me what happened then."

"To tell the truth, the convent was Jude's idea. He didn't want Mary to be on her own. She hasn't been eating or sleeping well. He didn't comment on the self-mortification. He seemed to accept that. If she's a saint, then we all have to accept that. Jude just explained to her that the nuns could care for her and she could feel safe and regain her strength. He made it sound very nurturing and peaceful, and that appealed to Mary. As though a mother would take charge of a sick child and whisk her off to bed with a hot water bottle and warm drinks, you know?"

"Mmmm," was James's only answer, although the imagery did appeal to him too. "What happened at the convent?"

"Fortunately, the Mother Superior was at home. But she wanted to speak with Jude and Mary privately. So I wasn't privy to all of that. Jude said when he drove me back to my car that she was very kind and gentle with Mary and agreed she could stay as their guest indefinitely."

"I don't like it, Ger," James said suddenly.

"What!"

"This convent thing. It's not natural."

"Natural? James, nothing in this situation is natural. Mary Dowd is a very special person. Special steps need to be taken regarding her."

"Ger, you're doing it yourself now. You're taking on a role. You're saying steps need to be taken *for* her, not *by* her. Did she ask to go to the convent?"

"No, but it hadn't occurred to her."

"It didn't occur to her because she was feeling safe in her own home! Now she's cut off from what little real life was left to her. She has lost her independence, and with it she will lose her self-regard. She is not master of her own situation now, Ger. Other people are controlling her."

"But you have to admit she couldn't go on like that."

"Like what?"

"Flagellating herself, for one thing. Doing penance!"

"Why not, if that was her choice?"

Geraldine stopped to consider his point.

"You let yourself be persuaded by Jude, just as Mary did. Who is he to make such decisions for Mary?" James added.

"Well, he explained to Mother Superior in front of me that he is Mary's confessor since the apparition."

"He mentioned that to me. But what does it really mean?"

"He is her spiritual adviser, he guides her prayer life, advises her on her reading, her meditative prayer and so on."

"No, no, Ger! He is controlling her. He's a Svengali!"

Geraldine's laughter was tinged with anger. "Honestly, James. You've met Jude. I've known Jude. He's not some stranger."

"Think about it, Ger. How well do you know the man today, not the young lad from the country years ago?"

"Look, James, he didn't put Mary away against her will in some asylum."

"No, but he put her in a convent when she is feeling weak and very vulnerable! It's the equivalent." James berated himself silently for revealing what he knew about Tim to Jude.

"No, it's not," Geraldine said sternly.

"She's free to come and go, then? Free to have visitors and so on?"

"Of course."

"And the convent—they will help her?"

"With what?"

"The self-inflicted pain."

"I can't know that. That's for her to decide with Jude."

"I can't believe this, Ger! Do you accept all this? Do you accept a young woman in the prime of her health and life is isolating herself, withdrawing from the world, occupying her time with arcane practices and some kind of prayer life!" James could not restrain himself. "Do you accept poor Mrs. Farley coming here and climbing hills on her knees! Do you accept that Nurse Hagan has seen the statue move! Come on!"

Geraldine sat back—stunned and surprised by his words. "I can't talk to you when you're like this."

"That's an easy way to end discussion, Ger," James said, trying to head her off as she picked up her purse.

"I have to go. You've reminded me that I have to drive Mrs. Farley and Nurse Hagan back to Dublin. Excuse me," she said, her voice shaking.

"I'm coming with you. I want to see for myself if anything has taken place."

"You can't judge that, James," Geraldine said as she hurried from the pub. "Even if she is not cured, we cannot, you cannot, know what spiritual benefits she's gained."

James fell silent as Geraldine drove as quickly as possible towards the grotto. Pushing through the crowds, she located her friends at the bottom of the hill.

"Sorry I'm late," she said breathlessly.

"Not to worry," Nurse Hagan said, "we have wonderful news. Look, Doctor, just look. Mrs. Farley, show her your arm now."

To James's surprise and perhaps dismay, Mrs. Farley shyly extended her arm, flexing her fingers.

"Thanks be to God," she said softly, so simply that James was moved. "The pain is gone, and the tingling in my hand and fingers. It's cured. It's cured."

A young couple in shorts and jogging shoes overheard the conversation and came closer.

"Your arm is cured?" the young woman asked in awe.

"Yes, dear. It is. I'd lost the use of it, and now it's back."

The young woman turned to her companions, a group of holiday-makers, James thought from the look of them, hoping the incident would stop with them. But within minutes more pilgrims approached, asking to see the cure. James and Geraldine began to retreat with the two women, hastily retracing their steps to the car. But not before fifty or more people began to follow them, calling for details, some clapping, some cheering. The four of them remained shaken and silent in the car. James stayed with them until Geraldine reached the fork in the road where she could take the main road to Dublin.

"Well?" Geraldine said with a half smile.

James, inhibited by the presence of the others in the car, was restrained. "All I can say, Ger," he whispered, "is that all of this is much deeper than it appears. Don't get caught up in it, all right? Just think about it . . ."

"You know, James," she whispered crossly, "you're not a cynic like your brother."

"I'm glad you see that."

"No, you're worse. You don't trust people. Maybe that's why they don't trust you in return. Why don't *you* think about that!"

James had barely shut the car door when she drove off in a huff.

Disconsolate, he turned in the direction of the rectory.

Was it true that he didn't trust people? he pondered as he walked. And if it was true, was that such a bad thing? It was not so much that he didn't trust, he decided, mentally arguing with Geraldine; it was that he'd learned that appearances could so often deceive. As he smiled at his pun, his thoughts segued to the issue at hand. That Miss Garrotty's death could lead to an increase of faith and so dramatically elevate the mood of the crowd at the grotto was, he observed, seemingly a good thing. A positive result from a sad and puzzling demise. Yet this was not James's reading of the situation at all: things were not what they seemed.

— *Chapter Seventeen* —

The mood was somber as Sergeant Molloy, Father Maguire, and James Fleming sat across from each other in the small kitchen of the old rectory with a pot of tea and a bottle of whiskey set on the table between them.

"Ah, God, this is bad," Father Maguire said, rubbing his face, the folds of dry white skin bunching on his forehead like old linen.

"Indeed it is that," Molloy said, placing his hat on the chair beside him. "Of course you understand that all of the findings are preliminary. All the tests aren't in."

"But the medical people are pretty certain?" James said, pouring himself a whiskey.

"Yes, they are. But I had been hoping myself, sad as it would have been, that poor Miss Garrotty had just passed away peacefully at the foot of our Holy Mother."

Sergeant Molloy looked over at Maguire, who nodded with an expression of sorrow more eloquent than words. James felt pity for these two old men nearing the end of their careers and now beset with such troubling issues of life and death.

"Could it not have been an accident?" Father Maguire asked softly.

"Indeed. What they are telling me is this: Miss Garrotty took too many doses of two different kinds of medication usually prescribed to lower one's blood pressure . . ."

"So she could have been merely, or should I say, unfortunately confused by the doses?" James said hopefully.

"Perhaps. But there are some problems." Molloy paused as he poured out some tea. "Firstly, we can't find any medicine bottles amongst Miss Garrotty's things. Secondly, the brothers didn't know of any medicines she was taking."

"That tells us nothing!" Father Maguire snorted.

Molloy nodded. "True. But neither can we locate any prescriptions at the local chemist's. We'll have to go farther afield, of course, to check this out, but is it likely that Rita went out of town to fill her prescription? Our local G.P., Dr. Reilly, hadn't prescribed for her. In fact he'd advised her on her *low* blood pressure over the years. He says, logically enough, that no doctor would have prescribed one drug, let alone two, to lower what was already a pressure that hovered around ninety over fifty-five! You remember how she used to, well, not complain actually, but just mention how tired she'd be? That was why. With the low blood pressure, she had low energy."

"Look, Molloy," James said, "it seems to me that what we *don't* have is very significant. No physical evidence of the medication, no evidence of a doctor prescribing the medicine, no real likelihood that Miss Garrotty would take high blood pressure pills given her condition . . ." James paused.

"Yes?" Molloy replied intently.

"I think she was poisoned, Molloy, and we've got another murder on our hands."

"God between us and all harm," said the old priest.

"We have to face it, Father Maguire," James said gently. "Obviously Miss Garrotty didn't own a wheelchair. Nor was it one of the wheelchairs Father Donnelly provided. She just didn't sit down in an empty chair to rest. Someone poisoned her and brought her there . . ."

"Ah, God, I didn't want to see it, Fleming," Molloy said, "But I have to agree. And dealing with it, Father, is why we've gathered here after all, right?" Molloy poured Maguire another strong cup of tea.

"There is one other possibility that we haven't looked at," James said soberly. "Molloy, do you think there is a chance that it could have been suicide? Everyone seems to agree that she seemed low, worn-out . . . the overdose of the medication might have been deliberate . . . Perhaps she wanted to die at the grotto?"

"Absolutely not!" Father Maguire exploded.

"I'm sorry, but I had to ask."

"Father, I think Fleming here is trying to eliminate all the possibilities. That Miss Garrotty accidentally overdosed, not understanding her condition; that she was murdered; or that she took the medicine in a state of depression . . ."

"I refuse to accept that notion!" Maguire said.

"Father Maguire, please," James intervened. "I too want to think her death was an accident, rather than suicide." He paused. "And too, it is horrible to think of someone murdering Miss Garrotty. Every version of her death is a troubling one in some way. But if it were not an accident, if it were not a suicide, then it must be murder. And we must—all of us—think fast, right now, we must work fast, to catch the killer.

"Accepting that she was murdered, we need to know what the motive might be for someone to kill Miss Garrotty. Generally we look at those people around the victim who had the most to gain from the victim's death," James said speculatively.

Father Maguire considered his words for a while. "I see. Well, in terms of the obvious, which is money, she had none to leave. She had a little insurance policy that would go towards her burial, and that's it. She owned nothing—no property. Not even a portion of the shop was hers. That's the way old Mr. Garrotty left it, unfortunately. Not too enlightened, I'm afraid. So her brothers have nothing material to gain from her death." Maguire was succinct as usual.

"In fact, her death is a real loss to them," Sergeant Molloy added, "because she was virtually unpaid labor in their house and the shop. She cooked, cleaned, slaved, and served behind the counter. They'll need three girls to replace her, and they're so tight with the money," he added dryly, "they'll never do it."

"And there was no ill will?" James said.

"No, just their pig-ignorance in taking her for granted, but no ill feeling toward her. And there's been no violence in that family. I know that."

"None we're aware of," Maguire interrupted. "People can do strange things, things that are out of character."

"That's unfortunately all too true in my experience. But besides her brothers, who else was near to her, close to her?" James asked.

"Well, she had a circle of women friends of her age in the parish. They've all known each other for years."

"Any male friends?"

"No, not a one, more's the pity. I've known Rita for twenty years, and I know she would have liked to marry. But there was no one," Maguire said.

"How about Devane!" James said, suddenly remembering Tim's words.

The reaction of the two older men was so abrupt that it was comical.

"Devane?" they exclaimed.

"Well, he's a widower. Not very old, after all. No children to think of. And they were thrown together recently. They did share the experience at the grotto."

"If there was something between them," Maguire said, smiling softly for the first and only time, "then they certainly were dark ones about it."

"But they'd need to be, wouldn't they!" James said. "Given what's happened to them in recent weeks."

"Of course, of course, they wouldn't have wanted any more prying into their private lives," Father Maguire added, giving this novel idea a little more credit.

"Right, then perhaps we could make some discreet inquiry. I spoke with Devane just the other day."

"More power to you," Molloy said, surprised. "He won't give me the time of day lately. Isolating himself up there at the farm with his guns."

"Understand me, Molloy. I'm not suggesting he killed Rita Garrotty."

"On the other hand, you were just agreeing that anyone is capable of violence if pushed . . ."

"Touché," James said. "All right. Now, leaving her immediate circle of female friends aside, and the supposition that Devane and she might have been involved, is there anyone else you can think of?"

After some obvious hesitation, Father Maguire spoke up. "I hate even thinking this, but given the mood of the crowd lately, they're latching on to this idea of a great sign."

"Go on, Father."

"Considering that and the fact that any kind of notoriety or public event in the Church draws large crowds, and among them some very troubled people, lonely souls, people who can get caught up into a frenzy of religious fervor— then perhaps some poor misguided soul saw that another death at the grotto, one resembling the first, would increase attention. It would further this idea that a sign had been given . . ." Maguire sighed after this unusually long speech.

"We could look at your idea from a slightly different angle," James interrupted, suddenly struck. "Such an act could bring scandal to the whole scene, could discredit the grotto itself. To murder a visionary—if one really believed her to be a visionary—surely would be blasphemous in the extreme. To interfere in the workings of the divine will by taking one of the seers away? Surely that would indicate an evil mind, a terribly malicious purpose. I think it would reveal someone violently opposed to, if not the visionary herself, then to the Church, or to the apparition, or even the Virgin herself!" James said, warming to his theme.

Father Maguire was nodding. "It could have been someone whose prayers or petitions hadn't been answered by the Blessed Mother, someone angered that a personal cure or miracle was not granted . . ."

Molloy caught at the idea. "So, out there in that enormous crowd of devout people there may be some unbalanced, very bitter person—angry at our Holy Mother and striking out at Her, by striking out at Her visionaries?" He stood up, pacing restlessly. "Any way you look at it, I think that Mary Dowd and Devane are now at risk."

"Am I interrupting something?" Jude petulantly said from the open doorway.

"No, no, Father Donnelly, come in," Father Maguire said. "We've been discussing the dreadful news about Miss Garrotty. We have to face the possibility that she was murdered. And if that is the case, it has occurred to us that the killer may have chosen her for one of two reasons. Either her death was to be viewed by others as a sign from God. Or her death was intended to redress some great disappointment or anger at a petition not granted." Maguire watched Jude's reaction impassively.

"I am shocked to hear you speak of Miss Garrotty's death as a murder," Jude said stiffly. "But I heard you mention Mary Dowd and Devane. Why was that?" he asked, sitting down at the table.

"We believe that they too might be in danger," Molloy replied.

"Well, at least I can vouch for Mary Dowd's safety," Jude said smugly. "I've just come from her and I've arranged that she is to see no one except myself."

"How is that?" Father Maguire said sharply.

"I'm forgetting that you don't yet know, Father. You see, I

installed her up at the convent earlier today. Mother Superior agreed to take her in for the duration. And I instructed them that Mary Dowd's visitors should be restricted."

"On whose authority?" James demanded.

"What do you mean?" Jude challenged.

"Why would you take it upon yourself to do such a thing? She's a grown woman. She can make decisions for herself."

"Look, Fleming, I'm not sure what concern it is of yours who she sees and doesn't see. I am her spiritual adviser—"

"Then stick to that! As I see it, you are interfering altogether too much in her temporal life, as you are fond of calling it!" James stood up.

"Gentlemen, please, sit down, sit down." Maguire's voice cut through their shouts like an elderly schoolmaster's. Only this master was pouring out two large whiskies.

Retreating slightly, Jude took the proferred glass.

"I apologize, Father. I only wanted to tell you that I was concerned for Miss Dowd's health and well-being. And I took appropriate steps. I also thought that the media might hound her. Or petitioners may seek her out in a sincere desire to enlist her aid. This way, no one can visit her except myself or someone to whom I have given permission."

James held his tongue, draining his whiskey instead. He had said his piece. Anything more now would reveal his own dislike of the man and his manipulative ways. Instead he turned to Molloy.

"Sergeant, tell me this—do you think the two deaths are related?"

"At first I didn't think so, when I had assumed that poor Miss Garrotty had died of natural causes. But now I am wondering. The two deaths are separated by only two weeks in time, which is significant in itself. More significant is that both bodies were found at the grotto. If we follow Father Maguire's thought, that the killer is demented, then perhaps the motive for the first and second murders was the same."

"So you are suggesting that the young lad was purposely killed and purposely left at the grotto?"

"In light of what's just been said, yes, I think it's a possibility, if it was a killer who wanted to discredit the religious movement developing here."

"So when the first death didn't have the desired effect, then he tried again? Only aiming at someone of more significance?" James said.

"Yes, and by that action, demonstrating that God and His mother cannot protect even those whom They have chosen," Molloy added in a discouraged tone.

Father Maguire stood up, obviously distressed. "This is very disturbing. The deaths in themselves are tragic. To be the result of this kind of warped thinking intensifies the tragedy. To think—oh God!—that twenty odd years ago Mr. and Mrs. O'Rourke built that little shrine, gave of their land, purchased the statue, and that I blessed it . . . All an act of homage, and devotion and veneration. That the statue was a beacon to all who passed by. Something at once homey and spiritual. She became to us all familiar, somehow comforting. Perhaps that statue became over time a feature of the landscape like the hills to the west. Not ignored," he said, turning to face them. "No, just the opposite. And if when our eyes glanced over at her as we walked or drove past, perhaps briefly we thought of her, or a small prayer passed through our minds. It was all so simple!"

He wrung his hands. "And now this. All that was familiar has been made strange."

"Yes, but by a miracle," Jude exclaimed, standing too.

"No," Maguire lashed out. "Made strange by death, by murder, by the evil and venomous heart of someone out there right now in Buncloda, in our village, Jude, in our very parish."

He looked at them all a little wildly. "Yes, someone whose darkness we have spoken with or brushed against, who is even now in our village, brooding, readying to strike!"

"Father Maguire," James intervened, "calm yourself. We

are speculating still. This person could well be someone who just snapped. Someone whose anger was tapped and then released by the tremendous crowds, the public attention, the atmosphere here that is sometimes so frenetic, so charged. There are many factors to consider. The numbers, for example. This person—if such there be—could easily be an outsider to your village."

"No, no, no . . . I know in my heart this is no stranger. This is someone from our village."

"Why? Why do you say that?"

"The quality of evil! These acts have been aimed straight at the heart of Buncloda. One who did not live here could not feel that kind of hate, that anger, that destructive intent. You may solve legal problems, James. You may have confronted the results of evil in your private cases . . . I have seen in your eyes a knowledge you should not have, of how the human heart can turn and feed on itself . . . yes, I see it there. And do you know why I can see it?"

James was now standing, growing pale, as if Maguire would blurt out his own hidden secrets. He stared back, bracing himself.

"I can see it in your eyes because I have listened to confessions since I was ordained."

He turned to Jude. "Yes, Jude, despite what you might think of me, I was young once like you, and optimistic." Maguire turned back to James. "When I came to this village years ago, people came to confession frequently . . . not like today. They came every Saturday, week after week, month after month, year after year. I was there, in the darkness, in that confessional with the purple velvet curtain. Listening to the murmurings of a thousand hearts, the sins of a thousand souls times a thousand. Weeping, grieving, angry, broken, sad, lonely. Mr. Fleming, as an outsider, can you understand what it is like to listen, to come to know your people only in the dark intimacy of their sins and their despair? Oh, there was sorrow and true repentance. And I pray they went away shriven and solaced. But afterward, I would kneel in that church, in the darkness, and try to put their darkness away from me . . . just so that I could go on."

"Father . . ." James said softly.

"No, James, I know sin intimately well. I know the human heart. This murderer is from this village."

Sergeant Molloy awkwardly stood up. "Perhaps you're right, Father, but remember, we had reports that the murdered lad was from Tipperary. He's been formally identified. The family is called Langan." He jabbed his head forward in his version of a nod to Father Maguire.

"Well then, Father, surely that might indicate the killer is not from Buncloda," James said in a heartening tone. "Right, Molloy?"

James hesitated, suddenly struck. "Listen, Molloy, you were just saying earlier that you thought the two deaths might be related, that there is only one killer. But surely this alters things?"

"Yes and no. If it was a local Buncloda person who killed the Langan lad, did he go out and seek a victim at random? And what was the Tipperary lad doing up this far? There had been drinking obviously, but that lad wasn't in any pub in this village."

"How about someone from this village out drinking elsewhere?" Maguire interjected.

"It's possible, of course. Yes, perhaps, but then my question still is: did he kill the Langan lad on purpose, just to leave his body at the grotto? That doesn't ring true for me. Yet I can't yet rule anything out."

James shook his head. "But Sergeant Molloy, look at the methods! A blow in a brawl in one case. A planned murder in the other?"

"I know, I know," Molloy said despondently as he reached for another mug of tea.

James returned to his theme. "If the killer were one and the same person, it indicates a person capable both of sudden violence and also someone prepared to plan to lie in wait, to bide his time."

This idea was worrying, James realized, because it gave no definite clue to the personality of the killer and thus no clue to his identity. And without that, no indication regarding potential victims.

But he couldn't escape the reality of the victims they already did have. A dead boy clutching a rosary at the foot of the statue. Rita Garrotty dead at the foot of the statue. If there were two different murderers, with different motives, then the potential victims and the possible killers would number in the thousands. Why not just look at the entire population of Ireland? James thought bitterly.

But what if the death of the Langan boy had been an accident, as they had speculated even from the beginning? What if the second murder was a copycat? Not so much in method, obviously. But what if that death, that disposal of the Langan boy's body at the grotto, had triggered off something in the killer of Miss Garrotty? Either way, whether one killer or two, the end result was the same—death. Either way, the two remaining seers were very possibly the next targets. James said as much aloud to the others.

"I agree, yes, of course," Molloy said. "Yes, yes, this is something to act on." He pushed back his chair and put on his hat. "If you'll let me use your telephone, Father Maguire, I'm going to ring Devane now to check on him. He's pretty vulnerable alone on that farm of his."

Maguire nodded as Molloy hurried from the room.

As James sat back in his chair, Jude stood up, pacing restlessly. "I think we should be doing more!"

"That's as may be," Maguire said dryly, "but before we go on, I have to tell you that the bishop of this diocese has asked me for a written report of recent events, including our handling of them, yours and mine. I am grateful it is a written report only: I've been dreading a visit, but apparently they are willing to wait for my notes on these two deaths. It was implied that there have been some inquiries from Rome on how this situation is being dealt with . . ."

Father Maguire rubbed his face again, and again seemed to age before their eyes. He looked over at Jude with an expression of hopelessness. "Jude, Jude, this situation cannot continue . . ."

"It is out of my control, Father Maguire. All these events have been determined, have been set in motion, by the apparition in May."

James noted that Jude's arrogance seemed to inflate at the rate that Father Maguire was withdrawing into himself and his desolation.

"No, Jude," Maguire said softly, "they are in your control."

"That's not accurate, Father," Jude said, flushing deeply, a fleeting expression of anger passing across his face. "Mary Dowd is calling the shots, to put it crudely," he added.

"No, no, no." Maguire was nearly whispering, and James was startled at the note of despair in his voice. "Jude, Mary Dowd is under your influence. It is clear to me even if it is not clear to anyone else involved, including Miss Dowd herself."

"I don't know about that, Father, but I do know the needs of the Church change from generation to generation. This is the modern era, Father. We are competing for the people's attention with cable television, media events, global communication, computer networking. People feed themselves on news, and on scandal and sensation in part. The Church needs this visionary manifestation."

"Oh, Jude——" Maguire said, putting up his hand.

"No, I will finish. You've implied so much since May, and hinted at more. Let me speak plain. I view this apparition in May here in our village in two ways. Yes, I've seen it as a great spiritual gift to Mary Dowd and the other seers, and, through them, to us—putting us in touch with the divine. But also I saw it as a great opportunity. You wouldn't see that, but *I* did, and I grabbed at it. I might have encouraged Mary Dowd to talk about her experience, but remember, please, it was *she* who had the vision. Yes, I might have spread the word, but only locally. If that word spread, then it was the people's need to hear it and to spread it, to repeat it and to recruit others to the cause.

"I didn't contact the media, but when they came, I welcomed them. The media was our route to the outside world. Father, people around the world have heard of Buncloda! Of the vision!"

"And of you?" James said bluntly.

"No, I have effaced myself." Jude grew redder. "This has nothing to do with me personally. I have been merely a tool. Think of it . . . people all over the world pick up a paper—"

"A tabloid?" James cut in.

"Perhaps, but nonetheless, for that minute they are raised up to consider something not of this world. Not the life of a movie star, a rock singer, but the life of a woman who was more than a saint, who was the Holy Mother of God."

"So these people are supposedly uplifted over their cups of coffee? Or on the train or the bus?" James sneered.

"Absolutely, no matter where they are. The information about the vision passes through their minds, however briefly. How do we know in whose mind and heart that information might lodge?" Jude spread his hands wide. "How many more people can be reached than the few hundred who attend Mass on Sunday here in our little old parish church!" He was dismissive.

"So you see yourself as facilitating all of this worldwide response, perhaps even coordinating it someday?" Maguire said dully.

"Why not? Look at Knock, look at Lourdes, look at Fatima. Why not here in Buncloda?"

"Why?" Maguire shouted. His vehemence was so unexpected that they both jumped. "Jude, why? Because we know nothing as yet. Three people, one of whom is dead, two who have willingly retreated, even fled, from the situation . . . Don't deny it. Rita? Dead. Devane? A recluse barricaded on his farm. Mary Dowd? In the convent, sick and distressed! No other witnesses. Certainly no proof beyond their words. No signs, as you've been urging and hoping for. And in the end? What? I'll tell you, Jude. No miracle!"

"That's not true! The apparition *is* the miracle. And there have been signs. I told you that Mrs. Farley's arm was healed . . ."

"Oh, please, Jude. A woman's arm hurts and then it doesn't hurt. Surely I am pleased for her, but what was it all about? Perhaps she was depressed and her depression formed an hysterical conversion. So? Her mental state was manifested in a physical complaint."

"A complaint that is gone now—because of her faith!"

"Because of the power of suggestion!"

"All right, but does that make it less valid a cure? Her faith made her open to the suggestion that Mary our Holy Mother could cure her arm. All right, then perhaps it meant curing her mind first. The healing of her arm was an outward manifestation of that cure. This is the modern world, Father, and the afflictions today are now of the mind: depression, loneliness, anxiety. Today we need to see things differently. It is not now a question of the dramatic physical cure: 'Take up your bed and walk,' as Our Lord said."

"Exactly!" Maguire cried.

"Father, those were limited times, illiterate peasants. The Lord had to use drama to make His message known. The miracles were physical, obvious, crowd-pleasing, so as to give the people reason to believe. Even when Our Lord cured the mind and spirit of the petitioner, he had to show those cures as demons being driven out of the body and mind and into pigs and hogs that then rushed off a cliff to their deaths! Imagine that happening in our new technological world. Father, *we* have to haul the Church into the twenty-first century. So now the miracles must be even more complex, less physical; they must occur within the mind, yes, that's it . . . The new miracle must address the modern condition of mankind!" Jude stopped, breathless, panting, yet obviously pleased with his speech. He poured out a cup of cold tea and tossed it back as Molloy reentered the room.

Maguire looked at Jude, shaking his head. "We have strayed considerably from our immediate purpose . . . Let's hear what James and the sergeant have to say."

"I can't get through to Devane," Molloy said. "And frankly I'm worried. I think James here is on the right track. The remaining two visionaries may well be at considerable risk, Father. I'm going to Devane's now . . ."

"I'm coming with you," James said, springing to his feet, caught by Molloy's urgent tone.

"Well, if that's your feeling, then I'm going to check on Miss Dowd," Jude said.

As the three younger men hastily left the room, the old priest crossed himself and closed his eyes, seemingly in prayer.

Chapter Eighteen

Despite the fact that Molloy was driving his official car, his journey with James across the town of Buncloda was painfully slow. As they drew near the mouth of the road leading to the grotto and beyond to Devane's farm, he was increasingly hindered by the pedestrian traffic.

"It's unlikely the killer would work so fast," Molloy said, half to himself.

"True, but I would feel better had Devane answered his phone," James replied, staring out the window.

He'd grown so used to the crowds, to the endless streams of people in Buncloda, that he barely took notice of them anymore. They were faceless, like the pedestrians passing on the pavements of Dublin at lunch hour. Yet as he watched, another feeling crept in on him, and he began to glance at the people, no longer faceless. He scrutinized their expressions quite openly. Some people caught his eye and looked away uneasily.

Was this man approaching the one? he wondered. Or the

older man behind him? Or the young teenager with the scruffy beard? Was he the one? Suddenly James realized how vulnerable they all were. The killer whom he had easily, theoretically, posited at the rectory seemed now much more real, and more threatening.

He was relieved when the crowds began to thin as they passed the grotto itself. The sky loured and the gray clouds were heavy with rain. The atmosphere was oppressive as the air grew still and almost fetid. Sweat stood out on Devane's leathery face as he urged the car forward.

"Not long now," he said as they approached Devane's property. James, damp with perspiration, noted again the Keep Out signs now hanging limply from the trees and hedges, the cardboard absorbing the dampness from the air. The ink on some was running, making black streaks beneath the letters.

As Molloy pulled in, James leapt from the car and attempted to open the gate to the driveway. No success. As before, it was double-chained and padlocked. He gestured to Molloy and together they climbed the gate and the inner fence and cow gate. They hurried up the winding lane towards the house.

"There'll be a storm, surely," Molloy said, indicating the cattle grouped together, heads lowered and all facing the same way. James scanned the scene, wondering in which field or barn they would find Devane, pondering where to begin looking. He could hear Molloy panting behind him.

"Devane! Devane! Sergeant Molloy's here. Halloo!" James shouted.

As they grew nearer he was pleased to see that in fact Devane was at home after all. He sat on his front porch.

"Look, Molloy, he's there. Asleep." James turned back to look at Molloy, who only shook his head in warning.

"Devane," James shouted again, wanting to wake him and yet not wanting to startle the man from his sleep and get himself shot in the process.

"Devane! It's Fleming and Molloy!" James waved, but Devane did not wave in return.

Molloy caught up to him and put a hand on his arm.

"Dead asleep," James said with sympathy.

"No, James," Molloy gasped. "Not dead asleep . . . he's dead."

"How is she?" Jude asked anxiously as the lay housekeeper let him in the convent's side door. As they walked through the maze of corridors, linoleum gleaming underfoot, the clean smell of wax filling the air, Mrs. Galvin merely shrugged.

"I haven't seen her, Father. It's the nuns who look after her. But I did turn away two poor souls from the door, as you told us to. They just wanted to see her, to ask her to pray for them. Poor things, I took down their pathetic requests."

"Did you know them? From the town?"

"Not locals, Father. Looked to me like a husband and wife. And then two young sisters came by, you know the type, in their twenties maybe. I told those two to be off with them to the palm reader in Wexford Town."

"Any men? I mean, on their own?" Jude said after she brought him to one of the small reception rooms near the chapel.

"Well, yes, there was. Only I didn't think of him like that," Mrs. Galvin said. "It was just Tim Kerrigan, Mary Dowd's friend."

"And?"

"Well, I just told him your rule, and then he was very rude, really. He was most put out."

"But he didn't come in?"

"No, he scribbled a note, and then later I went to her room, but she wasn't there so I kept it."

"May I see it? Perhaps I can give it to her now."

"Of course, Father. I'll get Mary Dowd, poor pet. I hope she got some rest . . ." Handing him the note, Mrs. Galvin left the room.

Jude glanced at the note and, folding it, put it in his pocket.

After a few minutes Mary entered the room, as pale as he'd seen her before, but with more animation in her face than earlier.

"Oh, Jude, it's so good to see you," she said softly as he took her cold hands in his.

"Are you feeling a little better, Mary?"

"Yes, I feel a great sense of peace here in the convent. The silence, the surroundings, but . . ."

"But what?" Jude said anxiously.

"I'm not complaining," she said, her expression becoming childlike. Jude's heart went out to her.

"Tell me, please. I am your confessor. You can tell me anything. You should know that now," he said softly.

"It's safe here, Jude, and it's peaceful. But Jude, it's lonely too."

"Lonely?"

"Yes, the sisters and staff have their work, Jude. And I think they're keeping their distance. Jude, it's been like this for me for so long . . . at home, at the school. People wanting me and yet keeping their distance." She looked frankly into his eyes. "It's that kind of loneliness. I feel cut off from normal life since . . ."

"Since May?" Jude supplied.

"Yes, yes, that's what I meant," she said almost shyly.

"Perhaps you are feeling the need to communicate with our Blessed Mother? Perhaps this is Her way of calling you to Her, and away from the world," Jude said.

Mary seemed to sag a little, and he moved to sit beside her on the small leather sofa. She put her head in her hands.

"Oh, yes, of course I feel that need to be with Her—as before. But Jude . . ." She hesitated, and he reached up and gently pulled her hands from her face. She looked at him then, her eyes sad, almost empty. "It's you, you here on earth who are the—" She stopped.

"Go on," Jude whispered.

"You . . . are the only one I can talk to. You are the only one who truly knows me, who can understand all that I have gone through, all that I am still going through. Even when Rita was alive I couldn't talk with her the way I do with you. Jude, without you, I'm not sure I could bear the strain. This is my life now, praying, waiting for Her to call to me . . . again."

"I see, I see . . ." Jude said thoughtfully.

"Perhaps I shouldn't have spoken." Mary stood up, suddenly withdrawing her hands from Jude's clasp.

"Why do you say that?" Jude asked, confused.

"I'm becoming a nuisance to you. You have your own life and your own work to go on with . . ." Mary walked to the window and lifted the curtain aside, but she stared through it without seeing.

"Mary, Mary, *you* are my life and my work right now. You must know that. Everything I've done since May has been for you and your cause. Our cause, if I can say that without offending you. I told Father Maguire this only today—that this was the case . . . my life's work."

Jude stood up as he sensed her withdrawing from him.

"Father Maguire?" She turned to face him, suspicion in her eyes. "And why? Why were you talking with him about me?" Mary seemed annoyed somehow. Her changes of mood were so quick, so transitory, that Jude was continually at a loss.

"Actually, that's why I'm here, Mary. Sergeant Molloy had news. Bad news . . ."

"What is it?" Mary clasped her hands to her chest.

"I'm very sorry to tell you that it appears that poor Miss Garrotty was murdered . . ."

"Oh my God," Mary said. Her body swayed and she braced herself, holding onto the table, her knuckles white with the pressure. Her shaking was so violent that the small bowl of June roses in the center of the table spilled water on the mahogany.

"Mary, sit down," Jude urged.

"No, no, I'm all right. Tell me everything."

"There's not a lot to tell. But Fleming and Father Maguire, and myself, we all agreed that it's possible some disturbed person may be directing his anger at you three: poor Rita, and Devane, and yourself."

"But why?"

"This isn't for certain, Mary. We are speculating, but nonetheless you may be at risk. That's why it is good you are here in the convent, for many reasons. But Mary, you must remember through all of this what your main vocation is now: your main role in all of this, despite the danger, despite the distractions, is to channel our Lord's grace through his Holy Mother here, to Buncloda. Have you . . . oh, how shall I put this?" He looked at her imploringly.

"No, Jude, I've had no sign from Her. But . . ."

"Please tell me . . ."

"I know that I'm having difficulty praying. And . . . and I felt a great need for you. Just in the last hour or so. I felt that . . ."

"Yes?"

"If I could be with you, who know everything, if you could be with me, I would receive some comfort, some relief from this terrible emptiness, this longing . . ."

"Of course, Mary. And I'm here now. Perhaps I was led here at this very moment when you feel the need for me."

As Mary moved her hands away from her breast, Jude saw a small dark stain on her blouse and he began to tremble.

"Mary, I did not speak up earlier, but now I feel I must."

She followed his glance and blushed a deep red.

"Why, dear girl, are you mortifying the flesh? What has put this into your mind? I'm not sure it's a healthy path to choose just now, when you are weak and distressed . . ."

"I'm not sure either. Oh Jude," she cried out. "I felt compelled to do it, to subjugate the flesh. To aid my concentration. I should not be thinking of earthly things, of

189

earthly pleasures . . . I want to be able to live without those needs, the needs of the body . . . I feel drawn to purify myself in your—in the Lord's sight . . ." She seemed caught up in her thoughts when she suddenly looked at him, afraid. "Is it wrong, Jude? Oh, how can it be wrong when I feel such need to do it?"

Jude was struck dumb for a moment as she stared at him, her eyes intense and wide.

"As your spiritual adviser I should be able to answer you, Mary. But I—I find I must consider this deeply. Please, just don't do it, all right? Until I can answer you. Try to resist, at least for a while?" He stumbled over his words as a look of disillusion seemed to pass across her face.

Quickly recovering a more commanding tone, he continued. "You said just now that you felt the need for me to be here. And here I am. Let us go into the chapel and see if we can pray together."

He moved closer to her. "We will work through this together, we will pray our way through it. And our Mother will surely hear us."

Jude took Mary's arm as she leaned weakly against him.

"I'm sorry I'm so weak, Jude, but this news about Rita is so awful. I can't believe that someone murdered her," she murmured as they began to walk towards the door.

"We will pray for her too, although I know she is with God after her great gift."

"Gift?"

"Of the vision. To know you are chosen. As *you* are chosen. You are special."

"You do think so? Lately I've had such doubt, Jude."

"Our greatest saints have had doubts. It is both a human and a divine challenge. The dark night of the soul. But they prayed, Mary. We will pray now."

They slowly walked towards the small chapel, Jude supporting Mary around the waist with one arm, holding her hand in his free one. Even more slowly they walked together down the center aisle towards the communion rail. The blond wood of the pews gleamed in the soft candlelight, and multihued roses were everywhere lending their sweet scent to the air. Daylight lit up the stained-glass window behind the altar, and Mary the Virgin shimmered before them in tints of blue and gold, her hands outstretched as if in welcome. The silence was complete.

Together they knelt. Mary bent her head until her forehead rested on the wooden rail, and she covered her eyes with her pale, veined hands. Jude's eyes were uplifted as he let the power of his faith and his hope fill his mind and heart. He focused his eyes on the depiction of Mary the Virgin, as have her many supplicants down the ages. Sweating from the strain of intense concentration, he prayed for the young girl at his side, a living, human vessel of all that was, for him, divine. His trancelike contemplative prayer might have gone on for hours if he hadn't been suddenly, mightily distracted. Mary Dowd cried out only once before she slid to the cold, gleaming chapel floor.

Molloy looked exhausted when he finally entered the kitchen of Devane's farmhouse. James had been waiting for some time as Molloy dealt with the demands of the situation.

"This is pretty bad, Molloy," he said somberly as Molloy sat down.

"God, I can't believe this."

"What can you tell me?" James said.

"Probably what you observed for yourself. Devane was seated on the bench, and he was struck from behind with the spade that was lying behind the bench. Simple as that." He sighed and took off his hat. "I'd noticed a few spades and rakes to the side of the front door on my previous visits. I'd say the murderer just picked up one of those and swung it. Quickly, and hard." Molloy wiped his face with a tobacco-stained handkerchief.

James tried, unsuccessfully, to block out the gruesome view he'd had of Devane's shattered head. He drew breath, trying to quell the rising nausea.

"Surely Devane would have fallen forward with the force of that blow," James managed to say at last.

"I agree. I think we can conclude that the killer pulled the body back onto the bench . . . perhaps to make it look natural . . . throw off suspicion if someone had glanced up the drive."

When they had found the body on the bench and he'd ascertained Devane was dead, Molloy had checked the house. Finding no one, he'd then used Devane's phone to ring for assistance. Keeping James away from the body, he'd made him wait in the kitchen near the phone. Molloy had finished his preliminary work when the forensic team arrived and took over.

"Can you tell how long, how long ago . . ." James watched Molloy's face to see if he shared his sense of guilt.

"I'm no expert, but I'd say not more than two hours, you know, from the condition of the corpse."

"You know, Molloy, his gun was across his knees," James said expressively.

"So why didn't he use it, you mean? My thought exactly, Fleming. My guess is that the killer approached him from behind . . ."

"He would have heard him . . ."

"Fleming, did you notice the tea things?"

"What?"

"On the grass, a little way in front of the body was a tray with mugs and a jug of milk. Two mugs. I think the killer was known to Devane and that's why he wasn't on the alert."

James looked around him suddenly. "God, Molloy! I hope I haven't destroyed any evidence. I don't think I touched anything in here. I've just been sitting here at the table."

Molloy silenced his fears, but with a gloved hand he lifted

the kettle: it was full and the metal was still warm to his touch. "It seems like it was boiled just a little while ago."

On the narrow counter abutting the refrigerator was a bottle of milk with the cap off.

"Someone was making ready for tea . . ." James murmured.

"And yet Devane was sitting down when he was struck?"

"The killer was making the tea, Molloy! Brought out the tray, returned to boil the kettle. Look, the teapot's here with dry leaves in it," James exclaimed.

"So the killer was about to pour the tea? And then went to the front door, caught up the spade and whacked it across the back of Devane's head!" Molloy was incredulous.

"And if the killer was making tea, then it means that Devane was comfortable with that person being in his kitchen. Oh, Molloy, this is madness."

"To kill someone while in the middle of making a pot of tea? I agree. It looks to me sudden, not premeditated . . ."

"What could Devane have done to unhinge someone to that extent—in midstream, so to speak?"

"Well, he didn't *do* anything, it seems, but sit there. It must have been something that he said, something so threatening to the visitor that the man caught up the spade and cracked his skull. Oh my God, Father Maguire will have a fit when he hears of this."

"I took the liberty of phoning the rectory. He was in the church, so I left a message for him to come here."

"Well done," Molloy sighed.

"Do I have to stay?" James asked restlessly. "Can you take my statement later perhaps?"

"Yes, of course, Fleming, but where are you headed?"

"Rita's dead, Devane is dead. Who do you think is next?"

"So you do think this killer is one and the same?"

"It fits our theory, Molloy! Two out of three of the visionaries—dead!"

"But it also looks to me like this killer knew Devane. Man, he let this murderin' bastard make tea in his kitchen!"

"That's still an assumption, Molloy. Perhaps there was an innocent guest, who fled. Perhaps there is a witness out there?" James added, but without conviction.

"It looks like Father Maguire was right," Molloy said, shaking his head.

"How so?"

"If Devane knew his killer, then it is certain that the killer is from Buncloda."

"If so, then at least it narrows our field, Molloy. It gives us some hope of finding him . . . but it must be soon! Look, I'm going to the convent now to check on Mary Dowd . . . I'm on foot, so I'd like to get going."

"Right, ring me as soon as you can."

James set off, averting his eyes from the dead body of Devane and the Wexford forensic team working feverishly around him. He loped down the driveway and ducked under the yellow tape marking off the crime scene, glancing at the young garda now standing watch at the entrance to the drive.

Too late, James thought—like locking the barn door after the horse has bolted. As he half ran, half jogged down the long road, he wondered what would have happened if they had acted sooner, if they hadn't sat arguing and speculating at the rectory. Just a few minutes could have made the difference, he thought, conscience-stricken.

It was with some sense of relief when he got in his car outside Mrs. Kehoe's and edged it back along to the main road and thence to the road that led to the convent on the outskirts of town. This time he would not dilly-dally. He had to reach Mary Dowd as soon as possible and begin to implement the plan now forming in his mind.

A sweet-faced little old nun opened the door cautiously and peered out and up at James towering above her.

"I can't let you in, sir," she whispered.

"But you must. It's a matter of life and death," he nearly shouted.

"I'm sorry." She started to shut the door, and he boldly placed a polished shoe between it and the doorjamb.

"Is Father Donnelly here?" he said, knowing Jude's car was sitting at the path.

"Yes?"

"Then tell him I'm here, please, and that I absolutely must speak with him this instant."

He removed his offending foot and she shut the door. Seconds later Jude threw it open.

"Fleming, what the hell?"

"I'll tell you, man, if you let me in. This is ridiculous. Where is Mary Dowd?"

"Lying down."

"Are you sure? Is she all right?" James asked frantically, the strain starting to show.

"Yes, of course. I just left her to come to the door. But she's not well."

Jude and James stepped into one of the anterooms.

"What do you mean?" he demanded, panic in his voice.

"We were praying in the chapel not more than half an hour ago, when she slipped to the floor unconscious. We had to lift her to her room, but she's come around. Mother is with her."

"What happened, why did she fall to the floor?"

"Look, Fleming . . . what is it? What's happened?" Jude looked frightened.

"I'm sorry, Donnelly." James threw himself in a chair and drew his breath.

"What's happened?"

"It's Devane. God, the poor old man . . . he's dead."

"What?"

"Murdered, and this time there is no doubt. He was dead when Molloy and I got up there . . ."

"You found Rita, and now you found Devane dead! What is this?"

"What are you implying?" James spat.

"Nothing, nothing. It's the shock. My God. Both of them

195

gone. It's a horror." He looked at James. "That's why you're here, isn't it? You think Mary Dowd will be next?"

James nodded. "I'd like to see her, Donnelly."

Jude was about to object when he was caught by James's deadly serious expression.

"I'll be right back," Jude said, rushing from the room.

─── *Chapter Nineteen* ───

Some minutes later James found himself sitting with Mary Dowd at a polished table as Jude handed around cups of tea that the lay housekeeper, Mrs. Galvin, had brought in. James waited until Mary had sipped hers, reviving from the shock of the news about Devane.

"I'd like you to talk to me, Mary, about Rita and Devane."

She nodded.

"I want you to recall the last few times you spoke with either or both of them. Any memories you have may reveal some clue, no matter how random it may seem to you now, or insignificant then."

Mary shivered and put down her cup with a shaking hand. "Jude just explained your theory of how someone, some very angry person, might want to kill those of us who saw the vision. And what struck me was . . ." She looked anxiously at Jude.

"The last few times I was with Rita, she was starting to say

197

that . . ." Mary hesitated again and her face began to turn a mottled red.

"Yes, go on," James said, noting her apprehensive glances.

"I think Rita was beginning to have doubts."

"Doubts?" Jude said loudly.

"Shush," James said sternly, leaning forward, trying to get Mary focused only on himself and not on Jude.

"Something like that," she mumbled.

"Like what, Mary?"

"Rita wasn't sure anymore, well not anymore exactly, but she wasn't sure all of the time . . ."

"Not sure about what?"

"About the vision. She said to me that some of the time she couldn't remember it clearly. It was becoming fragmented, I think she said."

"And?"

"And we talked about it a bit. I said I had doubts sometimes too."

Jude let his cup hit the saucer with a crack, and Mary jumped but did not look at him.

"But it wasn't the same for me," she said hastily. "My doubts were that I was so unworthy of this honor . . . but I could always remember my vision. I tried to help Rita to recall it, but she would say that her mind was going. You know, she was so tired all the time, and forgetful. I thought that was really the problem."

"What?"

"Her health."

"Of course, she was probably tired," Jude interjected.

James glared at him. "Did she tell anyone else about her doubts, Mary? Beside yourself."

"Perhaps. She mentioned Mr. Devane all right. And I assumed she might have spoken with you too, Jude?" She looked apprehensively at Jude.

"Not at all. I hardly spoke with either of them, Mary, you know that."

"Why was that, Donnelly?" James asked, puzzled.

"Well, I . . ." he stumbled.

Mary bowed her head.

"All right, this is very difficult to say in front of Mary, but my feeling has been all along that Mary was the true seer; her description was full of clarity and faith and truth. Rita and Devane seemed more reticent, perhaps being old-fashioned or a bit more limited . . ." Jude sought for the right words as James looked incredulous.

"What are you saying?"

"I think I'm saying that Mary was the most affecting."

"You mean as a public figure of sorts?"

"Yes, but that isn't a dirty word, you know, Fleming. And anyway, of the three, I was drawn most to Mary. We were compatible spiritually, I believe." He looked at her and as quickly looked away. "And with her innocence, her trusting nature, her youth and inexperience . . . she was more open than the others to my help and prayers. Right, Mary?"

"You mean your influence, Donnelly," James said, unable to restrain himself.

Mary intervened. "No, no, Mr. Fleming, Jude tried to help all three of us, but the others seemed so . . ."

"Nervous," Jude supplied, to James's further annoyance.

"Jude has helped me more than anyone in my life. He understood immediately how overwhelmed I was by seeing the vision. I felt . . ."

She looked at Jude, who nodded his approval.

"I felt very unworthy. At first I think I wanted to die, in a sense, to escape the burden. You see, I saw it as a burden. I could never live up to the ideal of being a saint who saw the Virgin, someone to whom she might speak or reveal a sign. Jude helped me to go on, to understand my own role, my own future . . ."

"All right, Mary, I accept you have a special relationship with Jude. You are saying that the others chose not to have this with him. And then over time they seemed to weaken in some way?"

"Yes, but I don't know if they told anyone else about their doubts."

"Of course not. I would have known," Jude added.

"Not necessarily, Jude," James said.

Jude leaned back in his chair. James could see that he had been hit hard by Mary's statements, or else was pretending to be.

"And you, Mary?" James said. "Are you certain you have not had similar doubts about the reality of your experience, about the validity of your vision?"

"I don't know about doubts . . . but today in the chapel I felt that—"

"Mary, please, we haven't talked about what happened in the chapel yet. I'd rather you waited."

Mary dropped her head yet again in deference to the priest's words, and James, maddened by her acquiescence, also realized he'd get no further with her as long as Jude was present.

"Just one more thing, Mary."

"Come on, Fleming!"

"No, let me finish, Donnelly. Mary, do you think Tim Kerrigan is angry with you?"

"That's enough!" Jude said.

"What? Tim?" she said, looking up. "No. Oh, I don't know. Really, I don't feel well. I'd like you both to go, please, so I can lie down." She stood up abruptly and walked quickly to the door.

"Mary," Jude called, "you realize you can't go outside, don't you? It's too dangerous now."

"If I need to go to the grotto, Jude, I will go," she said with surprising firmness. Perhaps a flash of the old Mary, James thought.

"But I will always go with you."

She closed the door behind her, leaving James and Jude with an awkward silence to fill.

"Why did you mention Kerrigan?" Jude said at last.

"Because he knows Mary, and because he's angry, as I

told you before." James prepared to leave. "Because I wanted to see her reaction . . ." James's impatience was showing. "Look, I've got to get going."

James was at his car when Jude caught up with him.

"Look, Fleming, I honestly forgot to give this to Mary." He handed James the note the housekeeper had given him earlier.

"'I must see you Mary. This has to stop. Ring me. Tim,'" James read aloud. "You mean he was here!"

"Obviously. Should I give it to her?"

James hesitated a long time. "Look, Jude, I'm starting to get an idea. Yes, give it to her, but ask her not to contact him until you tell her to. Will she do that for you?"

"You saw her, Fleming. She'll do what I say." Jude turned on his heel with a swagger and headed back to the convent.

James debated the propriety of laying just one right hook to Donnelly's jaw.

For once it was a relief to return to Mrs. Kehoe's. After an icy shower in the minute bathroom, and a change of clothes, James began to feel somewhat better. But Devane's death and Mary's safety weighed heavily on his mind. And hunger was gnawing at his concentration. Feeling like the boarding school boy he once had been, he went seeking food from this current matron.

Mrs. Kehoe, of course, had already heard of Devane's death and James's role in the discovery of the body. Sobered by the news, she reigned in her curiosity and forebore asking James all the questions ready at her lips. And, as hospitable as her avocation would have indicated, she made James an evening meal of comfort food: sausages and rashers, eggs and chips, black pudding and white. James wolfed it all down heartily and finished off with thick slices of Irish brown bread and butter and homemade black currant jam. He felt restored in body and soul and said so.

"Another cup of tea?" Mrs. Kehoe asked.

"Yes, please," James said. "But only if you join me." He

was feeling expansive; feeling, like Pippa, that all was right with the world—at least for the moment.

It was relaxing, James thought, after the strain of the last hours, to sit in the modern, bright, yellow and green kitchen. Such a contrast to the rectory kitchen, or to poor Devane's little kitchen, where he'd sat all those long hours ago. The appliances gleamed, the kettle was whistling, and the rich, comforting aroma of fresh scones wafted from the counter where Mrs. Kehoe was continuing with her baking.

"This is good, Mrs. Kehoe," he said simply.

"It's that I've hardly seen you, Mr. Fleming, you've been so busy over at the rectory . . . and elsewhere," she said slyly, and James sighed inwardly. "And I wasn't that sure how to get you either. I wouldn't go disturbing the poor fathers at home, and, as I always say to the da, I never disturb a man at his food. But you see, I had all these messages for you."

With his mug of sweet tea she handed him a stack of messages, all written, in the time-honored Irish tradition, on the backs of used envelopes.

Apprehensively scanning them, James realized that four of the messages were from Maggie: three about cases that his firm in Dublin was pursuing, and the fourth relaying a demand from his mother to ring her. The last two were even worse: one from Geraldine saying that she needed to speak with him, and finally one from Donald asking him to ring. Those two coming together seemed ominous to James, and he put them at the bottom of the pile.

"I couldn't help but notice their content," said Mrs. Kehoe innocently, "since I had to take them down. Trouble with the girlfriend, then?" Mrs. Kehoe was breathless with the need for some gossip, any gossip, and James, feeling tired and lonely, uncharacteristically obliged.

"She was once a girlfriend, I suppose you would think of her that way. But it wasn't that simple. A few years ago I had been working on a case which involved a friend of hers. In resolving that case, I needed Geraldine's help. But rather than asking her directly, I gained her assistance without her knowing what the potential outcome would be . . ."

Mrs. Kehoe looked puzzled and then her face cleared. "I suppose that's lawyer talk for the fact you lied to her, is that it?"

James reddened. "Yes, I guess so."

"But now you're back together?"

"Not really. I'm involved with another woman; Sarah . . ."

"But?" Mrs. Kehoe said shrewdly.

"But she's in America."

"So you've got some time for this Geraldine?" Mrs. Kehoe chuckled enthusiastically, pleased with James's confidences.

"In a sense, but . . . you see, she's dating my brother."

"That would be Donald?"

"Yes," James said, having lost his appetite for the rich, buttery scones she'd placed on the table between them.

Disappointed with his answers, Mrs. Kehoe succinctly acknowledged the quality of James's muddled love life. She stood up from the table.

"All I can say, Mr. Fleming, is that the phone's in the hall. Beside the coin container," she added as she took his tea things away with finality.

Fortunately for James's immediate plans in Buncloda, Maggie's questions, relayed from the other solicitors, were easily and expeditiously answered. Maggie was cool and professional and for once didn't tease him. This he found unnerving, and he felt bereft.

"Will you be so good as to ring Geraldine and Donald for me?" he asked forlornly.

"Is your dialing finger broken, then?"

"Maggie . . ."

"O'course if it is, and you had enough faith, you could get it cured down there in Buncloda, right?"

"Maggie, please . . . don't tease me," he said, yet that was what he had wanted. "And don't joke about this situation in

Buncloda." Quickly, he recounted the events around Devane's death, and Maggie was duly sobered.

"So you will ring them for me, then? Make my life easier?"

"Not on your nelly, James. I wouldn't touch your love life, or your version of it, with a ten-foot pole. And on that score, I have a new fax from Sarah, which reads, and I quote: 'Concert tour extended. No problemo!' End quote."

"Oh God . . . more slang," James murmured as Maggie rang off laughing at his pomposity.

Exhaustion and reluctance overcame him at last. The calls to Donald and Geraldine would keep, he decided, and forgetting to say good night to Mrs. Kehoe, he retired to his room, for once oblivious to its fecund interior decor. He slept through the night, letting rest repair his frazzled nerves, if not his fragmented love life.

When Jude returned to Mary with Tim Kerrigan's note in his pocket, he expected to find her lying down. Instead she was seated on a plain wooden bench in the corridor that led to the chapel. She looked up at him expectantly; like a naughty child, he thought.

"Why did you say that to Fleming?" he asked.

"What?"

"About the others doubting their vision. Such talk doesn't strengthen our cause, you must see that. I don't think Fleming will repeat it, but even so, it might raise questions in his mind."

"But they were weakening. Perhaps it was God's will that they were taken before they said so in public . . ." She put her face in her hands.

Jude moved to her side and hesitated slightly before placing a hand on her soft, gleaming hair. "Oh, Mary," he whispered. "You are the last. You have been left by God's divine will, to carry on alone. I'll do all in my power to protect you, to help you. But . . . I am afraid for you, Mary."

"Oh, Jude, please don't be." She looked up at him, her face full of emotion. "I know I'll be all right now . . . I have our Holy Mother's protection. And I have you. Now please! Let me tell you what happened in the chapel, please, sit down." She smiled with real joy and patted the bench beside her.

Her face was shining, and Jude was taken aback by her sudden energy, her glowing enthusiasm.

"I thought you had fainted in the chapel, Mary."

"I think I did, at the very end, but now I feel . . . oh Jude! If Mr. Fleming hadn't arrived, I would have told you all this. It's what we've been waiting for!"

"What are you saying, Mary, what are you saying!" Jude was breathless.

"I had a message, at last, a message. From Her."

"Oh, my God. What is it? Can you tell me? Is it all right if you tell me?" he said imploringly.

"Yes, yes, of course it's all right. I felt your presence beside me, praying beside me in the chapel. And then the feeling came to me—just as I began to faint. The words came into my mind. They filled my whole being."

"Yes, yes . . ."

"It is this: we must all pray on Sunday, this coming Sunday."

"Yes?" Jude said, the slightest hint of disappointment sounding in his voice.

"We must pray at the grotto—all the people, all the faithful—and if we all pray hard enough, the Blessed Virgin will grant us a sign."

"A sign? On Sunday?" Jude breathed with renewed hope.

"Yes, a sign!"

"Right," Jude said, leaping to his feet. "I must get to work, we must notify the people so that it can be done right. This is Thursday. Let me see. We don't have much time to get organized. Yes, I must get the word out . . ." He turned suddenly, catching a strange look on Mary's face.

"Mary, Mary." He grabbed her hands and pulled her to

her feet. "This is wonderful. It's what I've been waiting for, and I know it's all due to you. I'm sorry. I should have said that first."

"Oh, that's all right," Mary said softly. "Don't be worrying about me." As he turned to leave, he remembered the note and handed it to her. With barely a glance, he was glad to see, she put it in her pocket.

"I'd rather you didn't contact Tim right now, Mary."

"Of course not, Jude. Go on now, do what you must," she said as she gently pushed him towards the door. "I'll rest and pray here until you can return to me."

Chapter Twenty

It seemed like only minutes had passed when James was awakened by Mrs. Kehoe's voice outside his door.

"Oh God," he murmured, "what does she want now?"

"Mr. Fleming, it's nearly noon and there's a visitor to see you. She's waiting downstairs in the lounge. Mr. Fleming?"

"She?" James called as he leapt to his feet, straightening the clothes he'd slept in.

"That's what I said."

Quickly, James threw some cold water on his face and ran his electric razor over his black beard. At last presentable and awake, he raced down the narrow flight of stairs to the front sitting room Mrs. Kehoe insisted on calling 'the lounge.'

He threw open the door. "Ger!" he squawked.

She put down her magazine and smiled. "James," she said sweetly, "I'm glad I found you. I wasn't sure where you would be . . ."

"Ger!" James repeated, but he recovered. "What are you doing back here so soon? More patients to be cured?"

"Please, James, that's what I want to talk to you about, but not here." Silently she pointed at the half-closed door and the ever-present Mrs. Kehoe dusting the immaculate hall table. "I'm starving," she said in a stage whisper.

Laughing together, they took Geraldine's car and retreated to Reardon's Pub, now filled with lunchtime tipplers. This time, the stares of the patrons were frank and almost bold.

"What's going on?" Geraldine asked, uneasily noting the change.

"Mr. Devane . . . he was murdered yesterday, Ger, and I found the body with Sergeant Molloy." James paused to order two large gins and a plate of ham sandwiches.

"Oh my God," she said, "I hadn't heard. He was one of the three visionaries, wasn't he? The old farmer?"

"Yes," James said sadly.

"It must have been awful for you, James," she commented sympathetically. "Miss Garrotty, and now Devane."

"Indeed," James said, sipping his gin. "But obviously this terrible news didn't bring you down, Ger. So, why are you here?" James was not surprised to feel his heart racing.

"I rang you—through Maggie, that is—but you didn't get my message, I guess. It's just that, well, I wanted to apologize for my recent behavior . . ."

"What?"

"Nurse Hagan rang me with some news. And it made me think over my attitudes. I've been confused, James," she said sincerely, looking into his dark eyes. "Confused by my own longings and by the impact Buncloda has had on me."

"But you intimated that first weekend here, with Donald and me, that something happened to you?"

"I'm not sure anymore, James. Something came over me, of that I am certain. But whether it was divine, as I hoped and believed, or whether it was just my own desire to feel something that deluded me—well, I don't know yet. Maybe I'll never know . . ."

"Then choose to believe it, Ger . . ."

"Is this you, James Fleming? Saying that to me?"

"Yes, it is, Ger. I'm not a skeptic like Donald, I never was . . ."

"But—"

"No buts, Ger. Perhaps you don't know me as well as you think—and that's good, isn't it?" He looked at her, his dark eyes softening, and she glanced quickly away. "Perhaps I don't myself. It's been good to learn that I'm not set in my ways, fixed in stone like an old fossil—"

"Not so old," Geraldine said flirtatiously.

James blushed. "Go on, go on, tell me. I think there's more to this, isn't there?"

"Sadly, yes. To put it bluntly, Nurse Hagan phoned me to say that Mrs. Farley had a relapse as soon as she was at home, back with the children and the drunken husband! The pain, the stiffness in the muscles—it's all back," she said in a discouraged tone.

"And Nurse Hagan—how did she take it?"

"Oh, she's such a down-to-earth soul, she just thought it wasn't to be, and that maybe next time something would help," Geraldine sighed. "She simply has great faith, and nothing shakes it."

"I understand the distinction you are making, Ger. I've seen that kind of faith here since I arrived. But what about Mrs. Farley?"

"I did see her briefly, and she struck me as resigned. The pain seemed like a familiar friend. It was that, more than anything, that shook me up. And made me think . . ." She looked meaningfully at James.

"Her attitude?"

"Yes. She was disappointed. But no anger, no loss of faith. I hate to say this, but it almost seemed like it had been an outing for the day, a bit of a treat. Perhaps she liked all the attention. And then it was over." Geraldine sighed deeply.

"So you think that a certain kind of personality, one who craved attention, perhaps even power of a particular kind, could convince himself, or herself, that they'd experienced a religious, or should I say, a divine manifestation? Or crave to have just that kind of thing happen to them?"

"Yes," Geraldine answered slowly. "In this case, of course, it was brief. Mrs. Farley's moment in the sun. I haven't done my psychiatric rotation at the hospital yet, James, so I'm not up on this subject. But I know this much, just from growing up in Ireland, that in this country religion has a powerful hold on people." She paused and leaned back. "But why all these questions, James?"

"I've a theory, Ger . . ."

"Now why is it I'm not surprised!" She smiled wryly. "But before you go on, I want to say what I came here to say. It was because of me that you became involved in this situation here in Buncloda—involved with Jude, involved with the first death. Now you tell me it's not one, not two, but three deaths. James, you've been down here for days, away from your own firm . . . and I've been . . . thoughtless. I just wanted to say that I'm grateful to you for helping Jude. But beyond that, for helping all these people, this village. And if I can help you at all, I am willing. I've a few days off and, well, here I am."

James was truly moved by her words, and the residual anger he'd felt towards her melted away, as it always had where she was concerned.

"Dare I ask what Donald said about this?" he said neutrally.

Geraldine shrugged an eloquent shrug and then bit into her wafer-thin sandwich.

"Well?" James insisted, remembering that Donald too had rung him.

"He doesn't accept my feelings about Buncloda, let's say. And he seems to resent your involvement with this case too. He thinks, as he says, that you'll become involved in a publicity circus."

"Which might reflect on him! Typical," James said, and then stopped. "Well, you are here now and that means a tremendous lot to me, Ger." Hesitantly, he placed his hand over hers on the bar. Just a touch, less than a second, yet it brought them closer than they had been for a very long time.

"Now, is there anything I can do for you, for Mary Dowd?"

James pulled his hand away. "Why Mary Dowd?"

"All right, James, I admit I do have deep feelings about her and her vision. And yes, being near her, talking with her, affected me. But I'm also concerned as a physician at what she was doing to herself. Don't be so jumpy, James!" She laughed, a return to her old self. She knocked back her gin and lit a cigarette.

James was silent for a long time, and she looked at him curiously.

"What is it, James?" she asked at last.

"Are you sure about your offer to help me?"

She nodded.

"I warn you now, Ger. What I'm about to say will test our friendship." Fragile as it is, he wanted to add.

"James, I'm involved already and responsible for your involvement . . . so go on."

He took a deep breath. "Father Maguire thinks, for rather profound reasons, that the murderer is from this village. I agree with him for parallel reasons, let me say. And I believe this killer is acting to protect something . . ." James hesitated, wondering how honest he could be.

"I don't follow . . ." Geraldine said.

"I think that the first death, of the Langan boy, was what you suggested at the beginning: that he died accidentally, and his companions brought his body here in a panic. Perhaps that incident gave the murderer here in Buncloda the idea of killing the visionaries, gave him a way to conceal the murders. A way to cloak them, let's say."

"But what is this person's reason? Or motive, I should say?"

"Look at who has been killed. First Rita, then Devane."

"Yes, yes. Two visionaries. And it seems to me Miss Dowd may be next!" Geraldine exclaimed.

211

"Possibly. That is the theory Maguire, and Molloy, and Jude have agreed to. And initially I did too, but . . ."

"But what? You of course have a different idea?" Her voice was cool.

"Look, it's been suggested that the purpose of the killer is to strike out at the Church, at the Virgin herself. To discredit the apparition in May. Or to illustrate how God cannot protect his followers."

"That theory has its own internal logic, James."

"Yes, even a madman has his own logic. I'm glad you agree. Because if we accept that this is the murderer's goal, then my question is, why not strike at the most important visionary—"

"—Miss Dowd."

"Exactly. Why not attack her first, Ger? Strike at the heart, not the limbs. Why even bother with the others?"

"Well, perhaps she was harder to get at?"

"No more than the others. In fact, she lived alone until recently. As Devane lived alone, but he was a strong, fit man, and one used to guns. More threatening than Mary surely. Look at Rita. Living with her brothers, surrounded by people at the shop. She was hard to get to."

"All right, say the killer chose randomly, then." Geraldine was already frustrated.

"Perhaps. But I don't think so. Not after yesterday . . ."

"After Devane, you mean?"

"Right. Things began to take shape in my mind. Two visionaries eliminated. But not even an attempt on Mary Dowd."

"James!" Geraldine said in a warning tone.

"I went to see her straight away. In fear for her, Ger. Truly. I couldn't see her alone. Jude's got increasingly protective . . . or possessive, I'm not sure which."

"Can you blame him?"

"I'll get to that. I talked with her, with him there. But I listened too. And what she revealed was that Rita and

212

Devane were beginning to weaken in their own belief in the apparition in May."

He waited for this to sink in, but Geraldine merely shook her head. "So?"

"They were weakening to the point of having doubts, and expressing those doubts. Perhaps they were weakening to the point of recanting!"

"What if they did?" Geraldine said seriously.

"Think, Ger, what effect that would have. And who would be most affected . . ."

"Well, Mary, I suppose. It would cast some doubt on her too. By association. I imagine people would begin to wonder, to question the validity of her vision. If her two witnesses, I suppose *you'd* call them, turned around and denied it ever happened."

"Exactly. Their expressed doubts would weaken Mary's claims. And very publicly. This was no longer between them and herself. The vision has become public property now." He waved his hand, indicating the crowds of the faithful beyond at the grotto.

"So," he continued when she remained quiet, "who would benefit from these two weak links being silenced? Mmm?" he prompted, reluctant all of a sudden to say it aloud, the enormity of what he was suggesting striking him.

"You can't mean Mary herself?" Geraldine whispered.

James nodded.

"Oh please, James," she replied, shaking her head.

"Well, then. Who else who would be fearful of having this vision discredited? Who even more than Mary, and certainly more than the other two, has drawn attention to the vision? Who has made himself the indispensable tool of this incipient religious movement? This media event? Who else would suffer if the vision was debunked—losing face, losing influence, losing power?"

"No!" Geraldine said.

"Yes, Jude Donnelly."

213

Geraldine thought for a while, drawing heavily on her cigarette. James waited apprehensively. When she didn't speak, he continued.

"Look, Ger, these are just theories. But think: Mary Dowd found the body of the Langan boy. It could have inspired her to rid herself of the others."

"James, loads of people knew about the body, for heaven's sakes."

"Mary had access to Rita. They'd become friends. Mary could have encouraged her to take that blood pressure medicine."

"Yes, but Jude was also close to Rita since the vision."

"My point exactly," James said triumphantly. "Rita would never turn Father Donnelly away. She would heed his advice. And Devane wouldn't be afraid if Father Donnelly came to check on him at the farm."

"He wouldn't be afraid of Mary either."

"Right. Mary could slip out from the convent any time. Her visitors are restricted, but her own movements are not." He grew animated. "Look, while we were all four of us at the rectory, Mary could have got to Devane's farm and back—" He stopped suddenly. "On the other hand, Jude came in late to our meeting in the kitchen. He could have driven to the farm and back—"

"No," Geraldine cried. "Absolutely not, James. You're wrong."

"You've said that before," James said pointedly.

"Well, this time you're very wrong. I know Jude. And I believe in Mary Dowd."

"So . . ." he said slowly, "you won't help me then to prove this."

"On the contrary," she said with spirit. "I will help you disprove it. If you have some plan to expose them—whichever one you really think is the murderer—then I will help you. Because you will end up revealing the truth!"

That's the idea, Ger, he said sadly, but only to himself.

— *Chapter Twenty-One* —

As James approached the rectory on Friday evening, his heart was beating wildly. While fatigued from the day he'd already put in, he was also elated as he saw his plan to draw out the killer taking shape.

Mrs. O'Leary showed him to the priest's lounge, where he found old Father Maguire dozing in his chair, his mouth open wide, a sheaf of papers slowly dropping from his hands to the floor. James shook him awake.

"Sorry, Fleming. I was just trying to write out some notes for the bishop . . . Have you come to see me?" he asked, looking as though he might have forgotten an appointment.

"No, Father, I'm here to meet Tim Kerrigan, as we agreed you would arrange." For a moment James foresaw disaster.

"Oh, yes, of course. Yes, I set that up for you. And Father Donnelly told me to tell you he'd be in later. But listen," he said more animatedly as he came more fully awake, "Molloy just rang me. You haven't talked to him yet, have you?"

"No . . ." James said, sensing an excitement in the old man.

"He's had definite word from his colleagues in Tipperary. About the Langan boy, God rest his soul."

"Yes, yes."

"The police now have two lads in custody. And they've confessed to accidentally killing Langan in a drunken brawl. As the police suspected all along."

"You're sure they confessed?"

"Oh, indeed. Apparently they are very remorseful. God help them all." Maguire sighed heavily. "It's tragic for all those involved and their families—years of sorrow ahead of them."

"What about their leaving the body here at the grotto?" James asked, suppressing his own excitement at this final confirmation of the details of the first murder.

"There was no malice in that. He died in a punch-up over a local sports result. The boys were so terrified to come forward, they decided that the grotto was a safe place to bring him. A holy place, Molloy quoted one of them as saying."

"As Dr. Keohane and you yourself suggested, Father," James said.

"Oh . . ." Maguire shrugged. "I am just relieved the lad's death had no arcane purpose. Well, I'd best get this interim report to the bishop. At least I have something concrete to tell him . . ." He looked questioningly at James.

"I think I'm on to something, Father, regarding the other two deaths. But it's too early to say yet . . ." He looked apologetically at Maguire, the man who'd sought his help at the beginning.

"Well, good luck to you, then," Maguire said, and he left the room.

James paced restlessly. With the Langan murder resolved, his own theory was strengthened. Anxious to put it in motion, he checked his watch. There was one more suspect to deal with. And timing, as usual, was everything.

He heard the ring at the door and stopped pacing. Tim

Kerrigan entered the room, his open-neck shirt wet with perspiration from the clammy evening.

"Mr. Fleming," he said, shaking hands and sitting down in a direct fashion. His manner unnerved James. He had hoped for more dissembling or even anger.

"I've just a few questions," James said rudely, hoping to get a rise out of him. "Firstly, do you know where you were yesterday, in the early afternoon?"

"What kind of a question is that?" Tim said, annoyed.

"Do you?"

"Well, it was lunch. I took a run over to Gorey to see about a motorbike for sale."

"You drove?"

"Yes, the da's not well, as I've told you. I took his car."

"And did you buy the motorbike?"

"No, when I got to the house, there was no one at home. It was a private sale. I'd seen it in the paper."

"So there's no one who can verify your story?" James was antagonizing.

"No, no, there isn't. But I left a note in their letter box, to say I'd called and was interested."

"Pretty thin, Kerrigan."

"I don't know what you mean. Why should anyone have to verify my doings?"

"Because that was when Mr. Devane was killed up at his farm!"

"Why in God's name would I kill old Devane?" Tim shouted.

"You tell me. I think you may have killed first Miss Garrotty and then Devane—in order to frighten Mary Dowd into giving up her claims of a vision . . ."

"Why would I want that?"

"So she'd quit her new public role and come back to you. So that she would be frightened and fearful and need you again to look after her, to protect her."

"You're friggin' mad, Fleming," Tim said, jumping to his feet.

"Hold on, Tim! There's someone coming here you might want to see."

Tim looked around wildly as James waited. Voices sounded again in the hall, and Jude showed Mary Dowd into the room.

"Tim!" she cried out, startled.

"Hello," he said, more constrained.

"I only got your note a little while ago. I'm sorry they didn't let you in at the convent."

She walked shyly towards him and held out her hands. He took them and they sat down on the sofa.

"How are you, then? You look very pale," Tim said softly as Jude watched in surprise.

"Oh, I'm all right. But listen, Tim, I've had a message . . ."

"From whom?" he asked innocently.

"You know! From Her. Yesterday. In the convent chapel."

He dropped her hands as if stung. "Look, Mary, enough is enough. Give it up, why don't you!" he shouted. "Now, in front of these people. It can't go on."

She made a small low cry as she pulled away from him.

Jude interrupted. "That's enough of that, Kerrigan. You can't talk to Miss Dowd that way."

"And who's to stop me?" the young man cried, jumping to his feet.

"Sit down, Kerrigan," James said.

"No, I won't, Fleming. I've had enough of this nonsense. You are all stone mad." He turned to Mary. "I'm warning you. Get away from these people. Give it up." He looked her in the eyes. "And when you do, maybe I'll be waiting."

Jude moved to go after him, but James shook his head. He'd seen what he had wanted to.

"Did you set this up, Jude?" Mary said angrily.

"Me?" Jude was horrified. "No, Fleming asked me to bring you here, but he didn't say why. I thought we were going to discuss the murders. I hoped he had a plan to

218

protect you. Especially on Sunday when you'll be at the grotto."

"I'm sorry, Mary. I didn't think you two would cross paths," James interjected. "But on the other hand, you did receive a note from Tim, didn't you?"

Mary studied his face. "Yes?"

"Tell me, were you surprised to hear from him?"

"Yes, and I was pleased too. I thought he'd given up on me, but his note showed that he cared, or so I believed." She sagged back on the pillows. "Maybe he's right, though."

"No, Mary," Donnelly objected, "don't let that young man lead you astray. He has no faith! Look, just think what a fool he will feel—on Sunday."

"Why Sunday?" James demanded, addressing them both.

"We are all gathering at the grotto on Sunday—to pray. Mary has informed me that if enough faith and belief and prayer are demonstrated there on Sunday, then we can expect the great sign we've been waiting for. The sign from the Blessed Virgin herself!" Jude said triumphantly. "Perhaps this time she will speak to Mary. Perhaps this time there will be a verbal message we can promulgate throughout the world!"

James nearly smiled. Sunday! The timing couldn't have been better. Again the doorbell rang, and James felt his own tension mount. The next few minutes were critical to his plan.

"We're very busy tonight, aren't we?" Jude said pointedly. But James merely shrugged.

"Father Donnelly," said Mrs. O'Leary from the doorway. "It's Dr. Geraldine Keohane to see you."

"What?" Jude said. As the priest stood up, Geraldine came in and embraced him lightly.

She sat down, her pale, flowered rayon dress falling in folds over her long, shapely legs and delicate sandals. She looked both ethereal and in command.

"Hello, Miss Dowd," she said gently. "I hope you are feeling better?"

"Yes, thanks," Mary said distantly.

Jude sat down beside her. "What is it, Ger, that brings you here so late?"

"Oh, Jude," she said breathlessly. "I've just come from the grotto. I'd been there for these last few hours. I can't explain it, Jude, but I was compelled to come back here to Buncloda. I arrived yesterday and checked in at that little hotel . . ."

"You said 'compelled'?" Jude interrupted, quickly glancing at Mary and back at Geraldine.

"Yes, I was drawn here, Jude. You know, from the beginning I have had strong feelings about the grotto." She turned abruptly and looked at Mary. "Oh, Miss Dowd, it has been nothing like your own experiences, of course. But nonetheless significant, I think." She dropped her eyes. James paced slightly and then stopped himself.

"Go on," Jude said, whispering intensely.

"At the grotto, after I was there a few hours, I felt a message bearing in on me. I saw nothing, you understand?" She looked into his eyes.

"What was it, for God's sake, the message?" Jude cried.

"I think it was that there are to be great signs given here in Buncloda this weekend," Geraldine said in a low voice.

"I knew it!" Jude cried, slapping his leg with his open hand. He jumped up. "You were right, Mary . . ."

Mary looked at him, expressionless.

"You knew this, Jude?" Geraldine said, confused, glancing at James, who merely shrugged.

"Yes, yes, but no. I mean, tell me more. Is there more?"

"Well . . ." Geraldine hesitated, but only for a moment. "The message was that I was to pray at the grotto—alone—on Saturday evening. And then a sign would be given." Geraldine mumbled the last few words meekly.

"Saturday night?" Jude said wonderingly. "Saturday night?"

"Yes, this is the feeling that I had, the direction I believe I have been given."

"And alone, you said?"

"Yes. Why do you question me like this? Is there something wrong with Saturday?" Geraldine was peevish.

"Forgive me," Jude exclaimed, noting her exasperation. "I'm just surprised. No, of course there's nothing wrong with Saturday night. You must obey this summons, by all means. Please . . . can you tell me anything else?"

"Only that since I must pray alone, I realize it will have to be very late. Jude, to be honest, I'm feeling a little frightened by all of this." She sought his eyes with her own questioning ones, and James took a slight step forward.

"Oh, Ger," Jude said with feeling. "You must not be frightened. But I must think. This is very exciting, very wondrous news. I must think . . ." He fell silent, staring at her almost blankly.

James broke the awkward silence. "Really, Ger, you are a doctor, a woman of science and observation, logic and physical reality. I confess I'm more than a little surprised by all this. And I think it's a distraction from our purpose here."

"Hold on, Fleming. She has a right to express herself. And because she is a doctor, she makes a very valuable witness. For a woman in her line of work, scientifically trained, experienced, mature, if I may say that"—he flashed a smile at Geraldine—"and worldly, if I may also say that?" She nodded. "All this makes Geraldine a superb spokeswoman for our cause. I can see to that."

"Jude, Jude, I've come to you for your advice. I can't think ahead about being a spokesperson for anything. Tell me what to do . . ." Geraldine demanded, but she looked distressed.

"Of course, of course. First we must talk further. And pray . . . we must pray together for guidance and insight . . ."

"Pardon me, Jude," Mary Dowd said, as from a forgotten country.

Jude was startled.

221

"Pardon me," she repeated pointedly, "but I am feeling very tired. I think I have to go back . . . *now,* if you don't mind. You'll excuse me, Doctor?"

"Oh, I see . . ." Jude glanced about him as if confused. "Of course, Mary, of course you're tired and weak. You must rest. I'll call over to the convent tomorrow morning first thing . . . Look, Fleming, would you mind driving Mary to the convent?"

Startled by the sudden request, James glanced sympathetically at Mary's crestfallen face. "Miss Dowd, I'd be happy to take you back. It's on my way. And it'll give these two old friends time to discuss this"—he paused, searching for the right wording—"this news."

He took Mary's arm firmly, and as they left the room, they could hear Jude's voice murmuring intently.

"Mary, may I talk to you?" James said confidentially as he drove along the short back road to the convent.

"Of course."

"I've already told Father Maguire that I have to leave Buncloda. You see, a family problem demands that I return to Dublin, at least for a few days. I wanted to tell you and Donnelly tonight and advise you again that you are at risk. You must stay out of harm's way, Mary. I'd wanted to discuss all this with you and Jude, but then, well, obviously we were interrupted . . ." He let the statement hang.

"Dr. Keohane's visit was certainly a . . . surprise," Mary said dryly.

"Although she and I are acquainted, as you know, I'm not at all certain of the validity, let's say, of her feelings, her so-called experience. And I believe her news is an unnecessary distraction right now."

"Yes, I heard you say that at the rectory. What did you mean?" she asked softly.

"Well, Mary, it seemed to me that Jude was very taken with what Geraldine was saying. At a time when his attention needs to be focused on you as the last surviving visionary . . ."

James pulled the car in front of the dark and silent convent.

"My main concern now is your safety. Particularly on Sunday. Listen, as I said, I won't be back until Monday— it's unavoidable. I would really prefer to be here—but I will speak to Sergeant Molloy to ensure there will be extra police at the grotto."

Her silent smile was her only response.

— *Chapter Twenty-Two* —

Early the next morning James left Mrs. Kehoe's, much as usual. And he left town as announced. If he wasn't going to Dublin, that was not their concern. And as James drove out of Buncloda, Jude was even then closeted with Geraldine.

"And this is all I need to do?" Geraldine said for the second time.

"I assure you, Geraldine," Jude said, "all you must do now is pray, sincerely, and from your heart. I'd suggest you pray at the statue for a while this afternoon, and then return to your hotel for a rest before you visit the grotto again tonight." He cleared the remains of their lunch off the rectory's kitchen table.

"You're coming, aren't you?" Geraldine asked, pulling on her cardigan against the unseasonal chill.

"I'll stay for a while. You stay for as long as you feel compelled to be there. In fact we'll take both cars."

"What's wrong, Jude?" she said, suddenly suspicious.

224

"Nothing. It's just that . . . I don't think I should be seen with you. At the grotto, or elsewhere."

"What did you say, Jude?" Geraldine stopped in mid-stride as they neared their cars.

"It might arouse curiosity, questions. You know."

"No, I don't."

"Well, I've only really ever accompanied Miss Dowd to the grotto. If the people saw me with you, it's only natural they would wonder . . ."

"Wonder what?" Geraldine said, flushing red.

"If I had lost faith in Mary. And my presence there with you might preempt our plans for Sunday, as well as draw their attention to you. Ger, you've made it very clear that you must pray alone at the grotto on this evening. But if the people got wind of your expectations, then they could be streaming to the grotto in record numbers. You've seen for yourself what they're like." He continued persuasively, "But since Mary Dowd has requested the people to assemble on Sunday, they may choose to have an early night tonight, and that is in your favor. And with this oncoming rain, the grotto should be fairly deserted. You must see, Geraldine," he said sincerely, "I'm only being cautious—for your sake, and for the sake of our cause."

"Yes, all right," Geraldine replied, mollified. "But tell me," she added as an afterthought as she opened her car door, "will Mary Dowd be at the grotto this afternoon?"

Jude hesitated. "I don't know, I somehow doubt it. She didn't seem herself today. Listen, Ger. I will be near you at the grotto. Not physically by your side maybe—but spiritually."

Jude looked anxiously in her face and touched her lightly on the arm, encouragingly. He lowered his voice. "This is terribly important, Ger," he said, and then he ran quickly to his car.

Tim Kerrigan, despite all, responded to Mary Dowd's phone call with alacrity. Puzzled and impatient, he let the knocker fall heavily on the neat white door of her bungalow.

He was discouraged to see how pale and drawn she was looking.

"Come in," she said sweetly. "Thank you for coming, Tim. Please sit down."

He threw himself into a chair, not knowing what to expect.

"Seeing you last night, Tim, really upset me."

"Oh, please!"

"No, let me finish. After you left, things began to happen. I don't have to go into that now. But when I returned to the convent, I gave everything a lot of thought. From a fresh perspective. Tim, it was as though blinders fell off my eyes. And now . . . I feel like a great weight is off my shoulders."

"I don't understand," Tim said with rising interest.

"I've decided to call it quits, Tim!" She smiled warmly.

"You mean?"

"Yes, I want no more of this. You were right, Tim. I just couldn't see it. I had got caught up, swept up into something beyond my control. And now I see that maybe I was manipulated as well . . ." A frown crossed her clear features.

"I tried to tell you about that Donnelly character!" Tim was triumphant now.

"Please, Tim, let's not go into all the whys and wherefores. The main thing is that all of this is over for me. Now. And I want to get away from the grotto. From Buncloda! Tim, I'm not needed at the school until September. And who knows—maybe I'll move on to another school. There's nothing keeping me here, Tim. So, so . . . I've a great favor to ask of you. I know your feelings have changed, but for the sake of our old friendship—"

"Oh, Mary," Tim interrupted, getting up and taking her in his arms. "I didn't change. You did. I thought I'd lost you to this whole mad business. When the others were killed, first Rita and then . . . well, I must admit in a way I was glad . . ."

"Tim!"

"No, not glad they were dead. But I thought you'd get scared and give it up. I thought you'd come back to me out of fear . . ."

"I'm not afraid."

"I see that. And that's even better. You've made up your own mind. Right?"

"Yes, I have. Will you help me get away, Tim?"

"Of course. I've got the da's car. We can go to my digs in Dublin. Then we can take it from there." He hugged her to him. "I'll get the car now, okay?"

"No, Tim, not yet. I have things to do first—the house and all. I want to leave tonight. And I want you to meet me on the road on the far side of the hill . . ."

"What hill?" Tim said, still quick to mistrust her.

"The one behind the grotto?" she said sweetly.

"For Christ's sake, Mary," he exploded.

"No, listen. I am leaving, Tim. But I just want one final, well, one farewell prayer at the grotto. To round it off, you know. To end it right."

"And Donnelly? One final cozy farewell to him too?"

"No, Tim. Nothing like that. If I tell him, he mightn't even let me go. You see that, don't you? In fact, you mustn't tell anyone either. In case the people prevent me from leaving. I just want to get away quietly, after dark. You know these long nights, it's bright until eleven. All I'm asking is that you meet me. Around midnight. If I'm a little late, just wait for me . . ."

Tim considered this, but when he remained silent, she put her arms around his neck. "Believe me, Tim," she said, "you'll see that I've changed." She nuzzled his neck. "Please . . ."

"All right, Mary," he relented. "Midnight, tonight. And I will wait. Just don't . . ."

"What?"

"Don't let me down again, Mary. I couldn't take it this time. You understand?" He grasped her by the upper arms and peered into her face. "Right?" he said sternly.

"Right, Tim," she said seriously. "Tonight. And don't *you* let *me* down. Now let me get on with things here." She closed the door behind him with a soft smile.

While Geraldine rested that evening in her hotel room, preparing for her solitary visit to the grotto, she tried to push the doubts from her mind. She regretted letting herself, yet again, get caught up in James's convoluted thinking. He could be so convincing in person, so attractive when he needed her help. She looked at her watch. She longed to ring him. But there was no way to contact him. She rechecked her watch. It was too late now to back out. And not only that, she reflected, but her night at the grotto would prove to James how wrong he was about Jude and Mary. And the sooner this was over, the better.

Around the same time that Geraldine was suffering her doubts, Mary Dowd had summoned Jude to the convent. Dressed in white, she looked both spiritual and sickly.

"I can't stay, Mary," Jude said nervously as he walked with her in the garden.

"Why not?" she demanded. "I've hardly seen you today. We haven't talked. We haven't prayed together since yesterday, since before Dr. Keohane . . . Oh, please, Jude, I have something to tell you . . ."

"All right, all right, Mary. But you know Geraldine is going to the grotto. She may be there even now . . ."

"But I also know she means to go there alone, Jude. Don't tell me you are transgressing the good doctor's orders."

"Of course not. But I feel I should be nearby."

"What about tomorrow, then?" she said, changing the subject.

He relaxed. "It's well in hand. I've arranged for people to

lead the prayers hourly. In turn, you know. A group has volunteered to sing hymns, and I've scheduled them in too. Things should proceed in an orderly fashion. I'll lead the Rosary at fixed times throughout the day. The weather is to be good, they say, a blessing after this rain today. Oh, Mary, I will be there with you, for the entire time. My feeling is, though, that the message, the great sign, will be given towards dusk, as the cumulative power of the people's faith and prayers mounts up to heaven."

"And tonight?" Mary said. "You cannot pray with me tonight? To prepare me for all that's ahead tomorrow?" she pleaded.

"Mary, Mary! This news of Dr. Keohane's, the way I see it, it could be an important preamble to tomorrow. If she experiences something tonight at the grotto, it could serve as preparation for your role." He smiled inwardly. "She reminds me of St. John the Baptist—preparing the way. That's why I must be there tonight."

"Listen to me, Jude," Mary said passionately. "I've been meditating all day here in my room, and yes," she threw her arms wide and he winced to see the stains on her thin white blouse, "yes, mortifying myself. To prepare. To be worthy! I've prayed ceaselessly for direction . . . and now I know what it is!"

"What?"

"I'm going to the church now, to pray at the Virgin's statue there. The Virgin in her role of the Madonna, Jude. She is mothering me, Jude. I can feel it . . ."

"I understand, I do. Her statue there is a Madonna and Child. Oh Christ, help me!" Jude cried, throwing up his hands in confused supplication.

Mary waited in silence as he wrestled with his decision. But impatient, she spoke again.

"Maybe this is a test, Jude."

"What do you mean?"

"Maybe Dr. Keohane has been . . . perhaps she's being used?"

229

"By me?" Jude shouted.

"Of course not by you! Perhaps she is the Tempter in human form. Distracting your attention. Drawing you away from me in my hour of need. Come with me, Jude. Pray at the Madonna with me. Oh, yes, yes." She grew animated. "It would be a relief to have all of this resolved tonight. So that tomorrow could be the wonderful day that it is intended to be—that it *will* be!"

"Stop it, Mary. You must allow me to do the best I can. You were there when Geraldine spoke of her experiences. And you know that I encouraged her. I've promised I would support her through this night . . . God, what if something miraculous happened and I wasn't there!" Jude's voice was desperate.

"I see," Mary said finally. "But I will go to the church, Jude."

"It's not safe, Mary!" he cried. "You *know* that. I've told you. Fleming's told you."

He looked at her expressionless face. "Right, right." He paused. "This is what we'll do. I'll go over to the grotto and spend some time there, near Geraldine, but not with her. When I've . . . assessed that situation, I'll come back here to the convent and bring you to the church myself. We'll be together then, and you'll be safe. But you must wait for me, Mary. You understand?"

"Whatever you say, Jude," she answered stiffly, without looking at him.

"Good girl," he said, patting her hand. "We'll calm down and say a Hail Mary together." He murmured the prayer, lifting his voice only at the end in his haste. "'. . . now and at the hour of our death. Amen.' All right now? I'll be back." Blessing her, he walked away.

At the time Geraldine was pulling on her coat against the damp, and Mary was appealing to Jude to go with her to the old parish church, James Fleming and Sergeant Molloy were arriving at the grotto.

Again light drizzle had started to fall, and Molloy was cursing softly as they climbed the hill, finally concealing themselves behind some low bushes where they had a clear view of the area in front of the statue.

Molloy gathered his black raincoat around him and sat heavily on the ground.

"I'm only doing this because you asked me to, Fleming, but I think we're wasting our time . . . and gettin' drowned with it!"

James scanned the low scudding clouds rapidly passing overhead, darkening an already fading blue. There would be no moon, as he knew, and the drizzle had further lessened the diminished crowds at the shrine. There was no one on the hill to observe them. He turned the collar of his light black jacket against the water that was rolling down his neck.

"This weather's in our favor, Molloy," he whispered at last.

"I don't know what's put this into your mind at all."

"Look, Molloy, when you and your colleagues in Tipperary resolved the accidental death of the Langan boy, clearly you and I knew there was still a murderer at work—one from Buncloda, right? My reading of the situation was that it had to be a visionary or someone closely involved with a visionary . . . such as Tim Kerrigan . . ."

"What possible motive would Kerrigan have for attacking Dr. Keohane?"

"The same motive he would have had for Rita's and Devane's murders: to frighten Mary Dowd into giving up her visionary claims and coming back to him."

"That's pretty extreme," Molloy murmured.

"Murder usually is, and Tim is an angry, perhaps humiliated, young man."

"And what of your other suspects, Fleming? Donnelly's a priest, for God's sake, and Mary Dowd's a very religious girl. They've been told to stay away from the grotto tonight. And they will, mark my words."

"I wouldn't mind being proved wrong, Molloy," James said dryly. "But I do believe one of the three of them is the killer. Whichever one shows tonight . . ."

"But why tonight!" Molloy questioned as he cursed the rain again.

"Mary Dowd has declared tomorrow the big day. The Virgin will appear tomorrow. Donnelly has run with the ball. He's spread the word, he's organized the whole thing. Couldn't you feel it in the town, in the crowd—that buildup of suspense, of anticipation? The faithful have been primed, and tomorrow is the climax. The prize, if you will . . ."

Molloy sighed uneasily. "It's true we're expecting record numbers tomorrow, rain or shine."

"Exactly. The people have pressed for a sign. They've been told it will be given tomorrow. It will be Mary's great moment. But Geraldine has confused the issue by preempting tomorrow with her talk of a vision tonight. She's preempted Donnelly and Mary Dowd. She's put pressure on both of them. It seemed to me that any loose ends would have to be tied up by tonight. If Geraldine is perceived by either of them to be a threat, then—"

"Then you expect one of them might attack Dr. Keohane tonight."

"Yes. By using Dr. Keohane as the goat, I hope to draw that person out into the open."

"But why would Donnelly show? Surely it's to his advantage to have found another visionary?"

"I'm not sure, Molloy, but there's a vague uneasiness at the back of my mind about Jude and Mary. They share a common goal and thus may share a common motive. They seem, at times, like a couple."

"You think there's something between them?" Molloy was clearly shocked.

"Yes, but not sexual. He strikes me, since Dr. Keohane's arrival, as a man easily led . . . Hush! Look, look there."

Molloy followed James's pointing finger. He watched as a lone visitor climbed the now slippery rocky path. Hunched in a coat and scarf, she knelt before the statue. Molloy strained to see through the drizzle but could see no one else, standing or kneeling anywhere on the hillside.

In silence the two men settled down for a long wait.

The minutes slowly crept by and James felt sorry for Geraldine. He tried to imagine what was passing through her mind as she carried out this charade. He wondered if she were indeed praying. Would her conscience allow for that? he mused.

He shifted his position. The rain had left off but the sky was now completely black with cloud. It was increasingly difficult to see Geraldine. He felt the strain in his forehead and eyes.

There was a slight movement on the path below them. James checked his watch: half-eleven. He identified the dark figure as a man from his stride. He was alone. James turned to Molloy and, annoyed to see him dozing, poked him with his elbow.

Molloy's eyes widened in surprise. He and James stared at the ominous figure. The minutes ticked by when finally the man moved, indecisively at first; then, turning to his right, he climbed the hill towards Geraldine. He drew nearly level with them, unaware of their presence.

Molloy readied himself to spring.

"No, wait," James hissed, wanting the killer to show his intent.

The silence was complete. James stared hard at the man whose face was still hidden in the hood of his anorak. Almost unconsciously James became aware of a dull light on the horizon, beyond the motionless figure. It seemed to grow in intensity, and its brightness threw the town into a low silhouette. Molloy, still watching Geraldine, had yet to see it. But the candescent light continued to brighten and finally caught Molloy's eye too. The two men suddenly leapt to their feet. Startled almost to death, the figure of Jude looked first at them, and then in the direction of their stares.

"Oh my God!" A wrenching cry came to his lips. James

moved to his side. "Oh my God! Fleming, it's at the church! Mary went to the church. I told her to wait for me, but she must have gone ahead—without me! I should have stayed with her! Oh, I should have stayed with Mary! The Blessed Virgin Mother is appearing to her now—and I'm not there!"

James and Molloy stood, transfixed.

"Don't you understand?" Jude cried. "It's the sign! The great sign, Molloy! Just as Mary always said . . ."

He began to run down the hill, with James and Molloy following him headlong, caught up in the priest's frenzy.

"Donnelly, wait!" Molloy called out. "We'll take my car. Man, come with me. It's quicker . . ."

James saw a rush of flame rise up in the black sky, illuminating the spire of the church. This was no heavenly fire, not a version of the biblical burning bush, but an actual fire.

As the two other men raced down the hill and out of sight, James stopped himself from following. Whirling around suddenly, he looked up the hill for Geraldine.

Sounds of car horns and raised voices reached him on the drifting wind as he ran back up the slope, slipping on the wet stones in the dark, heart pounding. He could see her now, still kneeling, steadfast at her post. Suddenly a dark figure moved swiftly from the rocky base of the grotto itself. Just as swiftly it seemed to envelope Geraldine in a cloak of black.

"Christ! Geraldine!" James cried out as he ran the last few feet and lunged headlong in a rugby tackle at the struggling figures.

"No, No!" he cried out. He couldn't distinguish the two bodies, the hands, the flailing limbs. In the melee, he realized Geraldine was on the ground, facedown. He wrestled with the black figure, even then wondering wildly if he'd drawn out some demon; if he, in his deceit and deception of so many people, had opened the doors to the powers of darkness.

A hand shot up out of the dark, a white hand clutching a

candlestick, raised in the blink of an eye, poised to strike Geraldine's prone figure. James lunged again, grappling, finding his own bearings. He threw his arm around the attacker's neck and brought the struggling figure to the ground. Kneeling, one hand on the attacker's throat, he threw back the black veils, expecting the worst of what hell could offer.

It was Mary Dowd's face that looked back at him. Mary Dowd clad in a nun's black habit that had cloaked her so effectively in the dark.

"Mary!" a voice cried behind him. "Oh, Mary! What have you done?"

James, although startled, remained where he was, regaining his breath. He turned to see Tim Kerrigan's stricken expression.

"Mary, I waited. But when I heard the car horns and saw the fire, I came to find you. Oh, God, Mary!" Tim cried. "Why didn't you just come away with me . . ."

Mary Dowd closed her eyes against all of them and lay quite still on the ground. Not trusting her, James requested that Tim take over his grip on her arms. James hurried to Geraldine's side. She too lay still, but not by choice.

James rolled her onto her back gently and felt her head and face, felt the stickiness of the blood trickling down through her hair.

"Oh, Christ, Geraldine. Wake up." He lifted her as he would a child into his arms.

Sometime later, in the sitting room of the smoke-filled rectory, Sergeant Molloy described to Father Maguire the eerie *tableaux vivants* he had encountered on his return to the grotto. He'd been astounded to see Tim Kerrigan kneeling beside the statuelike figure of Mary Dowd. And James, holding Geraldine's limp body in his arms, his eyes cast up to the Virgin Mary high above them all.

Molloy explained that he had then taken all of them in his car, first bringing Geraldine to Mrs. Kehoe's house nearby.

Reassured by the local G.P. whom Molloy had alerted on the car phone, they'd left her there in good hands and come on to the rectory.

At this point in Molloy's monologue, Mrs. O'Leary, still dressed in her faded candlewick dressing gown with smudges of soot on her face and hands, brought in a welcome tray of whiskey and glasses. Taking the tray, Father Maguire offered a glass first to Jude, and then to James, who rivaled him in the grimness of his expression. Molloy shook his head, keeping a watchful eye on Mary Dowd, sitting motionless near the corner window.

"Where is Kerrigan, then?" Maguire asked.

"He's still outside with the volunteer fire brigade," Molloy answered. "They're checking for embers, for any lingering fire. Father Maguire, I haven't said yet how sorry I am . . ."

"It's nearly dawn, Molloy, and I'll know better then, but I think the stonework withstood the blaze. The wood beams and buttresses supporting the roof are charred and damaged though. It will take time to rebuild, obviously."

"Thank God you're safe," Jude said quietly.

"And I thank Mrs. O'Leary. It was she who spotted the glow. At first she thought it was dawn, but then she smelled the smoke. It was she who roused me and called the brigade."

"I can still hardly believe this," Jude said softly. He stood up and moved to the fireplace, leaning his head on his arm. Father Maguire moved to his side, patting him paternally on the shoulder.

"Father Donnelly, I'm sorry I ever doubted you," James said, "and that I used Geraldine as I did."

"She helped you in this plan you outlined to Father Maguire just now?"

"She only wanted to prove to me that I was wrong to suspect you or Mary Dowd. I set her up to act as a distraction for you. I thought if you were innocent of the two murders, nothing would induce you to leave Mary's side.

But if you were indeed the killer, then you knew Mary would be safe no matter where she was. . . . I thought if you were true, you'd stick close to Mary Dowd."

"I couldn't, don't you see? I was torn between them!" he cried out. "When Geraldine was at the grotto, I drove around, praying all the while, joining my prayers with hers. But I was overcome with curiosity. I was so anxious to hear if she had had a message, I couldn't resist. I went to the grotto. Secretly, even disguising my collar. I thought I might catch a glimpse . . . I thought that I too might see the Virgin."

"Oh, God . . ." Maguire groaned. Not one of the company looked at Jude as he spoke haltingly, humiliation in his every pause.

"And then I saw the bright light, the glow. My mind was in a terrible confusion . . . And as you heard, Father, I left the grotto and came here . . . with Molloy. Expecting to find Mary . . . expecting to see a vision of the Blessed Virgin surrounded by a great and divine light . . . never expecting to find the church, our church, in flames." He stopped, his voice choked with emotion.

Father Maguire was comforting. "We'll rebuild it, Jude. Together. And our people will come back to us. This fire was the fire of purification—for you who were led astray by misplaced longing and ambition, for me who let age wither my faith and my hope, for the parish who ran after phantoms and visions. All the trappings are burned away now, Jude. We will start anew. With true faith, with the simple practice of our Lord's commandments. We will love one another . . ."

But James could see that Jude was not hearing Father Maguire's inspiring words. Instead, the priest walked towards Mary Dowd, silent since her confession to Molloy in the car. Still dressed in the nun's habit, she sat as if struck to stone, her hands in her lap, head down, a small dark form. An incubus, thought James, in the corner.

Jude stood in front of her. "Was any of it true, Mary? Was

any of it real?" His voice cracked, sending chills down the spines of the older men. "I have to know."

Mary Dowd, clasping her hands until her knuckles showed white, did not reply.

The three men watched as the younger man began to confront his own role, his own actions of the last two months. They knew that three deaths, the injury to Geraldine, and the conflagration at the church were even now passing before his eyes. And they felt, pressing around them, bearing in on them, an overpowering awareness of the thousands of pilgrims and believers and suppliants who had lifted up their hopes and desires at the foot of the statue in the grotto of Buncloda.

— *Chapter Twenty-Three* —

The next morning, James sat gratefully by Geraldine's bed as she finished a light breakfast of tea and toast. Mrs. Kehoe, it turned out, made a wonderful nurse. And the local G.P., Dr. Reilly, who the night before had diagnosed a mild concussion and had prescribed an abundance of rest and relaxation, had just left after a second visit, pronouncing her well on the mend.

James and Geraldine had been talking on and off; she quite lucid, he more halting.

"So Mary Dowd didn't wait for Jude. She went on to the church by herself?"

"Yes," James replied, "Jude had left her at the convent because he desperately wanted to be at the grotto. Since he knew you had to be alone, he drove aimlessly for a while, trying to resist the temptation. But as it approached midnight, he couldn't keep away."

"He didn't want to miss out on anything, in case I . . ." She stumbled over the words, embarrassed still about her role in the ruse. "I don't know how I shall face him."

"All in good time, Ger," James said softly.

"So Mary Dowd set the fire? Why? And how?"

"She needed to distract Jude, and anyone else for that matter. She wanted to draw all attention away from the grotto. It was simple enough for her to set the fire. She'd an old paraffin heater of her mother's in the garage. And a full can of paraffin. She drove to the church and let herself in with a key Jude had given her in May, when he'd first become her spiritual adviser. She poured the paraffin on all the soft furnishings and hangings, and on the wooden pews and supports. Paraffin burns hot and fast, just like petrol. Within minutes the fire took hold. She grabbed the heavy brass candlestick and ran for her car. By the time the flames were devouring the roof, she, under cover of the darkness, was climbing up to the grotto."

"To kill me?" Geraldine shivered.

"Yes. My guess is that when she met earlier with Tim Kerrigan, Mary already had the idea to kill you. But she, at the same time, was going to give Jude one last chance. When she met with him she set Jude up with a choice: stay and pray with her in the church, choose to stand by her—the visionary who had brought so much into his life—or . . . choose you, the new seer, the blow-in. It was all or nothing. She was not to be fobbed off with a compromise.

"When he didn't make the right choice, in her jealous anger, she determined to eliminate you, the threat to her bond with Jude. She couldn't afford to wait to see if you'd have a vision or not. You were a childhood friend of Jude's, mature, attractive, worldly. And he had virtually said that you would make a better witness to a miraculous vision than even she did."

"He was just caught in it. He was . . . enthusiastic," Geraldine said a little defensively.

"That's right. And Mary Dowd saw it. She had always been daring. Remember what she had revealed to me and Jude after Rita and Devane were dead—that they had been having doubts about what they witnessed? This was to emphasize to Jude that she was left as the true visionary. And if it made me suspicious of Jude, it was a risk she'd take—since she knew he wasn't the killer."

"But why kill at all?"

"Oh, Ger. Her thinking had a logic of its own. It applied to her reality and not to ours. She saw you as a threat. Either you were a fraud, and being one herself, she knew that Jude was subject to being led by a deceptive woman. Or you were genuine. That was worse again. You might be real. And she told Molloy last night, she thought you might have been sent by God as a punishment to her. For all her deceit . . . and . . ."

James paused, deadly serious now. "You know, Ger, she felt less remorse for the murders than she did for disappointing the faithful."

"And the others? Rita and Devane. She actually killed them?"

"Yes. They were a threat of a different kind from you. They had told her of their doubts. She knew their recanting would rebound on her. But the whole visionary experience had evolved in her mind as a method of attracting and keeping Jude's attention. She was obsessed with him. Apparently she accepted they would never have what we would call a normal life together, even in her fantasy. Instead, she saw them as great spiritual partners in a magnificent religious endeavor binding them together for life: she, as virginal as a nun, he a celibate. They would be wedded together in some incorporeal yet powerful alliance. I'm unsure still if she ever had any genuine spiritual or miraculous experience at the grotto. Perhaps it was, if anything, something psychologically generated, and consequently real in that sense. Perhaps her desire was so strong it caused her to see an apparition . . ."

"And then she came to believe in its reality?"

"Yes. I think almost all of the time she sincerely believed it had happened. But as the pressure from the pilgrims grew . . ."

"As they demanded a sign or a miracle?"

"Yes, exactly. It was then, I think, her nerves began to give way. She grew anxious . . ."

"So the self-flagellation was genuine?"

"I think so. Don't you? Almost everything she did served a dual purpose. On the one hand, she sincerely believed she needed to make herself worthy of a genuine vision, a miracle. On the other hand, flagellating herself riveted Jude's attention on her yet again. You remember, it really was on account of that knowledge that he decided to put her at the convent. But just before that Mary had found out from Rita's own lips that she was about to go to Jude with the truth—"

"The truth being that she'd not really seen the Virgin?"

"No, the truth being that she'd been *persuaded* that she'd seen *something,* a light perhaps. My guess is that Mary's intensity and conviction at the time made Miss Garrotty think she saw at least that much. Think what even that experience would mean to that lonely woman! But over time she began to doubt, began to realize Mary had convinced her that she saw it. It would have taken courage for her to admit that to herself, let alone to others. The end of her dream . . ." James shook his head sadly, remembering Miss Garrotty.

"But how did Mary Dowd manage it?"

"She was still living in her own house. Her movements were unrestricted. Mary confessed to knowing about Rita's low and erratic blood pressure from their morning chats when they first started going to the grotto months ago. Mary had never disposed of her own mother's high blood pressure medication. She used to fill the prescriptions for her in Limerick—when she was at the teaching training college— on a routine basis. The chemist filled it for her again recently, having known Mary Dowd, the respectable, con- scientious student and daughter. The prescriptions were for two very powerful antihypertensive drugs.

"Mary Dowd invited Rita to her home and gave her a

massive dose of the two drugs dissolved in her coffee, which she always liked strong. Rita rather quickly slipped into a coma and then expired in the sitting room. Mary put her body in her father's wheelchair, which she'd kept in the garage. Heavily disguised, she pushed the body in the wheelchair, unnoticed by the crowds, up to the grotto."

"Look, James, this doesn't sound like a girl who suffered with nerves. This was a daring, imaginative plan!"

"That's probably the key word, Ger: imaginative." He sighed dejectedly.

"And Devane?" Geraldine asked after a long silence.

"Well, after Rita died, Mary went to see him. She thought he was still convinced, but she needed to make sure. But Rita's death had backfired on Mary Dowd. Devane had become frightened by the idea someone was gunning for the visionaries themselves. He was truly in fear for his life. He had decided to come forward and disavow the whole experience at the grotto. He thought that a public disavowal would keep him safe from a killer who only wanted to kill the seers, the true visionaries. Apparently, Mary Dowd acted on the spur of the moment—to protect herself and her story of the vision. She was making tea for him when he'd told her his plan. So she silenced him then and there."

James sighed, wishing he'd seen all of this sooner.

"But all along you were suspecting Jude?" Geraldine cut in, shaking her head.

"This is difficult to admit now, but it made sense to me. Jude had the most to lose if any of the seers recanted. One, and then another, seemed poised to do so. But with two tragically slain, Jude could have continued to develop Buncloda as a Marian shrine with no risk of recantation, obviously, from Mary, the remaining seer. And, knowing him—as I thought I did—I also knew he'd always live in the hope of a real, more verifiable, more impressive miracle occurring at the grotto. By introducing you into the situation as a potential visionary, one whom he'd known and liked and trusted as a child, I hoped to test that out. I had seen naked ambition in him, Ger, where you saw only immense faith."

"No, James, I too saw it. But it wasn't ambition. It was longing. In the last two days it was painful for me to see in Jude the heartfelt desire, the intensity of his longing to see a vision. I had to steel myself, just in order to keep true to your plan." Geraldine put aside her cup of tea and took a deep breath.

"Yes, my plan . . . I hadn't counted on Mary having such a daring plan herself. God, she even fooled Tim Kerrigan into thinking she would give it all up. But she was only using him to help her get away without taking her own car. That would have looked too obvious."

"But what did she imagine would happen today, her great Sunday?"

"Apparently she saw that you as a threat would be . . . gone. Dead. She too would be gone. She planned to disappear. But she was satisfied knowing that her role would remain the central one. In her fantasy she imagined the devotions at the shrine continuing, and that the faithful would see your death as punishment, and perhaps even imagine her disappearance to be miraculous. The weak had died, and she, the strongest of all, had disappeared, perhaps caught up to heaven as the great sign they all longed for . . ."

"Perhaps too," Geraldine said thoughtfully, "she knew in her heart, with or without a threat from me, that nothing would happen. What was left to her after such a crescendo of feeling? Life sequestered in the convent, a life of endless waiting for the sign, for something to happen. If only she had turned her thoughts towards life, and not towards death . . ."

"Oh, Ger," James cried, "I never meant for you to be in any real danger. Whether it was from Mary Dowd or Jude or even Tim Kerrigan. I knew that Molloy and I were right there at the grotto, near you, ready to protect you from an attack. And I thought when Jude arrived, that he'd betrayed himself as the killer . . . and then came the fire. I . . . we . . .

were distracted . . . obviously." James opened his hands in an expressive gesture.

"Well, Mary Dowd succeeded in one thing anyway," Geraldine said dryly. "She successfully distracted all of you."

"Oh, Ger, I am so very sorry. I can't apologize enough. You could have been killed . . . in fact I thought . . ."

James put his head in his hands.

Geraldine shivered again and pulled the blanket tighter. "You know, James, the power of the mind wedded to the power of intense desire can accomplish amazing things. I tried at first to keep a pure heart through this charade. Misleading Jude bothered me very much, but I believed that I was helping you to learn the truth. By disproving your theories, I believed I would help Mary Dowd. I thought once you saw she was an innocent, and that Jude was true, you'd focus your energy on finding the real killer. You would save Mary Dowd from her killer . . ." Geraldine's voice grew thin and tremulous.

"That was the higher cause for me, James, because I really did think Mary Dowd had been touched by God in some great divine and mystical way. I have to be honest here, James, because only brutal honesty will save all of us in this terrible situation.

"When I spent those long hours at the grotto, in the afternoon, and then last night, staring at that simple statue, I too really wanted to see something, feel something. And I did, James."

James's head snapped up.

"Yes, it's true, I felt a great sense of peace, a closeness to God. I'd never prayed for so long or so hard as I did these past days. The only way I could square my deception of Jude was to keep to my promise to him to pray and meditate. And I did. And alone in the grotto I made my peace with God. I still have that."

James watched as tears welled in her large blue eyes. Her face without makeup was white and frail. The tears fell down her cheeks and she brushed them away with the back of her bruised right hand. He wanted to take her in his arms.

And, for once, he did.

It was with a light heart that James paid Mrs. Kehoe and bid her good-bye. Even kissing her on the cheek, for good measure.

The word about Mary Dowd—speculative, sad, and confused—had of course spread with incalcuable speed. But his own role in the events that had unfolded remained obscure. James had always worked behind the scenes in his cases, and he wanted it to stay that way. He had spoken of this with Molloy at the rectory when the gardai had taken Mary Dowd into custody at last. And Molloy, James was glad to see, was clearly a man of his word.

As he and Geraldine drove off in the Citroen, he quickly saw that he would be unable to break into the endless queue of cars and vans. It seemed that every one of the hundreds of pilgrims had decided to depart Buncloda at the same time.

On impulse he pulled his car onto the verge and, after making an excuse to Geraldine for this slight delay, he walked against the tide of people. He climbed the denuded hill opposite the grotto, as he'd done that first day in what seemed another lifetime. Voices reached him, murmuring the now familiar phrases: ". . . Mother of Christ, pray for us. Mother most chaste, Mother inviolate, Mother most amiable, Mother of good counsel, Virgin most prudent, Virgin most venerable . . ."

James watched the few remaining faithful, whom he recognized as parishioners of Buncloda. Father Jude Donnelly, his long black soutane billowing around him in the breeze, was leading them in the Litany of the Blessed Virgin Mary: ". . . Mirror of justice, Pray for us. Seat of wisdom, Cause of our joy . . ."

Father Maguire, James noted, stood with Jude, lending his clear voice. ". . . Mystical Rose, Tower of ivory, House of gold, Ark of the covenant . . ." Yes, James thought, the rebuilding had already begun.

He strained to hear the ancient list of attributes, strained to see just once more the peaceful face of the weather-beaten little statue. It looked to him now so small and fragile.

The devout chanted on. "Gate of heaven, pray for us. Morning Star . . . Comforter of the afflicted . . . Refuge of sinners . . . pray for us . . ."

He lifted his hand in a silent farewell to the two priests he would never see again, and murmured his first and last prayer at the shrine of the Virgin of Buncloda.